The Cosy Teashop in the Castle

Caroline Roberts lives in the wonderful Northumberland countryside with her husband and credits the sandy beaches, castles and rolling hills around her as inspiration for her writing. She enjoys writing about relationships; stories of love, loss and family, which explore how beautiful and sometimes complex love can be. A slice of cake, glass of bubbly and a cup of tea would make her day – preferably served with friends! She believes in striving for your dreams, which led her to a publishing deal after many years of writing. *The Cosy Teashop in the Castle* is her second novel.

If you'd like to find out more about Caroline, visit her on Twitter, Facebook and her blog – she'd love to hear from you!

@_caroroberts
/CarolineRobertsAuthor
http://carolinerobertswriter.blogspot.co.uk

Also by Caroline Roberts

The Torn Up Marriage

Caroline Roberts

The Cosy Teashop In The Castle

Harper
impulse
we've got the love

Harper*Impulse* an imprint of
HarperCollins*Publishers*
The News Building
1 London Bridge Street
London SE1 9GF

www.harpercollins.co.uk

A Paperback Original 2016

8

A catalogue record for this book is available from the British Library

ISBN: 978-0-00-812541-7

This novel is entirely a work of fiction.
The names, characters and incidents portrayed in it are the work of
the author's imagination. Any resemblance to actual persons,
living or dead, events or localities is entirely coincidental.

Typeset in Minion by Palimpsest Book Production Ltd, Falkirk, Stirlingshire

Printed and bound by CPI Group (UK) Ltd, Croydon, CR0 4YY

MIX
Paper from
responsible sources
FSC™ C007454

Find out more about HarperCollins and the environment at
www.harpercollins.co.uk/green

For my wonderful friends.
And for anyone who ever had a dream.

'Our dreams can come true if we have the courage to pursue them'   – Walt Disney

'Tread softly because you tread on my dreams'
                                                          – W. B. Yeats

1

Ellie

Talk about flying by the seat of her pants. She hadn't really expected an interview. The ad had caught her eye in the *Journal*, and well, she'd been fed up, felt messed about by her twat of an ex, her bore of a job and fancied a change – of life, scenery, postcode, you name it.

So here she was, driving her little silver Corsa up the estate driveway that was lined by an avenue of gnarled-trunked, centuries-old trees. Her stomach did a backward flip as the castle came into view: blonde and grey sandstone walls with four layers of windows looking down on her – Claverham Castle. Did people really live in places like this? Did people really *work* in places like this? She felt like she'd driven onto the set of *Downton Abbey* or arrived in some fairytale.

The woman at the huge arch of an entrance did *not* look like someone from a fairytale, however; huddled in a huge fleece, dark jeans and wellington boots, and having a sneaky fag. She popped the offending item behind her back when she spotted Ellie pulling up on the gravel, but the wispy trail of smoke in the cool March air gave her away.

Okay, breathe, Ellie, breathe.

A quick check in the rear-view mirror. She hoped she still looked half-decent. She found her lippie and interview notes in her handbag, and tried to convince herself exactly why she was the right person to take on these tearooms as she popped on a slash of pale-pink gloss. It had all seemed such a good idea two weeks ago when she'd spotted the ad in the local press: 'Leasehold available for Claverham Castle Tea Rooms for the Summer Season.' A place to escape, and the chance to achieve the dream she'd harboured for years, running her own café, baking to her heart's content, and watching people grin as they tucked into fat slices of her chocolate fudge cake or strawberry-packed scones. A chance for change. So this was it! She *sooo* did not want to mess this up.

Her heart was banging away in her chest as she opened the car door. She stepped out with a pretence of confidence, aware of the woman still standing at the top of the steps. Sploosh! She felt a gloopiness beneath her feet, looked down. Shite! Her black suede stilettos were an inch-deep in mud and an attractive poo-like blob had landed on the right toe area. So much for first impressions.

She tried a subtle shoe-scrape on the grass verge, plastered a smile on her face and made her way to the castle entrance. A biting wind whipped at her honey-blonde hair, which she'd carefully put up in a topknot back at home in Newcastle-upon-Tyne this morning. Her black trouser-suit teamed with silky lime-green blouse was no match for the freezing cold. She hugged her arms around herself and headed for the door: a vast wood and iron creation – no doubt designed to keep out hairy, aggressive Border Reivers centuries ago.

The lady raised a cheery smile as Ellie approached, 'Hello, you must be here for the interview with Lord Henry.'

'Yes.' She reached out a trembling hand in greeting. 'Yes, it's Ellie Hall.'

'Nice to meet you, Ellie. I'm Deana.' The woman shook her hand warmly. She had a kind face, looked in her early fifties, with grey hair that hung in a grown-out bob. 'I'm Lord Henry's PA, well dogsbody really. S'cuse the attire, casual at the moment till the open season starts again. It gets bloody freezing here. Come on through, pet.'

Ellie relaxed a little; she seemed friendly. She followed Deana through the massive door to a stone inner courtyard, the sky a square of azure above. Wow – it was like some Disney set. And then into a circular stairwell that wound its way upwards – Sleeping Beauty or Rapunzel could well be at the top of that.

'There's no guests here at the moment,' Deana spoke with a gentle Northumbrian lilt. 'We close until Easter. So it's quiet. Come the spring, it'll be buzzing again. Well, kind of crawling,' she added with a wry grin, as though visitors were a necessity to be put up with rather than welcomed.

Ellie was offered a seat on a chair with a frayed red-velvet pad, positioned outside a closed door, which she imagined must be for Lord Henry's office. She could hear muffled voices from inside, formal tones.

Deana asked if she'd like a cup of coffee while she waited, said she wouldn't be long, and then disappeared back down the stairs. Ellie gathered her jacket and her nerve; it was bloody draughty there in the corridor.

Various artefacts stared down at her from the stone walls: black-and-white photos of the castle, the stuffed head of a weasel, or so she thought – ginger, hairy, teeth-bared, it looked pretty mean – a pistol in a glass case like something Robin Hood might whip out: 'Stand and deliver'. This was *so* unlike her white-walled, MDF-desked insurance office, she felt she'd been shuttled back through time.

A scraping of chairs brought her out of her reverie.

Footsteps, the door opening, and out came a plump middle-aged lady, dressed smartly in a Christmas party jewelled jumper kind of way, thanking the gentleman for his time, adding she hoped she would be back soon. She smiled confidently (almost smugly) as she spotted Ellie sitting there. Lord Henry, for that's who she thought the man must be, was smiling too. 'Yes, lovely to meet with you again, Cynthia. I've been impressed with your work for us in the past, and we'll be in touch *very* shortly.' His tones were posh and plummy, the vowels clearly enunciated. It all seemed very amicable, and very *settled*. Ellie felt her heart sink. Was she just being thrown in the applicant mix as a token gesture?

Deana appeared at her side with a tray and coffee set out for three – perhaps she was staying for the interview. She ushered Ellie into the wood-panelled office.

Well, this was it. Ellie took a deep breath to calm her nerves. Now that she sensed she hadn't a cat in hell's chance of getting the tearoom lease, she suddenly realised how very much she wanted it. It was what she'd been dreaming of for years whilst stuck answering call-centre queries for insurance claims in a vast, impersonal office. She absolutely loved baking cakes for friends and for family birthdays. Her football party cake for her Cousin Jack had gone down a treat, and a champagne-bottle-shaped chocolate cake that she did for Gemma, her close friend at work, had led to a flurry of special requests. Oh yes, she'd offer to fetch the doughnuts and pastries for the office at morning break, standing in the queue at the baker's savouring the smells of fresh bread and cakes, wishing she could be the one working in the bakery instead.

Deana set the coffee tray down on a huge mahogany desk, which had a green-leather top. It looked big enough to play a game of snooker on. She smiled encouragingly across at Ellie, then left the room.

Lord Henry had a slightly worn, aristocratic appearance. He looked in his sixties and was dressed in beige corduroy trousers, a checked shirt and tweed waistcoat. He stood to greet her from the other side of the desk, offering a slim hand, shaking hers surprisingly firmly, 'Lord Henry Hogarth. Please, have a seat, Miss . . .' he paused, the words drifting uncomfortably.

Great, he didn't even know her name. 'Hall, Ellie Hall.'

'Well, Ellen, do make yourself comfortable.'

She was too nervous to correct him.

He poured out two coffees and passed her one, pouring in milk for her from a small white porcelain jug. She took a sip; it was rich and dark, definitely not instant, then she sat back in the chair, trying to give the air of cool, calm and collected. She was bricking it inside. She hoped her voice would work normally. As Lord Henry took his seat on the other side of the immense desk, she tried out the word 'Thanks'. Phew, at least she could speak, though she noted that her pitch was a little higher than normal.

'*So*, how long have you worked in the catering industry, Miss Hall?' He leaned towards her, rubbing his chin, his brown eyes scrutinising.

She froze, 'Ah . . . Well . . .' *About never*. Seat of the pants didn't even cover it. What the hell was she doing here? 'Yes,' she coughed into her coffee, 'Well, I've had a few years' experience.' *Baking at home, for friends, birthday cakes, cupcakes, Victoria sponges and the like, not to mention her 'choffee cake special'. And, yes, she made the tea and coffee regularly at the insurance office.* 'I have worked in a restaurant.' *Saturday-night waitressing as a teenager at the Funky Chicken Express down the road for a bit of extra cash.* 'And I have managed several staff.' Where *was* this coming from? She had trained another waitress in the art of wiping down tables. Though, she had filled in that weekend for her friend Kirsty at her sandwich bar, when Kirsty's boyfriend went AWOL.

Ellie thought that had planted the seed. She'd loved those two days prepping the food, making up tasty panini combinations – her brie, grape and cranberry had been a hit. She'd warmed to the idea of running her own company after that, spent hours daydreaming about it, something that involved food, baking ideally, being her own boss. That, and her nanna's inspiration, of course, lovely Nanna. Ellie remembered perching on a stool in her galley kitchen beating sponge-mix with a wooden spoon. Nanna had left her over a thousand pounds in her will – it would give Ellie the chance to cover this lease for a couple of months. Give her the time to try and make a go of it. She was sure Nanna would have supported her in this venture. Ellie would have loved to have turned up at her flat for a good chat about the tearooms and her ideas to make the business work, over a cup of strong tea and a slice of homemade lemon drizzle. But someone else was living there now, the world had moved on, and Nanna too. She really missed her.

Ellie managed to smile across at Lord Henry, realising she ought to say more but not quite sure what. How did you capture those dreams in words?

'And if you did take on the lease for the tearooms, Miss Hall, how would you propose to take the business forward?'

'Well . . .' Think, *think*, you've been practising answers all night, woman. 'I've had a look at the current income and expenditure figures, and I'm certain there's room for improvements. I'd bake all my own cakes and scones. I'll look carefully at pricing, staffing levels, costs and the like, offering good-quality food at a fair price for the customer, and keeping an eye on making a profit too. But, most of all, I want to give people a really positive, friendly experience so they'd want to come back . . . And, I'd like to try and source local produce.'

Lord Henry raised a rather hairy grey eyebrow. It sounded stilted, even to her.

At that, there was a brusque knock on the door. It swung open. 'So sorry I'm late.' A man strolled in. Wow, he was rather gorgeous, in a tall, dark-haired and lean kind of way. He offered an outstretched hand to Ellie as he walked past her chair and acknowledged Lord Henry. He looked late twenties, possibly early thirties. 'There was a problem with the tractor,' he offered, by way of explanation, 'She needs a major service, but I've got her going again for now.'

He had a firm grip, long fingers and neat nails.

'Miss Hall, this is Joseph Ward, our estate manager.'

'Hello.' Ellie smiled nervously. Another interrogator.

The younger man looked back at her with dark-brown eyes, his gaze intent, as though he were trying to suss her out. Then his features seemed to soften, 'Joe, I prefer Joe.' A pointed glance was exchanged between the two men. Ellie sensed a certain tension, which had nothing to do with her. Joe sat down, angling his seat to the side of the desk. There was something about him that reminded her of the guy off *Silent Witness*, hmm, yes, that Harry chap, from the series before, with his dark-haired English-gentleman look. He must be over six foot, on the slim side, but not without a hint of muscle beneath his blue cotton shirt, which was rolled up to the elbow and open at the neck. He looked smart-scruffy all at once.

'Sorry if I interrupted you there. Please carry on where you left off.' His voice wasn't upper class despite his appearance, having the Geordie lilts of her home town. He smiled at her.

On closer inspection she noted that his eyes were a deep brown with flecks of green. Her mind had gone blank. What the hell *had* she been talking about?

'Local produce?' Lord Henry prompted.

'Oh, yes, I'd certainly look to use the local farmers' markets and shops to source good local food.'

'Hmn, sounds a good idea,' Joe nodded.

'Well, Mrs Charlton, the lady who's been running the tearooms announced her departure rather suddenly,' Lord Henry took up, 'She's had the lease here for the past twelve years and we were rather hoping she would be back to start the season again in a month's time. With Easter being at the end of March this year, we would need somebody quickly. Would that be a problem for you?'

'No, at least I don't think so. I'd hand my notice in at work straight away. I'm meant to give a month, but the company owes me some holiday, and I believe they are usually quite flexible.' Did that actually mean Lord Henry was interested in her? What about Supercook Cynthia from earlier?

'So, what *is* your current position, Ellie?' Joe looked right into her eyes as he spoke, unsettling her. *He* wasn't going to miss a trick, was he? Damn, and it all seemed to be going so well.

Deep breath, how to phrase this one? 'Ah-m, well, I have been working as an insurance administrator. But, as I was explaining to Lord Henry, I have been building up my experience in the catering industry over many years. My friend owns a bistro, where I regularly help out.' *Fill in sandwich bar here.* 'And I have worked at a local restaurant.' *Funky Chicken, as a waitress*, the heckler in her mind added. She was losing her nerve rapidly.

'I see.' Joe was mulling her words over, rubbing his fingertips across his chin, definitely unconvinced.

'Ah, right. Well then. I see.' Lord Henry was cooling too.

'And what formal qualifications do you have in catering, Ellie?' Joe.

She began to feel sick. *None, I have none.* Her voice came out small, 'I haven't anything formal other than the standard health and hygiene requirements.' *Liar, liar pants on fire.* Well, she'd be getting those as soon as possible. 'Much as I'd have loved to, I haven't trained profession-ally as a chef.' A lump stuck in her throat. She knew she shouldn't have come, what had she been thinking? The dream was slipping away . . .

'But,' she had to grasp at something, tell them how much this meant to her, 'I want this more than anything. The admin, the insurance role, that's just a job, a means of earning money. But I'm passionate about my baking. I cook fabulous cakes and pastries and scones. That's not just me saying it, either, my family, my friends are always asking me to bake for them. I can make soups and quiches. I've wanted to run my own tearooms since I was a little girl.' The words were gushing out now. 'Just give me a year. Give me this season and I'll show you. I can turn the business around, pay you a good lease, *and* attract more people to the castle to do the tours that I notice you do. We could plan themed open days. I could cook medieval-style food,' *She wasn't even sure what kind of food 'medieval' might be.* 'Try cream-tea afternoons. Link up with local charities, host a fundraiser, a summer fete. Halloween, why not? It looks spooky enough here.' She ran out of steam then.

Joe was giving her a wry smile. She wasn't sure if he liked what he heard or was thinking that she was totally bonkers. Where had all that come from? She hadn't actually thought of any of it till now; it certainly wasn't what she'd been rehearsing in her head all night. Some last-ditch chance at getting hired, probably. A final fling at her dream or else it was back home. Home wasn't so bad, to be fair. Her mum and dad were great, but it was a narrow life, living in a brick-built semi in Heaton, and working in an office block in the suburbs of Newcastle. She couldn't afford her own place. Well, not now anyway. *That* particular dream had been ransacked by

Gavin-bloody-tosser-Mason. She needed this *so* badly, this new start. And a castle, surely, wasn't a bad place to begin.

They were staring at her, an awkward silence forming around them. Then Lord Henry stood up, indicating that it was time for her departure. 'Well, thank you for taking the time and effort to come all this way, Miss Hall.'

There was no 'We'll be in touch very soon' like good old Cynthia had. Though Joe did add, 'We'll let you know something in the next week or so. We do have several candidates to see and there may be second interviews.' He stood up, his hand outstretched. His fingers clasped warmly around her own.

'Yes, we'll be in touch.' Lord Henry gave an inscrutable smile.

Out in the cool corridor, Deana caught up with her. 'Do you want to have a quick look around the kitchens, the tearooms? Get an idea of what you're in for?'

'Okay, yep, that'd be good.' Go on, just dangle that carrot, show her everything she was about to lose.

They wound down the stone stairwell. She could almost imagine an old witch up at the top with a spinning wheel; all ready to prick the girl's finger, send her to sleep for a hundred years, and then there'd be her knight in shining armour galloping in to kiss her awake again. It happened like that in fairytales, you see, oh yes, those heroic men would hack down a forest just to get to you. Where were all the heroes nowadays? She sighed – she'd obviously been fed too many Disney movies as a child. Back out to the courtyard again and in through a heavy wooden side door that opened with a creak into the kitchen. It was big, *very* big, with rather drab mushroom-grey-painted walls; you could cater for a function easily from here. Weddings and parties were flitting through her mind. It had obviously been designed for bigger things than a tearoom. She wondered if it had been the original castle kitchen, but there were no signs of anything pre-seventies, really, no old ranges or copper kettles, no Victorian bells lined up on the walls for the staff (*Downton* was still flitting around her head), just practical stainless-steel work surfaces, a two-sided sink, huge oven, modern microwave, fridge, chest freezer and dishwasher.

Deana waltzed through, pointing out the various equipment, apologising for the general state of the place, explaining that Mrs Charlton, the previous lease-owner, had left in a hurry at the end of last season, only recently announcing that she wasn't coming back – some family crisis, apparently.

On closer inspection the walls were a bit greasy-looking, and the convection fan had a layer of tar-like grime; it needed taking down, scrubbing and bleaching. But Ellie didn't mind a spot of cleaning.

There was a narrow passageway leading from the kitchen. Deana set off, Ellie following her through to the tearooms themselves. Now *this* was back in time, a real contrast to the kitchens. History smacked you in the face – high stone walls, leaded windows, a massive fireplace; they'd need whole tree trunks, not logs, on that grate. A huge pair of antlers was fixed high above the hearth; that would have been one hell of a scary deer, like something out of the ice age. Deana was chattering on about how different it was when the visitors were there.

'Are they real?' Ellie asked, looking up at the antlers.

'Replicas, I believe, but the originals were from a real animal, fossilised. Can't tell you when they were dated, but, yeah, that would have been a brute of a beast, wouldn't it?'

'You're telling me!' It was like Bambi on steroids.

The corridor had taken them from twentieth-century kitchen – it hadn't *quite* reached the twenty-first yet, back to some sixteenth-century vault. Well, the tearooms certainly had character: reams of it. There were about ten dark-wood tables with chairs, their floral-patterned seat pads frayed. It was an amazing place, but it all looked rather unloved.

Even so, she could picture it there with the fire on, posies on the tables, the smell of home baking, friendly waitresses in black skirts, white blouses and frilly aprons, and herself cooking away in the kitchen, doing plenty of Nigella spoon-licking, having to test all the cakes person-ally, of course – Ellie's Teashop.

Back in the car a few minutes later, she realised she was trembling. Maybe it was just the Northumberland March chill. Or perhaps it was the fear that this was the last she might see of this place. She wanted this so much.

2

Ellie

She pulled up, finding a parking space four houses down from her family home in Heaton. Rows and rows of brick terraces crowded around her. It wasn't a bad place to live; the neighbours were friendly, there were coffee shops and takeaways around the corner, a park near by and a ten-minute metro ride and you were in the lively city centre of Newcastle-upon-Tyne. But today she'd had a taste of something different; a castle brimming with history in the middle of the most stunning countryside, big Northumbrian skies, open space, a taste of freedom. And she wanted to taste just a little more of it, to live it, breathe it, cook in it.

Today had given Ellie a sense of her future. Made her want the job all the more. Yet she wasn't at all sure how the interview with Lord Henry and Joe had gone. Her inner interview-ometer was registering pretty low.

She got out of the car, walked down to number five, and wandered in for what might have been the thousandth time. Smells of polish and vegetables filled the air. She found her mum, Sarah, in the kitchen, peeling carrots. Onions, parsnips and a hunk of marble-fatted beef sat on a chopping board ready for cubing.

'Hello, pet . . . *So*, how did it go?' She turned to her daughter with a cautious smile.

'Umn, I don't know, to be honest . . . It was an amazing place . . . proper castle . . . big grounds. The people seemed nice.' Well, Lord Henry seemed quietly intimidating, but he was the sort of person it might take a while to get to know. Deana, she was just lovely. And Joe, hmn, gorgeous Joe, something about him made her feel uneasy, yet he seemed okay, a bit aloof, maybe, but then it had been a formal interview. His questions had definitely been more searching than Lord Henry's. She'd need to be far more prepared, do some full costings, a business plan and book her health and hygiene course, if there was to be a second interview or anything. *If* . . . a small word, *massive* implications. She plastered on a hopeful smile as her mother looked across at her.

'Well,' her mother's tone dipped into school-marmish, 'It is a bit out of the way up there. I'm still not sure why you're looking that far out? Just think of all the fuel. How long did it take you to get there?'

'About an hour.' Due north up the A1, then a maze of winding lanes. She wasn't thinking about travelling every day, she wanted to live there – the ad said there might be accommodation with the lease. But she hadn't mentioned that yet. No point getting her mum all wound up if it wasn't going to happen.

'Are you *sure* about all this, Ellie? It does seem a bit of a whim. I still can't grasp why you're thinking about giving up a good office job with a reasonable salary. What if it all goes wrong? You won't be able to waltz back into the insurance job again, you know – what with the recession and everything.' Sarah looked up from chopping carrots, her blue-grey eyes shadowed with concern.

'Well, thanks for the vote of confidence.'

'Oh, pet. It's not that I don't want you to do well. I just don't want you to fall down with this. Get caught up in some dream and then realise it's not all it's supposed to be. I'd hate for you to end up with no job at all.' She wiped her hands on her floral apron and gave Ellie an affectionate pat on the shoulder. It was as near a hug as she was going to get.

Her mother was sensible, cautious; she liked order and stability. Sometimes it drove Ellie nuts. Yes, the concern was no doubt born of love, but lately the family safety net felt like it was strangling her. When were dreams so

19

bad, so dangerous? The two of them got on alright, but often Ellie felt very different from her mother. They viewed the world through different eyes. Ellie felt that there was something more out there in the big wide world, something she hadn't found yet. And so what if it all went wrong? At least she'd have tried.

'It's not as though there are jobs on trees at the moment, Eleanor.' Jeez, her full name was coming into action now. Mum really was toeing the sensible line.

'I know that. But, I'd find something else if it came to it, Mum.' She'd waitress, clean loos or something if she had to, if it all went belly-up a few months down the line.

Sarah just raised her eyes to heaven and took the slab of meat to hand.

Ellie sighed. Nanna Beryl would have understood. But she wasn't here to back her up any more, bless her. A knot of loss tightened inside. She was such an amazing character, hard-working, fun, loving and wise. Nanna had inspired Ellie into this baking malarkey, many moons ago in her tiny kitchen flat – Ellie cleaning the mixing bowl out with big licks of the wooden spoon once the cake had gone into the oven. She had watched, she had learned, had her fill of sticky-sweet cake mix, and she had loved. She kept Nanna's battered old Be-Ro recipe book stashed in her bedroom, with Beryl's hand-written adaptations and extra recipes held within it. Her choffee cake was awesome – a coffee-chocolate dream: one bite and you felt you'd gone to heaven.

But bless her, she had died just over a year ago. Ellie still felt that awful pang of missing her. Hopefully she was up in heaven somewhere still cooking cakes and keeping all the angels cheery and plump. Yes, she was sure Nanna Beryl would have supported her in this, told her to go out there and give it a try. She could almost hear her voice, that golden-warm Geordie accent, 'Go on canny lass, diven' worry about your mam. She was born sensible, that one. It's *your* life, *your* dream.'

And she needed this change, especially with everything that happened six months ago with that tosser Gavin. Nah, she didn't want to even think about that. He wasn't worth spending thinking-time on.

Ellie popped her jacket in the understairs cupboard and came back to the kitchen offering to make the dumplings for the stew. She asked her mum about her day, glad to divert the attention and questions from herself. Sarah had a part-time job at the Co-op around the corner, as well as doing a couple of mornings' cleaning at the doctor's surgery. They chatted comfortably. Mixing the dumpling ingredients took Ellie's mind off things. She added dried herbs to the flour, then the suet and water, rolling the dough between her hands, circling broken-off lumps in her palms into neat balls ready to float on the stew.

Ten minutes later, the front door banged open and Keith, Ellie's father, appeared with a loud 'Hullo' and a broad grin, returning home after a day plumbing and handy-manning. He popped his head into the kitchen. 'Good day, girls! How did it go, then, our Ellie? Head chef already?'

'Not quite,' she smiled. 'There's a chance of a second interview. But I'll just have to wait and see.'

'Well, best of luck, bonny lass. Best of luck. Better go up and get myself changed out of these work things. Stew is it tonight, Mam?'

'Ah-hah.'

'Great. I'm starving.'

Things had been slower for him these past few years with the recession biting hard in the building trade, but he'd do odd jobs as well as the plumbing, anything really. He had a trade – he was lucky, he often said. Ellie listened to his cheery whistle as he headed upstairs to change out of his navy boiler suit.

Jason, Ellie's brother, sauntered in soon after, dumping muddy football boots in the hall. He was nine years younger than Ellie, seventeen to her twenty-six, and still at sixth form. In the main he tried to avoid schoolwork as much as he could, filling the gap with sport, occasionally interrupted by a crush on a new girl. This month it was Kylie of the white-blonde hair and dark roots from down the road. She was still giving out confusing signals, apparently, one minute sitting next to him on the bus to town, full of chat, the next giggling with her friends and hardly giving him the time of day.

'Jason, boots out the back, please. *Not* the hall. The house'll be stinking. I don't know how many times I have to tell you,' Sarah shouted, catching him before he drifted off upstairs, and the aroma of sweaty teenage footwear permeated the house.

An hour and a half later, they were all assembled around the kitchen table. Jay was famished, as per usual, and shovelled his stew down like there was no tomorrow. Then a normal night in the Hall household followed: telly – sport or soaps, *Coronation Street* being Mum's favourite, the boys swapping channels to any footie that might be going, general chit-chat, cup of tea, off to bed.

Ellie opted for an early night. The trip up north, the interview, had drained her. Lying there under her single duvet, within the four pink-painted walls – one cerise, three blossom, (she'd chosen the shades aged twelve) of her small bedroom, she thought about her day at Claverham Castle. Was there any chance they might offer her the lease? If so – *wildest dreams* – would they also offer her a room there? What might it be like, working there, living there? Her dreams felt like bubbles, floating iridescent in a blue sky of hope. But, then, wasn't there always the inevitable pop, then plop, when you came splatting back down to earth?

Her thoughts spun on, sleep elusive. She should have been better prepared, done her homework, thought about it all more thoroughly. *And*, she hadn't even mentioned half the things in the interview that she'd mentally prepped in bed the night before. Maybe her mother *was* right; doing things on a whim was never the best option. But something inside told her she was right to try for that interview today. She'd been so excited reading the ad in the job pages of the *Journal*, then ringing up, actually getting an interview, taking those steps towards her dream. She *could* make a go of it, given half a chance. The *if* dangled before her, her dream on a very thin thread, making her feel queasy in the pit of her stomach.

Concrete, steel, glass – Ellie's working world. Tuesday, the day after her tearoom interview, and walking into the impersonal open-plan insurance office made her feel flat; just serving to remind her of how the next ten years might pan out – the most exciting prospect being a promotion to claims supervisor, more targets to push for, deadlines to beat, staff to rally.

The other staff there were fine, to be fair. Her ally, Gemma, the only one she could trust with the truth about the interview and why she'd taken a day's holiday, collared her at the coffee machine.

'*So?* How was it?' her friend uttered in hushed tones.

She knew how much this interview meant to Ellie, and had volunteered a few days ago, half-jokingly, to become a waitress for her should it all come off. Gemma was a townie through and through, and dreaded the thought of leaving the city for *anything*.

'It went okay-ish . . . I think,' Ellie whispered back, taking a plastic cup in hand, positioning it and pressing the button. 'It's hard to tell. There's someone else lined up for it, though, I think.'

'Ah, but you never know. Good luck!' Gemma smiled encouragingly right through to her blue-grey eyes. She was tall with a lean, boyish figure and platinum-blonde hair cut in a short, choppy style.

'I'm just waiting for . . .' Ellie started.

'Morning, ladies.' Weasly William, a colleague in their claims team, shuffled up beside them, making Ellie jump.

'Morning, Will,' Ellie replied. Gemma just raised her eyebrows. He always seemed to appear just when you were chatting about something you shouldn't: sex or alcohol, in Gemma's case. She was sure he did it on purpose. Her theory was, and this had been giggled over on many a night out, that he was either a spy for the management, a perve, or just fancied the pants off Ellie.

Anyway, his presence cut their conversation short.

'Right, then, I'd better get back to work,' Ellie said cheerily, taking her coffee with her.

'Catch you later, El. Full details at lunchtime. I'll get us a Krispy Kreme.' Gemma grinned.

Back in from work, her feet throbbing from the walk from the metro station to the house – not ideal in two-inch heels on uneven pavements with a gaggle of commuters.

Her mum shouted from the lounge as Ellie's feet hit the welcome mat, 'There's been a call for you.'

Ooooh. 'Oh, okay, who?' She sounded calmer than she felt.

'Joe, somebody-or-other . . . Uhm, Ward, I think.'

A lump tightened her throat. So this was it – the decision. The rejection. She'd be staying at the insurance office for the foreseeable future, then.

'Any message?' *Deep intake of breath.*

Ellie was frozen in the hall, her mum behind the closed door of the living room, by the muffled sound of her voice.

'Just, could you call him back? He'll be there until six. I've jotted the number down on the pad.'

Deeper breath. She glanced at her wristwatch. OH MY GOD – she only had ten minutes left to ring him back. She wanted to know, but it was almost better not to. At least now, not knowing, there was still the slightest possibility that she might be in with a chance. Her stomach lurched. She was planted to the spot.

Right, Ellie May Hall, her mind gave her a kick, keep to the 3 Cs – cool, calm, collected. She kicked off her stiletto shoes, wriggled her toes. The relief was fabulous. And now for the phone. All this fannying about had already lost her, she glanced at her watch again, two minutes.

'Okay, then,' she spoke aloud to herself, in her best calming tone. 'Let's do this thing.' She grabbed the notepad, pen, handset. All she had to do was dial the number. Gulp.

She didn't want to. What if she broke down, couldn't reply at the 'Sorry, but' bit?

And there was this horrid nagging thought that this would be the last time she would hear Joe's voice, and then she could forget about ever seeing him again. And why did that matter? It was weird, unsettling. And now there were only seven minutes to go . . . He might have left a bit early . . . JUST BLOODY RING HIM!

So she did.

Dial-a-dream coming up . . . or was it Dial-a-disaster?

0-1-6-6-5 . . . every punch on the handset seemed to impact on her heart.

The dialling tone. Her pulse quickened.

'Good afternoon, Claverham Castle, Deana speaking.'

Aah, Deana, a friendly voice.

'Hello, Deana. It's me, Ellie . . . umn, about the job. Umn, I think Joe called earlier, when I was out at work.' She was babbling, she knew; it always happened when she was nervous. 'Anyway, is he still there? Could you put me through?'

'Yes, I think he's still in the office. Give me a sec, Ellie, and I'll transfer the call.'

The longest pause, it felt like her dreams were holding their breath. Then his mellow tone, 'Joe Ward speaking.' He sounded formal.

'Oh, hello . . . you asked for me to call back. It's Ellie . . . about the tearooms.'

'Ah, Ellie, yes,' his tone softened. Was he just preparing her for the blow? 'Right, well . . .'

Another second of agony.

'We'd like to see you again, for a second interview.'

'You *would?*' Her tone was slightly incredulous. She wanted to laugh, for some weird reason.

'Yes, this Thursday, if that's at all possible.'

Two days.

'Would you be able to make it for eleven a.m.?'

She would. Of course she would.

'Yes, of course.' She'd have to play a sickie, but she'd do it, needs must. Gemma would cover for her, for sure. 'That'll be fine.' Oh My God, she'd have to prepare herself more this time, apply immediately for a course for her food and hygiene certificates, and find some other evidence of how fantastic she might be . . . but what? Oh well, she had two days to think about it. Google was going to get a lot of hits.

'Well, that's good. We were impressed with you at the interview.' It sounded like he was smiling.

You were?

'And we just want to find out a few more details. Check your experience, perhaps get a couple of references, that kind of thing.'

Ah, the one second of elation was replaced by a sinking feeling at his last words. She wondered if Kirsty at the café would give her a reference, make her sound more experienced than she was.

Mum poked her head out from the living-room door, eyebrows raised. Ellie made a small thumbs-up gesture and then tilted her head sideways with a jerk, indicating the phone call was still ongoing, as if to tell her to disappear.

'Right, well that's settled, Ellie. We'll see you on Thursday at eleven, then.'

'Yes . . . and thank you.' She hung on the line, heard the click and silence. It wasn't a yes by a long way, but it was a definite maybe. *Impressed* – the word swum in her mind. And she'd thought all she'd done was gabble on like a loony at the interview.

She did a little dance into the lounge, where Jason lay draped across a sofa and her mum was making a pretence of watching the telly, 'Well, then?'

'It's a maybe,' she sung, 'Guess who's got a second interview?'

Jason managed a nod and the word 'Cool'. Mum was more cautious, 'Well, that's good news, pet', adding, 'Now don't get your hopes up too high,' with a knowing smile.

29

Ellie was undeterred, skipped out into the hall, punched the air and then wondered how the hell she was going to keep up the good impression with virtually no experience and no qualifications to show for herself. Her skipping slowed.

3

Ellie

Sickie pulled, she was heading north again. Ellie turned off the A1, away from the trail of lorries and cars, driving one-handedly at times, the other securing the cake box that sat on her passenger seat as the lanes got more winding. The box contained the choffee cake, Nanna Beryl's special recipe, that she had created last night. A batch of cherry-and-almond scones, baked fresh at six-thirty this morning, were nestled in a tub in the foot well.

She'd thought and thought about how she might impress Lord Henry and Joe, but with her 'on paper' lack of experience, the only thing she could come up with was to take a sample of her baking along with her and suggest a spot of 'afternoon tea' at eleven o'clock. It was her best shot.

Ellie had turned to Nanna's recipe for 'choffee cake' in her hour of need, mixing and baking, and decorating it with fat curls of white and dark chocolate and those lovely dark-chocolate-covered coffee beans (her own tweak on the original recipe). She had been up until the early hours, as the first attempt hadn't risen as well as she wanted. Her mum appeared in the kitchen in her dressing gown and slippers, bleary-eyed, wondering what the heck her daughter was doing at one o'clock in the morning still cooking; she had thought they were being burgled. Oh, yes, she was an intruder bearing a pallet knife and chocolate buttercream, Ellie had joked.

Anyway, there she was driving rather precariously along the lanes, whilst securing her precious cargo. There was no way she was going to risk the whole lot sliding off the seat, down into the foot well, ending up a smashed mess.

She was on a long straight now and she relaxed a little. The panorama panned out ahead of her; sheep were scattered across rolling green fields, clusters of small villages, the foothills of the Cheviots. Cattle were languidly grazing, the odd shaggy head lifted and gazed across their domain. Could it be her domain? For a city kid she was curiously drawn to the countryside. When she was smaller the family used to come up for picnics to the Ingram Valley once or twice a year, park the car on the chewed-down grass of the river bank and spend the day in shorts and T-shirts paddling in the icy brown waters, damming up a small pool area. Finally coming out, to be wrapped in towels when the shivers struck, to munch away on cheese-and-ham sandwiches and packets of Mr Kipling angel slices or mini apple pies (her mother had somehow missed the baking gene). They'd often track down some other kids along the river bank and have a game of bat and ball or rounders, if there were enough of them. Then, the hour back down the road to Newcastle-upon-Tyne, tired and happy, leaving the sheep and the bracken in peace once more.

Her little Corsa wound its way down into the valley below, through a small village: stone cottages, a village pub, a friendly nod from an old man with his dog. She'd bet they all knew each other around here. Turned off at the sign for Claverham Castle.

That was when the nerves hit.

How the hell was she going to convince them that she could run a successful teashop and afford to pay the lease, when she wasn't even sure of it herself? She didn't even have any qualifications. She'd been chatting with Kirsty at her café, and she knew some of the basic health-and-hygiene and food-handling requirements from when she had worked there that time. And then there was the health and safety side of things to consider, customer service, staff issues – it seemed a bloody mine-field. If she hadn't spent half the night baking these bloody cakes, and the thought of her mother's 'I told you so' ringing in her ears as she landed back at Fifth Avenue, then she might have turned around right there and then.

Thankfully her optimistic alter ego took over, in fact the voice in her mind sounded very like Nanna Beryl's, 'You've got this far, girl, keep going. Just try your best and see what happens' and the warm flicker of her dream gave her the courage she needed to drive on. Turning into the castle driveway, she slowed instinctively to take it all in this time. Crocuses and snowdrops lined the grassy verges, making way for the tight yellow-green buds of daffodils just about to bloom; she'd hardly noticed these a few days before. Tall gnarled trees lined the track, dappling the road with shadows and light. Then the majestic outline of the stone castle itself, curls of smoke from a couple of its chimneys, the turrets along the rooftop. It was regular in shape, four storeys high with the main door bang smack in the middle and four square towers securing its corners; like a castle a child might draw. She wondered briefly what might have happened between its ancient walls, what trials and tribulations – the joys, the pain, loves, births, deaths?

And her own little bit of history about to unfold, would she ever be back? Was there a glimmer that her future might be here, for a while at least? What would it feel like to come here every day to work, to be baking cakes and scones, prepping sandwiches and soup in the kitchen, serving customers, dealing with Lord Henry, Joe? Her heart gave a tentative leap. If only she'd get the chance to find out.

She parked up, gave her hair a quick brush, then twisted it into a loose knot and popped it up in a clip at the back of her head. The last thing she wanted was a stray strawberry-blonde strand attaching itself to the chocolate buttercream of her pièce de resistance. She'd decided on wearing a dark-grey trouser-suit with flat black suede shoes this time – the high heels having proven tricky before, *and* she was going to have to carry the choffee cake and scones.

There was no sign of Deana or anyone at the front steps, so she would have to carry the goods all by herself. She took one last look in the rear-view mirror, slashed a little gloss over her lips. She'd have to do, it was ten to eleven, so she'd better get out and get on with it. Deep breath. Car door open. Check for muddy puddles – all clear. Phrases she'd practised were whizzing through her head, the likes of 'I am organised', 'a team player, with leadership skills too', 'able to take the initiative', 'sole responsibility of bistro/café', 'good business mind' (passed GCSE in business studies, got a B no less). Walk round car. Open passenger door. Hang the bag of scones from wrist. Lift cake box *very* carefully. A slow shift of the hip to close the passenger door. Proceed with caution to castle steps.

The main door was closed. There was an old-style bell button apparent, but how the hell was she going to press it without dropping the cake? She was starting to feel flummoxed when a crack appeared between the two heavy wooden doors. A gruff male voice said 'H'lo?' The crack widened to reveal a young man with a gappy grin and shorn-short hair, dressed in camouflage-style jacket and trousers.

'Hello, there, it's Ellie.' She was just about to add that she was here for an interview when Deana appeared at the lad's shoulder.

'Ah, Ellie, lovely to see you.' She was smiling broadly. 'Well, don't just stand there, James, let her in. And maybe give her a hand with that box. You can see she's struggling.' Deana's tone was bossy but not unkind; it seemed the young man needed help to understand what was required of him. Though he looked adult physically, there was something in his face, his eyes, that suggested to Ellie that his mind wasn't quite as advanced.

He made to grab the box. Ellie didn't want to reject his help but urged, 'It's a cake, be careful with it. Please hold the box flat, thanks.'

He nodded, holding the box like a fragile gift, his eyes lighting up at the word 'cake'.

Deana smiled again, 'If it's to be cut and there's any

left later, we might just save you a bit, James, if that's alright with Ellie?'

'Yes, of course. I thought it might be a good idea to show Lord Henry a sample of the kind of things I'd like to be baking for the teashop.'

'Hmn, now that sounds good.'

They followed Deana into the courtyard and then into what seemed to be her office on the ground floor. It was small and crowded with files and paperwork.

'Can I have a peek?' Deana asked.

'Yep, go ahead.'

Deana got James to lower the cake down onto her desk, then Ellie lifted a corner of the lid. They all peered in.

'Wow! That looks amazing. Well, there goes my diet if you get the job. I'll not be able to resist. It looks a darned sight better than anything Cynthia brought out at the end of last year when she was standing in, I must say.'

James stood there gazing in, eyes wide. He looked like he might actually drool.

'I'm sure there'll be some spare, James. Just ask Deana later,' Ellie said.

He grinned widely, showing the gap in his front teeth.

'Right, I'll just give Lord Henry a call and see if they're ready for you yet,' said Deana.

Ellie felt the nerves tightening inside her. The clock on the wall said five to. James was standing quietly.

'Thank you, James. Why don't you go and see Colin in the yard. He had some wood for you to chop for kindling.'

The young man nodded and left, with a last longing look at the cake box. Once he was out of earshot, Deana began to explain, 'He's a nice lad. Lives in the village. He had an accident on one of the farms when he smaller, never been quite the same since. He's a hard worker, mind. Lord Henry likes to give him some work when he can.'

That seemed a nice thing to do. Her opinion of Lord Henry lifted. He didn't seem quite as scary.

As Deana dialled through, Ellie looked around the office. There was a portable gas heater that looked like something out of the seventies; she seemed to remember Nanna having a smaller version in her flat years ago. A romantic novel was open, pages splayed face down, on the antique wooden desk; it looked as though Deana had been reading just before Ellie had got there. There was also a mobile phone, a computer monitor, a small framed photo of what looked to be Deana and her husband, and a half-empty cup of coffee with a pink lipstick mark on the rim. Behind Deana's head, on the wall, was a pen-and-ink print of the castle in former days, and a stuffed red squirrel in a glass box. The room was a curious combination of old and new.

'Just letting you know that Ellie Hall's here.' Some

muffled words came back down the line, 'Okay, I'll send her up, then.'

Deana gave a small thumbs-up signal, then placed the handset down.

'You're on. Good luck, pet. Can I give you a hand up those stairs with that cake? And I'll make a fresh pot of tea and coffee and bring them up after, shall I? I assume you've brought the cake and scones to try, they're not just for looking at?'

'Yes, that was the idea. Thanks, Deana, that would be lovely. Perhaps if you can take these scones, I'll manage the cake.' She didn't want any accidents at the last.

'Of course.'

Ellie sensed that she had someone on her side. Back across the courtyard they headed up the stone tower, Deana first, to the second-floor study again. Ellie took each step cautiously. She was glad of the black polo neck she'd popped on under the grey suit, and the cerise-pink scarf gave her a splash of colour as well as warmth – she was learning.

Well then, this was it, Round Two.

'Good luck.' Deana's smile was warm and genuine as she knocked on the office door, opened it, and gestured for Ellie to go in. Ellie tried to look her most confident, smiling as she placed the box carefully on Lord Henry's desk. Both he and Joe raised their eyebrows inquisitively. Joe then gave her a small grin. She felt a little flip inside. Deana said she'd be back with some tea and coffee, taking the scones back with her to plate up. The two men stood up at the same time. They were roughly the same height. Lord Henry shaking Ellie's hand first, 'Good morning, Ellen.'

'Morning.' She still didn't have the nerve to correct him. Then she turned to Joe.

'Welcome back,' the younger man's tone was warm as he took her palm in his own for a second or two, which gave her a weird, tingly feeling, probably just the nerves. 'Did you have a good journey?' he continued.

'Oh, yes, fine.' She held back a grimace; if only they could have seen her wrestling with the cake box around the corners. 'Except for some interesting cake-balancing in the lanes at the end,' she added, deciding to break the ice with some humour.

'Aah, I see.' Lord Henry smiled.

'Hmn, I hoped there might be something along those lines in there.' Joe was smiling too.

'Well, I thought you might like to actually taste my work, rather than me just tell you about it.' *Cos there isn't much to tell.* 'Give you an idea of what I might be serving in the tearooms, should I be lucky enough to obtain the lease.'

They were nodding as though that were a good idea, so Ellie warmed to her theme, 'Well, anyone can say they're a good cook or baker, but as my Nanna always used to say, "The proof of the pudding is in the eating".'

'Indeed,' agreed Lord Henry.

Right on cue, there was a knock at the door and Deana reappeared with a tray laden with a teapot, cups and saucers, the scones piled enticingly on a plate, with a mountain of butter in a dish beside them, forks, tea plates, the works.

'Thank you, Deana,' Lord Henry's tone was warm but still formal.

Ellie took this as the cue to unbox the choffee, spotting that Deana had thought to bring both a cake slice and large knife. 'Wow!' Deana exclaimed convincingly, despite having already seen the cake, 'That looks amazing. You lucky devils.' She grinned at the two men, in a show of envy.

Thank you, Deana. Ellie appreciated the support.

'Well, I'd better be on my way. Enjoy. It looks delicious.'

Ellie sliced the cake carefully. It was deep, moist and very chocolatey. The chocolate-coffee frosting was more or less intact, as were the chocolate curls and decorations, even after the zig-zag journey. 'Would you like to try some?'

Her hand was trembling a little as she placed a slice onto a tea plate.

'Certainly,' said Lord Henry. 'Yes, please,' Joe added.

'Choffee cake,' she announced, 'A favourite family recipe.'

The 'mmns' that accompanied their eating cheered her,

though she had no appetite and hadn't taken any for herself, her stomach still suffering from the nerves that had gripped it for days now. Joe poured them all some tea.

The two men sat back in their chairs after polishing off the slices of choffee. Then the more intense questioning began.

'Right then, Ellie, what do you know of the health and safety and good hygiene requirements for running a catering outlet?' Joe. 'And do you have the relevant certification to show for this?'

Gulp! *Hold your nerve, girl.*

'What experience do you have of dealing with and managing staff?' Lord Henry.

'How will you keep an eye on the accounts side of the business?' Joe.

'Have you taken any business advice?' Joe.

Questions were fired like bullets. She tried her best to answer honestly yet positively. It was like an interrogation, far more searching than last time, and Ellie's initial confidence surge from the high of the cake-tasting was plummeting fast. But she did have some kind of answer for every question: the nights spent fretting had meant she'd already gone over much of this in her mind, and she'd done a lot of research in her breaks at work. Yesterday, she had also got in touch with the small business advisor at her local bank for advice. Google had helped no end, too, and what she didn't yet have in the way of certification she'd already got her name down to take as soon as possible – her only white lie of the interview.

By the end of all the questions her head was spinning, she felt drained and was wondering once again how the hell she ever thought she could run a teashop? Having a dabble on Google, getting some advice and making a decent choffee cake didn't amount to a lot.

The interview drew to a close after she'd had the chance to ask some questions herself. She'd remembered to ask about the terms of the lease and how that worked. How long it would be for? (One season, initially, as a trial, from Easter through to the end of October.) And she asked if there were any tearoom staff expecting to return to their jobs from last year? She'd need help with waitressing at least. There were two apparently: Doris and Nicola. Ellie thought she saw Joe's face look a little strained as he mentioned Doris.

As they stood to shake hands, the interview drawing to a close, Ellie felt utterly exhausted.

'Thank you for taking the time to come along today,' Lord Henry's words and thin smile were unreadable – Ellie reckoned he'd make a great poker player.

Joe's dark eyes held a flicker of warmth as their hands connected in a farewell grasp. 'The cake was delicious,' he said encouragingly. She managed a hopeful smile back.

She stared a second too long, lost to the green flecks amongst the intense deep-brown of his irises, then stood back as his grip released.

Cool, Calm, Collected – her mantra back in place. 'Thank you very much for asking to see me again,' she managed, 'I look forward to hearing from you.'

4

Joe

Well, he hoped Lord Henry wasn't going to be a stick-in-the-mud about this one . . . That cake was bloody delicious. She could cook, she seemed organised, had good ideas for the future of the business, she was intelligent, hardworking . . . and, she was pretty. Yes, she *was* attractive, wasn't she – lovely green eyes and that honey-blonde hair piled on top of her head. He wondered what it would look like loose, how long it would be? Christ, what was the matter with him, thinking about her looks? Anyway, that was all beside the point, though being attractive would certainly help draw in the clients. Definitely be more damned appealing than that Cynthia-bloody-Bosworth woman, with her hips that stuck out at right angles to her body: she could probably use them as trays.

And, it wasn't as though they'd had a queue of applicants for the job.

Oh, but Henry could be so bloody-minded and set in his ways, insisting on carrying on with the 'same old' just because it had always worked alright. Alright? Didn't he want anything to work better? Joe felt that for the past four years he'd been trying to drag his boss kicking and screaming into the twenty-first century, when in fact Henry was only just getting used to the twentieth century. He'd only just managed to persuade him to get Deana a computer three years ago. There had been paper ledgers and everything was being handwritten, which wouldn't have been quite so bad if Lord Henry's handwriting had been legible in the first place. Deana had done her best to get the administration in order, but Joe had realised that much of the paperwork had been left to flounder when Lady Hogarth had passed away.

One of the earliest tasks that Joe had set himself was to set up a website and get the castle some internet presence – other than the tourist information centres and the occasional drive-by, no one really knew they existed – which was probably how Lord Henry preferred it. But the castle needed income, and quickly, if it was going to survive. A chap called Michael, from a marketing company in the nearby town of Alnwick, had helped set up the website and designed some new brochures and adverts to attract the tourists. Trying to get Lord Henry to realise that most businesses these days had a web presence, and to commit some funds to that, was like drawing blood from a stone, but he and Michael got there in the end.

Everything seemed a battle, but over time Joe had learned how to handle Henry – introduce the idea and the reasons why it would be beneficial, for example, why they should take Ellie on, and then leave Henry to it, so in time he began to think it was his own idea after all. The 'gently, gently' approach seemed to work, and 'slowly, slowly' . . . but they didn't have a lot of time with this one, Easter was less than three weeks away. The tearooms would need a freshen up before opening, staff would need to be in place, deliveries supplied . . . There was a massive amount of work to do in a short time.

'So what do you think?' Joe put the question out there as the two of them sat in the study after the interview.

'Hmn, I might just have another slice of that cake. It was rather good, I must say. But I do still have one or two reservations. She seems very young and there is a real lack of experience there.'

'But the cake's pretty damn good, isn't it, and the scones? She's proved she can cook. I can always advise if there are any management issues. At the end of the day we need good food, good service and a clean venue. And if the food is right, then people will come along, recommend us and come back. That's what we need.' He was sticking his neck out. But he really didn't want to be dealing with Cynthia, her grumpy attitude and her tasteless lumpy cakes. She'd covered a couple of weeks last year when Mrs Charlton had taken a fortnight off for a bunion operation. And in that short time she'd managed to upset the waitresses, Doris and Nicola – though upsetting Doris was an easy enough thing to do – not to mention a couple of their regular customers.

'Ellie is pleasant, she seems well organised, a hard worker, ambitious, with some good ideas too,' he continued.

Lord Henry gave him a sour look. Dammit, he realised he'd overstepped the mark. New ideas were always suspicious to Henry. They were not tried and tested.

'And how will a young girl like that manage the staff?'

'She's worked in a team for a long while, and seems to have managed well when she had responsibility for her friend's café. And anyway, it didn't take Cynthia very long to upset Doris and Nicola, did it?'

'Hmmn,' was the answer he got. Then Lord Henry started with, 'Cynthia doesn't need to give notice.'

'Well, that's only because she's unemployed at the moment. So that's the best reason to take her on, then, is it?' He couldn't hide the hint of sarcasm in his tone. 'Look, I think Ellie will be good. I like her,' were Joe's final words on the matter.

Lord Henry merely pressed his lips together.

There was no more to be said just now, so Joe got up

to leave. The older man was never going to make a decision that quickly, not with the girl just five minutes out of the room. Joe was already by the door. He turned, saying, 'We can't leave it too long, Henry. We've interviewed them both twice now, and it's not as though there's a queue of applicants. Easter is just over three weeks away, and I don't know how to cook a batch of scones, do you?' He challenged his boss with a stare, as if to say over to you, but I'll be arguing my case.

Lord Henry's stare back didn't falter, 'I'll see.'

Deana came in through the part-open door to clear the crockery. Joe guessed that she was rooting for Ellie too. Hopefully she would set to work on Lord Henry as well. A double-pronged fork action – that might just do the trick. But he could be such a stubborn old bugger. Joe was sure Deana had warmed to Ellie; the way she had helped with the tea and coffee, laid out the scones. She was on Ellie's side. The last thing she would want was another bossy middle-aged woman in the castle . . . She was enough herself, and would be the first to admit it!

'We'll speak later.' Joe walked on out the door. He had loads to do. He was getting a new flyer made up to distribute around other local attractions and the tourist information centres. He needed to organise an advert too for the local *Gazette* as they were doing a special 'What's On Over Easter' section. And he had to call in some contractors to look at repairs to the roof after last week's storms; some missing tiles had caused a leak in the Edward I Room. God, this place was falling apart, and, boy, did they need to pick up their visitor numbers this year and improve their income! The repairs and staff bills alone would eat up any chance of a profit they might make. And the farm side of the estate was only just covering its costs. Yet he'd grown fond of this place, this crumbling crazy castle that he thought of as home, and had built up over these past four years. He didn't want to see it fail now, be sold off to some property developer and made into flats. Surely Lord Henry didn't want that either, but the whole damn place was at risk of turning to dust.

Joe wound his way down the stone stairwell and headed for the great hall, which was the quickest way to get across to the opposite wing, where his own office and apartment were. There were two huge fireplaces in the hall, and an immense mahogany table that virtually filled the room. There must have been thirty-six chairs set at it. Deana would lay it all out with crockery and glasses just before the Easter visitors were due, ready for the banquet that never happened. The tourists could only look at it. But why couldn't it be used, why couldn't they move on to doing functions; weddings? Ellie seemed the sort of ambitious businesswoman who could drive that forward; the castle might be able to do function catering. That would surely bring more income in. Yes, they'd get booking fees, they might even let some of the bedrooms out as guest suites and bring these rooms to life once more. Give this place a future not just a past.

But would he ever manage to persuade Lord Henry?

*

Five days . . . five days it had taken, of arguing his case, then backing off a bit. The 'softly, softly' approach. But they were desperately in need of getting someone into the position. Lord Henry couldn't make *any* decision in a hurry, oh no, and the poor girl and that awful Cynthia woman were left hanging by a thread, no doubt wondering what was going on.

Well, at least he was making the call now.

A lady answered the phone, middle-aged by her tone, definitely not Ellie. He introduced himself and then heard her shout away from the receiver but still pounding in his ears, 'It's for you, Ellie. That Joe chappie from the castle, I think.' Must be her mother, he mused, with a wry smile.

He was sure he heard a little squeal in the background, of excitement or fear; he wasn't certain. It made him grin. He could picture her dashing to the phone – it was a nice image. He couldn't help but notice at the interview that she had generous boobs, they were sure to be bouncing. His heart rate cranked up. God, what was he thinking?

He was usually very professional about these things, and he would continue to be. Image removed promptly.

'Hel-lo,' her pitch was higher than he remembered. She sounded nervous.

'Hi, Ellie, it's Joe Ward here. I'm just calling to let you know . . .' He sensed her holding her breath. He could drag this out, but that wouldn't be fair on the girl. 'Well, I'd like to offer you the lease on the Claverham Castle Teashop for the season.'

Silence for a second, then her voice, 'You *would*?'

'Yes, I would.' There was a hint of amusement in his tone.

'Oh . . . My . . . Goodness.'

It wasn't quite the response he'd expected, but it made him feel good, nonetheless. He'd obviously just made her day. And her genuine enthusiasm and warmth gave him even more confidence in his decision, though she'd have an awful lot to pick up in a short space of time . . . but he could help; he'd seen how the tearooms had worked over the past couple of years, and the improvements she could easily make. As the landlord, and his experience in running the estate, he knew the ins and outs of health and safety, insurance requirements and the like, he could put her on the right track. And then . . . functions . . . the future. His mind was rolling along. Yet, there was no further response down the line. Was she still there?

Come to think of it, she hadn't actually said 'yes', had she? 'Oh My Goodness' wasn't exactly a yes, he realised. 'Would you like some time to think about it, Ellie?'

'Oh no, well yes. The answer's definitely yes.'

'Great . . . Well, we'd like you to start as soon as possible, to get things up and running before the Easter weekend opening. But I realise you will probably have to work some notice with your present company.'

'Oh, I've already looked into that. I officially have to give a month, but I had an off-the-record chat with my supervisor, you know, just in case, and I'm already owed a week-and-a-half as holiday, so she said she could let me go in two weeks. That'd mean I could be with you at the castle a week before the opening weekend.'

She seemed to have thought things through and be organised. He was pleased she was already living up to expectations.

'Okay, well that should be enough time to get the place ready, *just*,' he added with a smile.

'Great.'

'And if you have any particular questions and queries in the meanwhile just give me a call. I deal more with the day-to-day running issues at the castle, so best to ask for me rather than Lord Henry.'

* * *

Ellie

Any questions or queries? My God, she had a running list in her mind . . . But they *wanted* her, she had the lease. Wayy-hayyy! She was having trouble keeping still, bouncing on her toes in the hallway of their terraced house. She was going to be her own boss, under the watchful, not unattractive, deep-brown eyes of Joe Ward, and she was going to be working and living (hopefully!) in . . . a . . . castle. Were there any pressing questions? She couldn't possibly ask all the ninety-seven that were bouncing in her head!

'Thanks . . . Actually, yes, there is something. You mentioned at interview there might be accommodation with the role. Umn, is that still the case?'

'Oh.' He sounded as if he was thinking on the spot. 'Well, we can sort you out with one of the guest rooms in the castle. I'll get Deana to get it all organised for you. Does that sound okay?'

'Ah, yes . . . And would that be included in the lease payment, or will I have to pay extra as rent?' She was a little concerned as to how far Nanna's money was going to have to go.

'Umn, maybe a nominal fee but nothing too much, don't worry. I'll have a quick think on it and let you know, if that's alright.'

Again she had the feeling he was thinking on his feet.

The previous tearoom leaseholder had probably lived locally. This seemed to be a new prospect for him.

'Okay, well thank you. And thanks for giving me this opportunity . . . I won't let you or the castle down.' She had the feeling it was more his decision than Lord Henry's that she had the offer. She just hoped that in reality she could keep that promise.

'I have every confidence in you, Ellie. We'll speak again soon.'

'Thanks again. Bye.'

'Goodbye, Ellie.'

Oh wow, she was going to be living in a castle in two weeks' time. She was bouncing again. She suddenly felt like Cinderella.

5

Ellie

'Just one more flight,' Ellie tried to sound cheery against the noise of her father's huffing and puffing. She *had* rather overloaded that case. Thank heavens he was well built and strong, but she'd need plenty of clothes, and the jumpers and cardigans were essential this time of year, especially here.

It was cold and draughty in the stairwell, though her dad was dripping with sweat, balancing her massive suitcase against his broad chest as he wound his way up the spiral staircase to her room. Jason was following with a huge black sack of shoes, and her mum was tottering behind with a cardboard box full of kettle, mugs, tea, coffee and basic food essentials to start her off.

Deana had showed Ellie and her family up to her new

lodgings ten minutes earlier. They all stood nodding appreciatively, taking in the room. It wasn't hotel grade, but it wasn't bad, considering Joe had asked a mere £100 a month for it – which was some relief. It was a medium-sized bedroom with a high ceiling, white-painted walls, a double bed with black-metal bedposts (like something out of Mary Poppins), a simple dark-wood dressing table and stool, wardrobe, cosy armchair in burgundy velvet – there seemed to be a lot of red velvet around the place – that had seen better days but was extremely comfy when she tried it out, and a small fireplace that was set with kindling and coal but not lit. The only other source of heat was a solitary Victorian-looking radiator that was merely lukewarm. Dad set about trying to adjust the valves, letting some air out with a radiator key he'd had in his coat pocket – the joys of being a plumber.

In all honesty, the room was a bit drab and Mum looked nonplussed. The small window served to highlight the fact it was grey and drizzling outside, and that didn't help matters either. But Ellie was determined to stay positive, setting out a few nick-nacks from her room at home, and installing a small TV on the end of the dressing table (was there an aerial point?), and she had her new double duvet to put out (thank heavens she'd gone for the toasty twelve-tog). She'd chosen red-and-cream country-style plaid covers with red scatter cushions to match. It'd be fine. She'd make it feel homely.

Deana had set out a kettle and tea bags, mugs and biscuits for them. Ellie was touched by her kindness. It was lovely that she'd made such an effort to welcome her.

'Thanks for the tea stuff,' Ellie remarked later, passing her office with armfuls of gear.

'Oh that's no bother, flower, thought you'd need a cuppa after tripping up and down those stairs with all your stuff. Do you need a hand with anything?'

'We're fine, thanks,' Dad answered, passing by with a stack of DVDs. 'We'll manage won't we, Son,' he clipped Jason's ear, who shrugged his shoulders with embarrassment.

'Okay, then. But if there's anything you need, Ellie, just pop in and give me a shout. Joe's about somewhere too. I expect he'll drop by at some point. And really . . . don't be afraid to ask if there's anything you want, or we can help you with. Welcome to Claverham Castle.'

Dad and Jason headed back to the car to unload the next lot of luggage, while she and her mum took the new bedcover set out of its packaging, tugging it over the duvet and pillowcases.

'Are you sure you're going to be alright here?' Sarah began tucking the sheet in, muttering 'Well, this has seen better days,' as she eyed the mattress with caution.

'Of course, Mum. Look, it's what I really want to do. And I just need a change, to get out and do something different. I've never really enjoyed the insurance job.'

'Well yes, maybe with everything that's happened these past months . . . I can see that, but to move right away, from your family and everything. Won't it just make things harder?'

Ellie didn't answer that question. She wasn't sure whether it would or not yet. 'I'll show you the kitchen and teashop before you go.' She quickly changed the subject. 'So you can see where I'll be working.'

'Oh, pet, I do hope it all works out for you. But you know you can always come back if it doesn't. It's such a way out up here. Won't you find it lonely? You know your dad and I can be here within the hour if you need us.'

'Mum, thanks for your concern but I have a car, I'll not be stranded and there are other people here. It's not just me. It'll be fine, I promise.' And even if it wasn't, she wasn't going to be giving up any time soon; she'd already promised herself she'd stick the full season out, *whatever happened.*

A black sack on legs wobbled at the door. 'Give us a hand, Ells, this weighs a ton.' Jason nearly fell into the room. It was her books and CDs. She loved reading and had a great selection of cookbooks, baking manuals and, of course, her nanna's beloved Be-Ro book (that one was packed safely in her case). She managed to catch the front of the bag from Jason before they all tipped out. Dad appeared with a second suitcase, more clothes; she'd packed for winter, spring and summer, though summer seemed a long way off. On a day like today it was hard to imagine the castle as anything but cold and grey.

'I'll make us some tea then, shall I?' her mum popped the kettle on, while Ellie checked out the adjoining room – she'd spotted a white wooden door, thick with layers of paint, leading off from the bedroom. It opened onto a small shower room, with a basic white sink, shower cubicle and loo – at least she had an en suite. Very posh. On closer inspection, the cold tap on the sink had evidently dripped over the years and left a metallic green trail on the porcelain. The window had condensation inside, and there didn't appear to be a radiator in there – that didn't bode well. It'd be freezing of a morning, for sure. 'Bathroom,' she announced chirpily as she stepped back out.

They had tea and biscuits – three of them perched on the bed, Dad in the armchair – chatting on inanely about the castle. It's just *so* old, Mum kept repeating. *What did she expect?* Her family commenting on her room – general consensus *not bad*, the weather, the journey. Then they had a quick tour of the castle, via the rooms Ellie had already seen, on the way to the tearooms.

She stood there, bigging up the huge kitchen space she had to work in, and explaining that it would all look different out front in the teashop when it was up and running. It had an air of shabbiness about it at the moment that certainly wasn't shabby chic. She made a mental note to go and buy new oilcloths for the tables and some posy vases – for spring flowers on each table – that would perk things up a bit for the customers on the Easter weekend. She tried to distract her mother from the grimier parts of the kitchen – buying disinfectant, rubber gloves, and scrubbing the place from top to bottom would be her main priority tomorrow. Ooh, and placing an order for all the food she needed for the coming week (she had no real idea of quantities – she'd ring Kirsty in the sandwich bar later). Joe had mentioned in a phone call that they used Breakers for most of the supplies, and that they delivered daily. She wondered where he was – hadn't seen anything of him as yet today. She had so much to think of, her mind was spinning.

The time was approaching for her parents to leave, the late-afternoon light thinning outside, and Ellie began to feel a little strange. She'd holidayed with friends before, been away from home for the odd week or two, but had never lived away for any real time. Okay, so she was twenty-six, and for all her bravado that she was doing the right thing and would be fine, it still felt odd. An elastic twinge of vulnerability pulled inside.

'Well then, lass, we'd better be setting off shortly.' Her dad grasped her to him in a big bear hug. Oh shit, there was a mist of tears in her eyes, better not let Mum see, or they'd have her whisked back home to safety in the back of Dad's van.

'Yes, pet. It'll be coming in dark soon enough,' her mother agreed, 'We'd better be going. Now, are you sure you've got everything you need?'

'She's brought half the house, Mam. We'll probably find we've got nothing left when we get home,' Jason joked, softly punching his sister in the ribs.

They left the dim light of the tearooms and walked out into the courtyard and towards the main doors. The elastic band in her gut was pulling tighter.

'Make sure you ring, now, and tell us how you're getting on. We want regular updates,' Mum said, her voice waivering.

'I will, of course.' Stay *cool, calm, collected.*

'And you'll pop home and see us sometimes too.' Dad's eyes looked a bit misty.

'I promise. I'm only an hour away, and I'm sure I'll get the odd day off. Once I've settled in and got things up and running, I'll come and see you all.'

'See ya, Sis.' Jason put an arm about her shoulders with a squeeze.

There was a knot forming in her throat now.

'Oh, and we'll come up to visit you too, no reason why not,' Dad grinned. 'Come and sample the food here! It'd better be good,' he laughed. Then he began fishing in his back pocket, pulling out banknotes. He counted out a hundred pounds and handed it to Ellie. 'Just in case, pet.'

'Oh, you don't need to, Dad. I've got savings.'

'I know I don't *need* to pet, but I *want* to. Take it.'

'Aw, thanks, Dad.'

'Where's mine, then?' Jason jested.

'Yours can wait till *you* leave home. It might give you an incentive. Just think of the peace and quiet we'll get then, hey, Mam.'

They all laughed, a little too loudly, anxiety feeling its way through the four of them. The family dynamics were about to change.

At the main castle door now, Ellie pulled across the heavy metal bolt, turned the latch. And there she was, on the threshold of her new life. Hugs, kisses and 'Byes'. They were walking away, the rest of her family, back to Dad's white work van. Waves and more goodbyes shouted from wound-down windows, a toot of the horn, and she watched with a lump in her throat and tears in her eyes as the van got smaller and smaller, until it was swallowed up by the vast tree-lined driveway.

Well, that was it. She was on her own now, and she had to make damned sure this new life and her teashop dream worked out.

6

Ellie

She was lying on the bed, having emptied one case, which filled the whole wardrobe before she had even opened the second. She had crammed her books onto two shelves that were set into an alcove in the wall, the overflow pile stacked under her bed. Hmn, storage was going to be an issue.

There was a knock on the door.

'Come in,' her voice sounded strange and echoey in this high-ceilinged room.

Joe popped his head around the door. 'Only me! Just thought I'd see how you were settling in. Sorry I didn't get chance to come a little earlier and meet your family. Deana said they've gone now. I got held up – bit of a problem down on the farm.'

So, there was a farm to deal with on the estate too; Joe

must have a lot to keep up with here. He was hovering on the threshold. She suddenly felt awkward lying there on the bed, so sat up briskly, 'Come on in.'

He walked to the armchair and perched on the edge of it as though he didn't intend staying long. 'Is the room okay? Do you have everything you need?'

'It's fine, thank you.'

'I'm afraid you might find it a bit chilly. The central heating system's a bit antiquated through the castle, seems to have a mind of its own. There is the coal fire. I'll get James to fetch you up some more coal and logs if you'd like.'

He must have spotted the blank look on her face. She hadn't a clue how to keep a fire going, she was worried she might end up setting the room alight – they had an electric flame-effect affair in the lounge at home in Heaton, and toasty hot radiators throughout.

'Actually, I'll bring you down the electric heater from my office – that'll take any chill off.'

'Oh no, it's fine. You might need it.'

'It's okay. I'm hardened to the cold by now. No, I'll bring it across, honestly by the morning you'll be glad of it.'

'Okay, then, thank you.'

'Well, we'll have a proper meeting tomorrow, talk about the tearooms, any questions you might have, information you might need, all that kind of stuff. For now, I'll let you settle in. Oh, and if you want to cook for yourself just go ahead and use the kitchen in the tearooms. And if you think of anything else, or you need anything, my rooms are on the floor above you, this wing. Just go one more flight up the staircase and knock on my door. It's got a sign saying Keep Out on it.'

She laughed, 'That sounds very welcoming!'

'Oh yes,' he grinned. (He had a lovely smile, which made his eyes sparkle, she mused.) 'Well, that's just for the tourist season, they tend to wander off the recommended route in the guide book and get everywhere, and think they can barge in wherever they like just because they've paid a fiver to get in! You might think about getting a sign for your door before the weekend, and don't forget to keep it locked once we're open. Other times it's fine, you can trust the staff here with your life, they're a great bunch, but the tourists . . .' He shook his head, but was still smiling.

He seemed much more friendly now they were out of interview mode, Ellie noted. 'I'll bear that in mind.' She smiled back.

He stood up, as though he were about to leave.

'Oh, Joe, is there a TV point or anything?'

'There is an aerial socket in the corner here.' He pointed behind the small table, where Deana had left the kettle and cups. 'Good luck with reception, though. It's a bit hitty-missy.'

Sounds like the bloody radiators, she thought. 'Okay, well, I'll give it a go and see how I get on.' What the hell would there be to do here of an evening if there was no telly? Well, at least she had her iPod and laptop. There was always iPlayer. And then another thought dawned on her, 'Any wi-fi?' *Please, please.*

'Now, there you are in luck. But only because you're in this wing, Lord Henry doesn't have a computer his side of the castle, but I'm pretty sure the wi-fi router from my room will connect through down to here. Try it now and we'll see.'

She took up her laptop case and started the computer up. As she tried to get into the internet there, to her delight, was the wi-fi symbol, and a message asking her for a password. Joe spotted it and then his cheeks seemed to colour. He said nothing for a second or two, just gave her a funny look.

'What is it?' she asked.

'You need a password.'

'Okay, *and?*'

He pulled a face, 'Okay . . . it's Batman.'

She stifled a giggle.

His brown eyes crinkled with an embarrassed smile. 'Well, don't you like Batman? Those films are great.'

In fact, she had liked the films, when she was about twelve. But she just hadn't expected a superhero crush from him and not at thirty, or whatever age he was. But it made her smile widen, shifting her view of him from the nice, slightly scary and far-too-intelligent boss as per the interviews, to someone far more human. As she shrugged her shoulders with a grin, he ducked for the door. 'Okay, well, I'll fetch that heater for you.'

Later that evening, she lay in bed, with her zebra-print onesie on and thick socks. It was bloody freezing in that room – the radiators must go off at night. If she got out of bed, she could put on the electric heater that Joe had brought down for her. But she didn't fancy getting out at all, the cold air would blast her the minute she lifted that duvet, so she just snuck further down under the quilt, listening to the lonely sound of an owl hooting. There had been a weird cry outside earlier, too, probably a fox or something. It was high-pitched like a baby's wail. Ooh, she hoped the castle wasn't haunted – don't be daft, she chided herself, what a load of old nonsense. Get to sleep, Ells-bells. Jason's nickname for her floated around in her head. You've got a big day ahead.

She lay there thinking, finding it hard to settle. It was nice that Joe had given up his heater for her. She liked him. He actually seemed quite down to earth and approachable, was probably very clever and had a nice smile. She remembered the Batman thing and grinned in the dark. As she thought of him, a warm glow flooded her. It surprised her. It was the first time she had felt that in an absolute age. Oh well, there'd be nothing in it, of course: a) there was no way she was going anywhere near men or relationships for the foreseeable future, and b) he was her landlord and they'd be working together – and getting involved in the workplace was never a good idea, a total no-no in her book. Gemma at work had done the boss thing at her previous workplace – big mistake – ended up having to give up her job in the end, all got far too messy. And the 'man' thing, well, she didn't want to dwell on that. Onwards and upwards, or as bloody far away from all that relationship stuff as possible. Still, a little glow in Joe's presence might be allowable. Just in terms of eye candy, that was all. But what she really had to concentrate on was getting the teashop venture up and running and making a success of it.

There was just so much to organise: clean the kitchen from top to bottom – main priority tomorrow – then meet up with Joe and go through everything. She'd need to order food in and ingredients, find the local suppliers, check if there was crockery and cutlery to use, buy those oil-cloths she fancied and find some posy vases and a florist to supply flowers, something cheap to cheer up the tearooms, bake like a mad thing, menus – bloody hell, yes, she'd need menus – she'd have to draft something on her laptop, meet the wait-ressing staff, the list droned on in her fractious mind. And she only had four days in which to do it! Tomorrow was Monday. They opened to the public on Friday at ten o'clock, Good Friday. It'd be Easter weekend and Go, Go, Go! Aaagh! Had she bitten off so much more than she could chew?

She finally got off to sleep in the early hours, to the sounds of the owl hooting away like her night watchman, rain tapping on the glass and the drumming of her heart.

7

Ellie

She was up a ladder, yellow rubber gloves on, washing
down the tiled walls that were grimed with a layer of
cooking grease. She'd found an old-fashioned portable
radio that had been left on a shelf and had tuned in to
Radio 1, and set herself up with a large bucket of steaming
water and disinfectant, some all-purpose cloths, a mop,
and currently Ellie Goulding as background music.

The check list of to dos was still running through her
mind. She needed to plan her menu ASAP. She'd keep it
simple for now – test the waters, see what sold, make
homemade soups, jacket potatoes, paninis and sandwiches, a selection of her yummiest cakes, scones, yes,
and maybe some cookies. Exactly *when* she was going to
actually bake all these before Friday she wasn't quite sure,

but as her baking needed to be fresh she could envisage a very long day and *night* on Thursday.

She scrubbed away, humming, taking a scourer to the particularly gungey bits. Her mind was back on the food order. What quantities would she need? Bloody hell, she didn't have a clue. Twenty jacket potatoes, thirty, fifty? Paninis – twelve, thirty-six, seventy-two? She may as well put the numbers in a hat and do a lucky dip. She suddenly felt extremely naïve and unprepared, and had a little wobble on her ladder. Right, focus. She'd check how often the suppliers delivered – see if it was just the weekend she was catering for, and she could ring her friend Kirsty at the café. She'd surely have some idea.

She could speak with Joe, but she didn't warm to the latter idea, not wanting to appear inept before she even got started. She didn't want him to regret his decision to back her.

One wall scrubbed and finished, Ellie was on tiptoes by the window, trying to get a signal on her mobile phone.

'Hi there, Kirsty.'

'Ellie, is that you? Hi, how's it all going out in the sticks? Are you up and running yet?'

'Friday's D-Day. Look, are you busy? I just need a bit of advice.'

'No, I'm okay for a sec. My customers are all served. Fire away.'

'It's the ordering – likely numbers I'm catering for,

what to buy in? I haven't a flippin' clue. I can't believe I'm such a numpty.' She could hear her mother's warning tones, *I told you so*, running in her ears.

'Ok-ay,' even Kirsty sounded as though she wondered what the hell Ellie had taken on. 'Right, well, look you've got to get an idea of numbers of customers to start. Decide on your menu, and then I can help with what to order. But yeah, numbers, bums on seats . . . Did you get any paperwork or accounts when you applied? Can you get figures now?'

'Umn, well I have the accounts. The Easter figures looked pretty good, but how the hell do you convert pounds profit into how many bloody jacket potatoes and cakes sold?'

'Hmn, right. Well, they must take a record of visitors to the castle, surely? If I were you, I'd ask if they have some idea how many people tend to call in at the tearooms. It's worth a try, and should give you some indication at least.'

'Yeah, I suppose so.'

'And buy in stuff that won't spoil too quickly or can freeze. You can even freeze some of the cakes if need be, as soon as you've baked them, so they're nice and fresh. Take them out as you need.'

'Okay, that sounds a good idea.'

'Oh, hang on . . . Yes, sorry, a latte . . . and a cappuc-cino, no problems. If you just take a seat I'll bring them over . . . Ellie, sorry, I'm going to have to go. Ring me back in a while, and try and get that info.'

'Will do, thanks.' Right, she needed to have a word with Joe, or maybe Deana. It looked like Deana took the admissions for the castle; her office was right on the main gate. Ellie was seeing Joe shortly anyhow, but how could she confess to not having a clue about the ordering? Oh well, she'd scrub the next kitchen wall, that'd be two out of the four done, and then make herself a cup of tea. She'd take five minutes time out to think carefully, and write down a list of everything she needed to ask Joe, to get herself organised. Ooh, and she'd have a look and see what kind of freezer and fridge storage they had. She'd noticed a couple of big chest freezers out in the corridor as well as the one in the kitchen; they must be to do with the tearooms.

She went out to the hallway. Jeez! They hardly needed freezers out here, it was bitterly cold. She opened the lid of one of them. Jesus Christ! What the hell was that? She dropped the lid down in shock, pinching her finger in the seal. 'Shit!' Then raised it slowly again, just a few centimetres, peering in tentatively. Well, that certainly wasn't loaves of bread or spare milk!

Antlers – it was friggin' antlers! Attached to fur and a head. Some poor deer, by the looks of it, its head sealed in a clear plastic bag. What the hell? It made her feel sick. Bambi's bloody dad was stuck in her freezer. What was with this place and deer? Ice Age Bambi on steroids in the tearooms and now this. At least it wasn't a human body, she mused. Well, that was certainly going on Joe's list for the one o'clock meeting: freezer space, why the hell is there a beheaded deer in what I presume is one of the tearoom freezers, and please can it be removed to make way for my paninis and spare milk? Back to the task in hand. The disinfectant was beginning to smart her eyes by the end of the third wall. She was sure she'd reek of it. She was going to mop the lino floors with some bleach next, and then she'd have another cup of tea and add some more to that list.

Deana popped her head around the door. 'Hi, Ellie, how's it all going?'

'Not bad thanks. I'm on a major cleaning session.' She clambered down off her ladder, happy to have a short break. Ellie mentioned the visitor records. It was a relief to find they did take that information, and Deana promised to get it ready for her in time for her meeting with Joe. One hurdle over at least. But she had a feeling there were going to be plenty more.

'Have you got time for a quick cuppa?' Ellie offered.

'Only if you have, pet. Looks like you've got a lot on.'

'Well, five minutes won't hurt, and I was ready for a cup anyhow. I'm parched and my tongue tastes of disinfectant.'

'Okay, then. Thank you.'

Ellie popped the kettle on and set out a teapot for the brew.

'Deana, do they have any strange habits here I should know about?' She was still thinking about Bambi's dad out in the corridor.

'Oh, yes, for sure. Lord Henry's often a little quirky, but are there any particular ones you're interested in?' Deana had a wry grin on her face.

'The freezer, that's all. There's something *unusual* in there.'

'Oh God! He's not saving stuff for the bloody taxidermist again, is he? What's he got in there this time?'

Ellie wasn't even sure what a taxidermist was – not someone who gave you a lift anyhow, but she had a feeling Deana knew exactly what was going on.

'Animal?'

'Yep.'

'Which?'

'Deer. A stag I think.'

'Ah, it'll be for stuffing and wall-mounting, not my kind of thing. But each to their own. It's a country, hunting thing. But I've told him before not to use the bloody tearoom freezers. It probably didn't fit in his own, that's all.'

Hunting trophies. Collecting animal heads. That was just weird. Country life was certainly odd!

They had a quick cup of tea and a nice chat, Deana

mentioning some of the other castle workers who she might meet in the coming days. Then she said she'd better be getting on, and leave Ellie in peace.

'Just give me a shout if you need anything, though. Ring a nine for the office.'

'Okay, thanks, Deana. Will do.'

Then Ellie set herself away with the mop and bucket once more.

It was five to one, and she realised she hadn't had any lunch and her whole body was aching. She still had the two ovens to clean, the microwave, and then all the working surfaces needed a thorough going-over with antibacterial spray. But it'd have to wait till later in the afternoon now. She needed to see Joe – armed with her million and one questions. She peeled off her rubber gloves, already with a sticky leak in the right index fingertip, and set off across the courtyard, up the stairs, past her own room and up again.

Standing before the Private Keep Out sign, it dawned on her, unfortunately just *after* she had knocked, that she was wearing an old tracksuit sporting bleach marks and her hair was scraped back in a ponytail. Damn.

His 'Come in' was formal. He was on the phone as she went in, so she took the seat opposite him quietly and looked around the room, pretending not to be listening in. It was more modern than Lord Henry's office, the desk more like something from Ikea than the Georgian period. The room was tidy, there was a small grey-and-brown tartan sofa set to one side, the desk with in-tray, laptop, phone and pen, his black leather chair, and another comfy black chair where she sat down. The shelves on the back wall held a neat selection of books: *Business Management, Stately and Country Homes*, a few crime thrillers, mountaineering, skiing, no Batman annuals that she could see – hah! There was a door ajar off to another room. She wondered if he had a suite, and if that might lead to his private quarters.

His voice raised. She turned her focus back to him. He looked rather stern. 'What do you mean you can't come until Friday? That's too late. We're open then. The contract clearly states you would be here to do the work on the Wednesday.' He listened a while, raising his eyebrows in frustration at Ellie as a tinny voice rattled on. Then Joe stated, calmly but with a don't-mess-with-me tone, 'Look, I don't care what your issues are at that end, I need the service I have paid you for and I need it by Wednesday afternoon at the latest. Ring me back when you've sorted it out.'

He switched off the phone, looking right at Ellie, 'Incompetent buggers.'

Ellie broke into a nervous smile. She wondered if she might be placed in that category very swiftly, especially when he realised she didn't have a clue about how much food to order in.

'Right, sorry, we've a lot to go over, haven't we?' Luckily his grumpy mood had dissipated, and he seemed fairly patient with her as she ran though her *long* list of queries. He had questions to ask her too: yes, she had organised the public liability insurance, *costing her an arm and a leg*, yes, she'd contacted the two existing waitresses, who were coming in tomorrow afternoon to make themselves known to her, and to chat about their role.

He brought out two sheets of A4. 'The admissions figures for the Easter weekend last year. Deana said you wanted them?' His last comment came out as a question.

She gulped back a little knot in her throat; did she dare explain her ordering dilemma? But surely it was better to be honest now than cock up the whole launch weekend by either over- or under-ordering.

He was gazing intently at her, as if he was waiting for her to say something. Eventually he spoke first, 'And you've got the phone number for Breakers, the suppliers, haven't you?'

'Yes,' her voice was timid, on the brink of her revelation that she was an incompetent fraud.

His dark eyes fixed hers.

'Okay,' she started tentatively, 'I have a bit of a confession, I'm really not sure what quantities to order in.' So there it was, her lack of catering experience out in the open. He'd probably rue his decision now; they'd have a dreadful Easter, the food would run out and he'd be left handling numerous complaints . . . She could see it all now. He'd have to cancel her contract and that'd be it.

'I see.' He ran his fingers through his dark floppy fringe and let out a slow sigh, a look of concern crossing his brow. 'Ellie, I thought you had experience in catering? You'd certainly led us to believe that in the interview.' He paused, while she sat feeling more and more uncomfortable. 'Well, those figures will tell you who came into the castle but not who ate at the tearooms or what they ate. I'm afraid I don't have the details of the previous tenant's ordering.' He held her gaze, then continued, 'We really need the tearooms to run well over Easter. It's the reputation of the castle that's at stake.'

'I know.' Her voice was small. She felt terrible.

'Ellie, I've gone out on a limb here to secure you the tearooms' lease.' He was frowning.

Okay, well there was no need to be quite so miserable about it. She was new to all this and had never pretended to be Jamie Oliver or anything. 'I was only asking for a bit of advice.'

He said nothing, just looked at her.

'Right, well I'll just find someone else to ask. I do have other contacts.' She got up to leave. She'd sort it somehow.

'Ellie,' his voice stopped her at the door, 'What I'd suggest is when you call up Breakers, who incidentally supplied us last year as well, you ask if they keep details of back orders and find out exactly what was ordered for last Easter. I'm sure they'll have that information.'

She felt the heat flush up her neck. Could it really be that easy? And why the hell hadn't she thought of that? What an idiot. It seemed obvious now. She wondered what he must think of her. Totally inept came to mind. Though his opinion was hard to read. He seemed to have a deeper side to him that shielded his emotions, but at least he was trying to help her, if only to save his own bacon in front of Lord Henry.

'Oh, and get a little more of everything in just in case,' his tone lifted. 'I've got a feeling your food's going to be far more appealing than Mrs Charlton's last year,' he added, which made her feel marginally better. 'Okay, well, if there's nothing else, I have a rather busy afternoon ahead.'

'Actually, there is one more thing. I was going to ask you about the freezers. Are they for the tearooms? The ones out in the corridor next to the kitchen.'

'Oh, yes. They are yours to use.'

'Right, well, there is a bit of a problem with the far freezer?' She paused, 'A problem with antlers on. I mentioned it to Deana when she popped in earlier.'

'Oh, Christ, it'll be Henry's hunting trophies again, for sure. He shot a stag on the estate last month. I bet he's waiting for the taxidermist to collect it. I'm sorry. I'll get it moved . . . I'm never quite sure what he's going to do next. Eccentric doesn't cover the half of it,' he grimaced.

'Thanks. And look, I–I'm sorry about the confusion with the ordering, I'll be fine once I get everything up and running.' She stood, crossing her fingers behind her back.

'Yes, well let's hope so.' He echoed her concerns. His confidence in her had obviously been dented. Well, she'd just have to prove herself, wouldn't she? Get this first order right. Cook some great food, and keep the customers happy.

'Right, well, I suppose I'd better get back to my cleaning duties. I'm on to the ovens now.'

'That won't be a pleasant job, for sure. Oh, and I hear you're meeting with the waitresses tomorrow. Best of luck.' He said no more as she rose to leave.

Hmn, would she be needing luck with that, then?

She'd made a batch of cherry-and-almond scones: a) to test out the kitchen ovens, which seemed to be fine, except the main one had a mind of its own when you were trying to put stuff in or out – the door swinging to a close (she had the burn mark on her forearm to show for it), and b) to offer to Nicola and Doris, her waitressing staff, as a welcome gesture. They were due to appear any minute for a quick hello and general introduction before they started work officially on Friday morning. Ellie felt nervous; she wasn't used to dealing with staff, well not as the boss, anyhow, and wanted to appear friendly but also efficient.

She was testing out the ancient filter-coffee machine that looked like a relic from the seventies, when there was a brusque knock on the teashop door.

'Come on in,' she called.

A fifty-something, short-but-wide lady marched in, with brown, grey-tinged hair set in a rounded bob, wrapped up in several layers of winter clothing, followed by a timid-looking girl of no more than nineteen, who was tall, slim, with curtains of straight dark hair that flowed past her shoulders – she had the palest skin.

Ellie smiled and said 'Hello' as she offered her hand to greet them, 'I'm Ellie.'

'Doris,' the older lady announced. She took Ellie's hand with quite some grip, 'And this is Nicola.' The young girl didn't get chance to introduce herself. Her handshake was gentle. As she looked up, Ellie saw she had the most amazing blue eyes; with her dark hair she looked unusual. She had a gothic air about her, and more than a hint of Morticia. Well, they were certainly a contrasting pair. As long as they worked hard for her, that was all that mattered.

'Right, well, nice to meet you both. I was just trying to work out the coffee machine here. I've made some scones. I thought you might like something while we have a quick chat. They're cherry and almond.'

'Hmn,' Doris's nose was raised, sniffing out *change*. 'Vera Charlton used to make sultana or cheese scones, *traditional* she was,' her tone was accusatory, 'Had a lot of experience.'

'Well, they sound nice. I'll try one.' Nicola was more positive, at least.

'Okay, I'll just get this coffee on.' Ellie fiddled about with the old-fashioned coffee maker, trying to work out where you poured in the water. She'd filled one of the two glass jugs, and placed the empty one on the hot plate, she'd even found some sachets of filter coffee left in the kitchen, only just in date, and a couple of filter papers.

'I'll do it, shall I?' Doris muscled in, with a tut, her tone not in the least bit patient. 'Look, the water goes in there, Missy.' There was some kind of grated hatch at the top.

And *Missy?* Ellie tried to keep her tone light. 'Okay, yes, I see. Not used one of these before. Right, I'll fetch the scones, shall I?' This wasn't going quite as she had planned.

Doris had taken her Michelin-man padded coat off by the time Ellie got back with the scones and butter, all laid out nicely on a tray. The coffee was filtering through, and Ellie popped scones onto plates, setting out the nearest table for the three of them. As they sat down, Doris announced, 'I'd rather tea with scones,' with a bright, testing smile on her face.

Ellie had the feeling she was being played. 'Well, I can make a pot of tea if you'd rather.' She tried to keep her response light and breezy. *Cool, calm, collected*. Christ, what would Doris be like with the customers? She'd be scaring them away! But finding someone else at this short notice would be tricky, and Lord Henry had insisted that Ellie give the previous staff a chance, which seemed only fair. Mind you, she'd make it bloody clear they were on a six-week probation period. She even had a contract ready for them to sign up to cover herself, thanks to Kirsty, who'd had some nightmare issues with staff in the past.

'Oh no, don't trouble yourself just for me, just saying that I would normally have tea.'

'Coffee's good for me,' piped up Nicola, showing some support. That seemed to shut Doris up, though she gave her waitressing colleague a sideways look as if to say remember whose side you're on.

Ellie poured out filter coffee, which smelled rich and roasted, and they took their scones and started eating as they chatted. 'Well, obviously you've both worked here before. So you know the general set-up.' *More than me*, she was thinking with a hint of panic that she kept down. 'I'm not planning to change too much initially. I've just moved the furniture around a bit, as you can see.' The waitresses nodded. 'And I intend getting some oilcloths on the tables – easier for clearing up, and some flowers to brighten the place.'

'Sounds nice,' Nicola commented.

Doris was nodding quietly, waiting for her moment to strike, no doubt.

'I'll be doing the majority of the cooking. I'm trying to keep most of it homemade. And I'd like you to concentrate on serving, clearing the tables, just being friendly.' *Would that be possible for dour Doris?* 'I thought we'd take orders at the counter. So people can come up and see the cakes and what we have on offer.'

'*Come up to order?*' Doris made it sound like Ellie had just suggested they waitress in bunny-girl outfits. Ellie tried to push away the image that was forming in her mind – Doris in a . . . no, no, no. 'Well, that'll never work. We *always* used to take orders at the tables. Proper waitress service, that is.' Her moment was evidently here. 'Our customers *like* that. Feel they are being looked after.' She was shaking her head at Ellie and tutting away like Skippy the kangaroo.

Ellie knew she'd have to stand her ground. She was the one in charge, after all, 'Well, I believe it gives the customer a chance to see what cakes and treats there are on offer, which is helpful for them and will surely lead to more sales. They can order quickly, take their teas and coffees, and then take their seats and relax, as we'll still be serving them thereafter. It happens in lots of places that way, and most people seem very happy to do that.'

'Well, it didn't happen here,' Doris grumbled on.

'It will from now on, Doris.' Ellie felt she were drawing battle lines, staking her claim on her authority.

Nicola sat quiet, her eyes low, finishing the last of her scone, clearly not wanting to get involved with the heated discussion.

'Right, I'd like you both to start at nine-thirty on Friday. You'll be doing five days a week, nine-thirty till four-thirty. I'll be staying after that time to tidy up. You'll be paid by the hour. I'll be able to keep your wages the same as last year. Joe told me you were paid at £7 per hour. I hope that's still okay. Now, I understand the castle is closed on a Wednesday. I'll need you both in on the weekends, but you can choose another day off, either on a Monday or Tuesday. I'll let you decide between you.'

'Sounds fair enough,' Doris appeared to concede. 'Though I think you'll find that a Thursday and Tuesday are the quieter.'

That wasn't what the admissions figures she'd now looked over showed. 'Well, we'll see how things go on. We'd need to be flexible, if that's the case.'

'Yes, I'm fine with that,' said Nicola, who seemed happy to agree with everything, 'I don't mind which days off I have. Doris, you can choose.' Nicola smiled, adding, 'And the scones are lovely, Ellie.'

'Hmn, not bad,' came from Doris.

'Any other questions, ladies?'

'How will we get paid, then? Weekly? Cash?' asked Doris.

'Yes, I'll do a weekly pay packet for your both. And when you come in this Friday there'll be a contract for you to sign.'

Doris's eyes nearly popped out of her head. 'We never had no contracts before. And I ain't signing nothing till I've had chance to read it.'

'Fair enough. I'll have them ready for Friday, so you can take them home and read them. That's fine. You can sign on Saturday. It's all straightforward stuff, just some basic conditions, health and safety regs to adhere to, that kind of thing.'

'Hmn, I see. *Well*, I'll have a read of them first.'

'That's no problem, Doris.'

'So where was it you worked before then, anyhow? In Newcastle, was it? Somewhere we'll have heard of? Some fancy restaurant or something?' Doris was quizzing her now.

Ellie knew the truth had better not come out now, or her hard-earned authority might be very short-lived.

'Oh, just a small bistro. I doubt if you'll have heard of it.' White lies, skin of teeth. Smile. 'Well, then, I've got lots to do still, so I'd better get on, unless you have any other questions?'

Doris seemed to be thinking, but said, 'No, no not for now. We'd better be getting on too, hadn't we, Nicola?'

'Well, nice to meet you both. See you on Friday.'

Friday. D-Day.

8

Ellie

She was exhausted, her hands were sore from kneading dough, her body was aching, and her brain felt all fuzzy. She glanced at the old wall clock in the kitchen, nearly seven-fifteen pm, Thursday . . . and she still had *sooo* much to do, but all she really felt like was a nice lie-down on a cosy sofa.

Yesterday, she'd taken a drive through to Kirkton along winding lanes, the hedgerows thick with honeyed prim-roses, past wide-open fields with skipping lambs. The spring sun was finally out and the glow gave the whole landscape a new look. Ellie had gone to source a butcher for ham for her sandwiches, and had put an order in for fresh bread rolls to go with the soup at the bakery – she'd have loved to have made her own, but there were only so many hours in one day.

She had also found a cute little flower shop on the high street – she'd wanted to buy spring posies to put on the tables for over the Easter weekend. The lady there was lovely, introducing herself as Wendy, suggesting Ellie stick with carnations and freesias as they would last a bit longer, and putting her off the daffodils she was keen on, after hearing it was for a food venue. 'Those yellow carnations will last far longer, and put with the colourful freesias they'll look really pretty, *and* smell gorgeous. Daffodils can smell a bit piddly, pet, once they're on the turn.' She'd also put her straight as to where she could pick up some oilcloths in the town. Ellie headed there next, while Wendy made up the posies, ready to pop straight into the little coloured-glass vases she'd promised to sell Ellie at a discount, seeing as she was buying several. When Ellie got back to the flower shop, Wendy wanted to hear all about Ellie's new venture taking over the castle teashop, saying she'd put in a good word for her around the town and drum up some local business.

Ellie had driven back with a smile on her face and had set about baking several cakes ready to freeze in advance.

Today, Thursday, found her baking another five cakes, including, of course, the famous choffee, a double batch of cup-cakes to turn into Easter extravaganzas with mini chocolate eggs, crumbled Flake bars and hundreds and thousands for the topping, *and* chocolate-chip cookies. The scones would have to wait till the morning, fresh every day; her nanna wouldn't have had it any other way. She'd still need to make a huge batch of coleslaw, and scrub all the jacket potatoes ready to go in the oven in the morning too. Two pans of soups were simmering away on the massive stove – a leek and potato and a tomato and lentil, a last-minute ingredient change after another trip to the tiny supermarket in Kirkton and the realisation that she wasn't going to get fresh basil in the small local town.

Oh dear lord, tomorrow was Friday, the Easter weekend – she really didn't know what to expect. Would it be really busy? Would she be running around manically like a blue-assed fly? Or quieter than she imagined and she'd be left with loads of stuff? She just had to do as much prep as possible as she really didn't know. But now it was getting late and she'd lost her energy – bad timing. There was no way she'd be getting an early night tonight. And there wasn't going to be a lot of rest over the next few days either, with the teashop open.

A knock on the kitchen door startled her. It swung open. Joe stood there with a grin on his face. 'I saw the light on, thought you might be working late. Pizza? Do you fancy any? I'm going into town – can't get enthused about cooking tonight.'

Hmn, with his dark, floppy hair and wicked smile – he really was rather attractive. At least he had seemed to have thawed a bit since their meeting in his office . . . Ellie, behave, working relationship alert. 'Ah, yes . . . yes. That'd be great. I don't think I've eaten since, oh about twelve.' And that had only been a packet of crisps. No wonder she was feeling a bit drained.

'Wow, it looks pretty impressive here.' He scanned the rows of cakes, cookies, pans of soup. 'Looks like you've had a busy day. Well, I'd better get going, leave you to crack on. The pizza – any special flavours? Toppings?'

'Hawaiian.'

'A ham-and-pineapple girl, hmn.' He eyed her thoughtfully, 'I'm a Sloppy Giuseppe man myself.'

She stifled a giggle. It made him sound like some kind of scruffy Italian, which kind of fitted, looking at his ruffled brown hair that was a touch too long in the fringe and neck line. 'Is that the one with the spicy beef and peppers?'

'That's the one, though at Kirkton it tends to come out more like minced beef and onions. Still tasty, mind.'

Ellie couldn't agree more, and found herself blushing.

'Right, well, I won't be too long.'

'Thanks.'

* * *

Joe

He was balancing two pizza boxes in the crook of his arm and two bottles of cider in the other hand as he pushed back through the kitchen swing door.

Wow, she'd been damned busy: cakes, cookies and more were piled on every surface. She was obviously a hard worker. He just hoped she could cope once they were open. He'd had a few doubts of late; she seemed less experienced than she'd led them to believe in the interview, not even knowing how to order the supplies. The food looked fantastic, though. With any luck the visitors would be in for a treat. Thank God, as Lord Henry was still going to take some convincing. The old chap would be watching her like a hawk over the coming weeks, especially as Joe had had to twist his arm to take the younger girl on.

She looked up at him. She'd been mixing something in a big plastic bowl and had a cute smudge of flour across her nose and cheek. Laying the pizzas on the last free section of work surface, he resisted the urge to walk across, reach out a fingertip and brush the flour from her face. She was pale, he noticed, looked pretty tired; she must have been working from the early hours.

'Pizzas,' he announced, 'Time for a break.'

'Great, thanks. I'm starving. That's crazy, huh? All this food here and I've hardly eaten all day.'

'I bought some cider, too, just in case. Do you like it?'

'Yeah, I do. I'm thirsty, that'll go down well. How did you know I liked cider?'

'Lucky guess, I suppose . . . And I like it, so I figured if you didn't I'd just have to have the two.'

They smiled at each other. She wiped her hands on her apron that clung just *sooo* nicely across her breasts. He quickly removed his gaze, hoping he hadn't been caught in the act of staring. *What was up with him?* Come on, Joe, you know you always keep things professional at work at all times. He'd never had any trouble with eyeing up the staff in the past, but then Cynthia and Vera didn't leave an awful lot to be desired, to be fair. Just some male instinct triggered, that was all. Best ignored. He knew when to leave well alone.

'Mind you, I'd better not have much of that cider or I'll be asleep before I get finished here,' she muttered, not seeming to have noticed his loitering gaze.

Should he stay? Would she like some company? She seemed pretty busy. He'd leave her in peace.

'Umn, well, here's your Hawaiian.'

'Great, thanks. How much do I owe you?' She moved to fetch her purse from her handbag.

'Oh no, it's on me. You look like you've put in a hard day's work.'

'No, Joe, I couldn't.'

'Of course you can. And, looking at this lot,' he eyed

the cakes on the counter tops, 'I'm sure there'll be a time when I'm desperate for a slice of your cake or something.' The thought of *something* made him feel rather hot under the collar. What the hell was up with him?

'Alright, then, thank you. But I'll make sure I return the favour.'

'Right, well I'd better let you get on.' But somehow, he didn't fancy going back to his quiet rooms just yet. The place had been like a ghost town over the winter. It was, in fact, meant to be haunted, but he'd never seen a hint of anything spectre-like – might have provided a bit of drama at least. But no, nothing.

'Actually, I could do with a short break. So I don't mind if you want to stop to eat your pizza. I've been on my own all day. It gets pretty quiet here, doesn't it? I must admit, it's a bit strange at night thinking it's just you, me and Lord Henry here in this bloody big, ancient place.'

'Oh, well, it'll all change tomorrow, I tell you. Visitors in every nook and cranny. You'll be glad for Wednesdays, our closed day, to come to get some peace and quiet. Henry hates it all really – having to open up the castle.' Joe took a slice of pizza from the cardboard box and bit into its cheesy-meaty base. 'In his eyes it's a necessary evil to earn an income to keep this old place up, that's all. He'd much rather shut it all off and live like a hermit.

But it won't pay the bills, unfortunately, or keep the rain out of the roof.'

'Oh,' she suddenly said, 'Is Lord Henry having any pizza? Should we take him some up?'

It was sweet that she thought of Lord Henry, but no, he'd never once mentioned about eating with Joe, preferring his own company, and, to be honest, Joe wasn't sure that Henry would be the kind of company he wanted in his downtime. It made for a very quiet life at the castle, though. He suddenly realised he'd been living a bit like a hermit himself of late. 'No, he's not that sociable and I shouldn't think pizza's his kind of thing anyway. Prefers traditional food, I think.'

'Does he cook for himself, then?'

'Not often, no. Since his wife died a few years back, Deana tends to make him some meals up and leaves them for him to re-heat. We don't really see much of each other of an evening, just keep to our own space. I suppose we're both quite private.'

'Like a pair of hermits,' she smiled, echoing his thoughts. 'How do you find it here? It seems a different way of life. Have you always lived in this area?'

'No, I'm from Newcastle, actually. Byker way.'

'Oh, that's not far from me, Heaton.'

'Yeah, I know it . . . Anyway, what made you want to give up the city life and come out here to the sticks?' He steered the conversation back to Ellie – safer ground.

'A change.' She looked uncomfortable.

The pause was telling. He sensed she was holding something back.

'Well, my job wasn't inspiring me any more,' she continued, 'I'd got stuck in a rut. I wanted to try something I love doing, not just something that paid my keep. So, here I am . . .' She let the words drift, then tucked into a second slice of pizza, the oil from the cheese greasing her upper lip, which looked kind of sexy. Dammit.

'Yes, here you are.' He raised a cider bottle. 'Opener?'

She rummaged in the cutlery drawer and found a bottle opener, passing it to him.

The cider fizzed as the tops came off, an appley aroma filling the air. He passed her one and they clinked bottles.

'Cheers,' he said. 'Well, here's to a successful starting weekend for you.'

'And a great season for you and the castle too.' She took a swig.

He couldn't help but smile, watching her. She seemed a nice enough girl, easy-going, maybe a bit naïve. But he'd just keep a friendly distance. He wasn't used to having anyone else living here at the castle, apart from Henry.

'Just to give you more idea of the set-up here, by the way, I'm generally behind the scenes when we're up and running. Deana's front of house, taking admissions, dealing with the day-to-day issues. There are also a couple of guides who come in, they keep an eye on the main rooms and do the tours: Derek and Malcolm. I'll introduce you to them tomorrow, though I'm sure they'll make themselves known and pop in for a cup of tea early on.'

'Okay. No problem.'

'And you've met your waitresses?' He raised an eyebrow.

'Yeah,' Ellie didn't know quite what to say about that meeting.

'Don't worry about Doris, her bark's worse than her bite.' He knew how the middle-aged dragon might come across, but he wanted to reassure Ellie too, 'They are both hard workers, honestly.'

'That's good to hear.'

The pizzas were nearly gone. Ellie leaving several crusts in the box, Joe noted, as he polished off his last slice.

She looked across at him, 'Do you like working here?'

'Yeah, I do actually. Although it's halfway to falling apart, it's an amazing place. I recognise the castle has to run as a business, unlike Lord Henry. And I want to give it a future not just a past. And though he hates to admit it, Lord Henry needs help with that. I try to keep things as unobtrusive as possible for him, so it can still be his home, but you have to have a business angle. And you need to have visitors in. It takes a lot of money to keep this place running, at the end of the day, just to stop it decaying and becoming a crumbling wreck. But yeah, it's a good place to work. It's different. I like it. It's certainly not boring. It's not like any other job or place of work I've ever been in before.'

'Have you been here long, then?' She took another sip of cider.

'Four years now. Been the estate manager for the last two.' He went quiet for a second or two, looking around. 'Is that . . .'

There was a scent of burning.

'Shit, my last batch of cup-cakes.' She flew off the stool she'd been sitting on and grabbed the oven gloves, taking out the baking tray, cursing. Joe could see all the cakes to one side of the tray had gone a dark shade of brown. The oven door did its swing just then, catching the bare skin of her arm just above the gloves. 'Shite,' she muttered under her breath, as she felt the skin singe. He couldn't get there quick enough to stop it.

'Are you okay? Put the tray down and we'll get some water on that burn.' He ran to turn on the cold tap. 'I'm sorry, Ellie, I've been interrupting you.' She placed the tray down carefully, some of the cakes looked as though they might be salvageable, and walked to the sink, where he gently took her forearm and placed the reddened mark under the stream of cold water. 'It'll need a good few minutes in running water.' He could see an angry welt developing.

'I'm alright, honest. The oven door's just a bit temper-amental.'

'Christ, you should have said. I'll get it adjusted first thing in the morning, get our handyman in to look at it. Bloody typical, everything's archaic here. I'll get it all checked over. Should have done it before. I'm sorry.'

'It's okay. It's just one of those things. It'll heal. But, yeah, if you could get that door fixed that'll be great.'

He held her arm under the cool water a while longer. He didn't like the look of that angry mark – felt it was his fault, the dodgy oven and the fact he'd been chatting and distracting her. 'I'm sorry, I should have had the equipment double-checked before the start of the season.'

'It's fine, honest. Look, I'd better get on.'

She'd probably have to make another lot of cakes now. So much for him trying to help her by fetching her some supper. But he should have known better than to get involved on any personal level with any staff, even if it was just a pizza delivery. He felt irritated with himself, released her arm and backed off, ready to go.

'Thanks again, Joe. That was really nice of you, getting the pizzas.'

'No worries. Sorry about the damned oven. I'll get it checked first thing.' He'd better get out of her way. Let her get on with her job. That was what she was meant to be doing here, and he shouldn't have been interfering with that. He probably shouldn't interfere, full stop, chatting with her like they were friends; what was he thinking? The swing door left a cold draught in his wake.

9

Ellie

Beep. Beep. Beep. Beep.

What the hell was that? Bloody noise. Beep. Beep. Beep.

She surfaced from under the duvet. Pitch black. Beep. Beep. Alarm. She prised her eyes open as she fumbled for her phone and the off button. Six-thirty blinked at her from its screen. Aagh . . .

It was today.

Ellie's teashop opened *today*. Her dreams kicked off *today*.

She had two batches of scones to make and a heap of salad to prepare – that's if the Breakers' order arrived in time. She flew out of bed and into a cool shower, which freshened her to the point of chill. Not from any decision to have lukewarm water, more that the castle's ancient hot-water system hadn't woken up yet either. And she was off, down the winding chilly staircase, dressed in sensible flat pumps, black trousers, a comfy pale-pink T-shirt and essential cardigan. Her hair was piled up out of the way in a practical bun, for health and hygiene reasons. That reminded her, she'd have to make sure Nicola tied back her long hair too. Doris's was short enough in her bob, no problems there. Ooh, she hoped they'd be cooperative today, especially Doris. She just wanted it all to go well, to be able to work together as a team. She'd have to wait and see.

She'd also like to get the fire going in that huge grate. May as well give the tearooms a cosy glow this time of year. She'd ask Deana if the young lad, James, might pop in and help before they opened, but as she reached the cobbled courtyard she remembered just how early it was. There was no light on in Deana's office; she'd pop back later, once her first batch of scones was safely out of the oven.

Entering the teashop she held her breath and paused, suddenly feeling the enormity of the task ahead. It looked good in there, she had to admit, the sort of place she'd like to sit and while away a half hour with tea and cake – the old stone walls and latticed windows gave it character, the tables all set out with the new rose-patterned vintage-style oilcloths she'd found, and the fresh flowers in their posy vases. The freesias filled the room with a lovely fragrance, a good match alongside primrose-yellow carnations and a sprig of greenery; Wendy had been really helpful. Ellie would definitely call back and see her again.

Well, this was it, opening day. Her chance to prove herself. But she was so afraid of getting it wrong. What if no one turned up – she had the monthly lease and the staff to pay, what about trying to eke a living out for herself? What if they did turn up but didn't like her baking? What if Doris and Nicola hated her and made her life a misery and peed off all the customers? What if she'd sold out by lunchtime and had nothing left to serve – an unlikely scenario considering the volume of food in the kitchen! Her brain was in full spin.

Right, focus, a voice in her mind snapped her out of it. Make the damned scones. Have a bite of breakfast or you'll never make it past ten o'clock, and just get on with what you have to do. 'Yes, ma'am', her dithery-self replied. It was funny but the bossy voice sounded very much like that of her nanna. It calmed her; she'd keep listening out for her.

Ellie cracked on. The smell of warm doughy scones filled the kitchen. The first batch of cheese-and-herb scones were out; she glanced at her watch, seven-forty. She'd make herself some tea and toast and then she'd pop out and see if anyone was about to get the fire going.

*

She phoned Deana's extension a while later. She might be in by now. It was nearing eight o'clock.

'Hi, is that you Ellie? All alright there? Ready for the off?'

'Just about. Umn, I was wondering about lighting the fire. But I'm not sure how to really. There's logs and stuff ready here. Can James or someone have a look, do you think? Is he in today?'

'Yes, no problem, he's on a little errand for Lord Henry at the moment. Should be back in ten minutes or so. I'll send him across then. Oh, and good luck today, pet. I'll pop across a little later and see how you're getting on.'

'Thanks, Deana. Come and have a coffee and cake, or something.'

'Don't tempt me, or I'll be in every day.'

'That's fine with me,' replied Ellie warmly.

'Not with my waistline, though,' she chuckled.

'Deana, do you know what time the Breakers' delivery normally comes?' She was waiting on potatoes, all her salad stuff, paninis, sliced bread for toasties and fresh milk. *Pl-ease* let it arrive before opening time.

Deana glanced at her watch. 'Ooh, they're normally here by now. Might be busy, I suppose, delivering for the bank holiday weekend. I'll keep an eye out for them. Though they usually come straight around the back. There's a side entrance for deliveries. If you go along the corridor from the kitchen, you'll get to it.'

Oh great, and no one had thought to tell her. So while she was here in the kitchen the delivery might have been and gone! Surely they'd think to call at the front entrance if there was no one about, or to leave the supplies, at least. Ellie could feel mounting panic swelling inside her. She'd go straight back and check.

She whizzed along the corridor where the freezers were, there was a right turn, and then the side door. Nothing left inside it. She tried the handle. Ah, it was locked, turned the key, poked her head out. No boxes, no van. She held down her fears, but oh, if this lot didn't come there'd be no toasties, paninis or jacket potatoes. Her lunch menu was going to look very limited indeed, or it would mean a flying visit to Kirkton at least, and there *really* wasn't time for that. *Okay, Ellie. Keep calm. Give them chance. It's only eight-ten.*

Ten minutes later, James turned up with an armful of kindling, newspapers and matches, just as there was a loud knock that sounded as though it was coming from the corridor. *Could it be?* She left James to set the fire and dashed to the side entrance. There stood a stocky man in a white overall bearing a box of lettuce, cucumber and tomatoes. *Yippee.*

'Where do you want these, love?'

She could have hugged him. 'Yes, along in the kitchen, if you don't mind.'

He set the cardboard box down on a work surface,

then went back to his van for the bread and other items.

On his return, she offered him a coffee, but he said he had a hectic day, and maybe another time. She signed for the delivery, after a quick check that it all seemed to be there. And he was on his way, whistling chirpily as he went.

'Thank you,' she called after him. One small hurdle over, at least. Right, time to prep the salad, then.

James popped his head around the kitchen swing door. 'Done it. It's all lit, miss.'

'Thank you, James, that's really helpful. Would you like a cookie or some cake while you're here?'

He shook his head while glancing longingly at the cakes that she'd been setting out earlier on the counter. He seemed shy.

'You sure?'

He still shook his head.

'Well, okay, some other time maybe.' She'd leave something in Deana's office for him later.

He nodded and left the room, seemingly eager to be away.

Five minutes later, while she was scrubbing potatoes for the jackets, Ellie noticed a grey film filling the air in the kitchen and an acrid scent; she thought for a second that she'd burned more scones, but then realised there was nothing in the oven at present. Just as the smoke alarm set off in the kitchen, she dashed through to the tearooms to find them filled with choking smoke. Shit! That had been a dozy idea, hadn't it? The fire probably hadn't been lit for years and the chimney must have been full of soot. The tables were already grimy with dust. She quickly opened every window she could, climbing precariously on wobbly chairs to reach them, then wondered about putting out the fire in the hearth with a jug of water, but the flames were beginning to flicker into orange licks and the smoke had begun to dissipate. Oh well, she'd just have to wipe down all the tables *again*, and her lovely freesia scent had turned into smoky barbecue. It was bloody freezing in there now, too, with all the windows open – so much for a cosy glow.

She was on a stool, broom in hand, back in the kitchen prodding at plastic buttons trying to silence the bloody smoke alarm, as Joe marched in, concern etching his brow. 'Are you okay? I heard the alarm. Christ, it stinks in here.'

'It's all in hand,' she muttered, trying to look in control perched on her tiptoes, backside in the air, broom uplifted.

'What the hell happened?'

'The real fire. James set it away for me. Probably not been cleaned all winter. Sorry. Think it's settled down now.'

She finally wafted enough fresh air to stop the alarm sounding. 'All fine now.'

Joe offered her a hand as she got down from the stool. His grasp was firm. His anxious-grumpy look was turning to a thin smile. 'Well, at least you're okay and the kitchen's not on fire. I thought the whole place was going up in smoke for a moment there. Right, well I'll have to go and make a call to the fire station now. We're linked into them, so if any of the alarms go off here, they get an alert too. I'll let them know it's a false alarm.'

'Oh gosh, I'm sorry.' Another cock-up! What must he think of her? And she hadn't even opened the teashop doors to the public yet!

'How's the arm today?'

'Bit sore, but I'll manage.' She'd put some antiseptic on it this morning. It wasn't too bad, just a bit red.

His hand was warm around hers from helping her down off the chair. He glanced at the burn. Then he loosened his grip suddenly, as though he felt awkward.

'Right, well I'd better get on. I'll just have a quick check on that fire on my way out, but it seems to have settled now, doesn't it?'

'Thanks for looking in.'

'Didn't have much choice, did I? What with all the castle fire alarms going off . . . Oh and, watch yourself teetering on stools. You'll break your neck. We do have safety ladders for that kind of thing.'

'Yeah, of course. Didn't have time to think, that was all.'

Ah, could she not do anything right? There was so much more to this than baking cakes.

After the door closed on Joe, her mobile, which was

propped for signal in the windowsill, buzzed into life. Ellie picked up.

'You alright? Everything going well?'

Ah, typical. It was her mother. How did she manage to sniff out a mini-crisis from fifty miles?

'You haven't been working too late, have you?' she continued. 'And are you remembering to eat and sleep?'

'Yes, Mum. I'm fine.' *Knackered but fine.*

'Well, good luck then, pet. Big day today, isn't it? Ring us back later and let us know how you get on.'

'Will do.'

'Oh hang on, here's your dad. He's just off to work.'

Her dad's rich, warm tones filtered down the line, 'Good luck, sweetheart. I know you'll do well. Hope you get lots of happy customers, and make a mint.'

'Thanks, Dad.'

Then in the next ten minutes there were texts from Kirsty at the café and her brother Jason. Aww, it was so nice to have their support. Five minutes after that came a call from Gemma, 'Good luck, hun! I know you'll be busy, I'll not keep you long. But make sure to fill me in on all the craic soon. Have a good launch weekend! Love you!'

'Thanks, Gem. It's all fine, just finding my feet really. Been a bit manic, but I'm looking forward to getting open and starting for real now.'

'Well, very best of luck! You'll do brilliantly!'

'Thank you! I hope so.'

10

Ellie

Nine-thirty came around fast. Ellie was busy setting up the filter-coffee machine in the teashop, hoping she'd done it right this time, when there was a rap on the door and the waitress duo marched in, ready for their first day of the season. At least they were bang on time.

'Morning,' Doris's tone was flat.

'Morning, Doris, Nicola. You both okay?' Ellie kept her tone bright and breezy.

'Fine,' they chorused, as Doris's beady eye scanned the room, assessing the new table arrangements and self-serve counter facility that was laid out with a large selection of the cakes and biscuits that Ellie had made.

'Right, well if you wouldn't mind wrapping some

cutlery. I've bought in some new paper napkins.' Nice-quality red ones.

'We never used to do that, mind.' Doris was off already. 'We used to lay the tables out with full cutlery.'

'Well, that seems a little wasteful to me. If people are just having cake, then all they need is a fork and spoon, or a single knife for a scone.'

'Right, well, as you say.' Doris's tone belied the positive words she spoke.

Ellie was determined to stay upbeat. 'Well, then, I think everything else is just about ready. But if you think of anything, just let me know. There are new notepads to take orders at the counter.' She spotted Doris's eyebrows twitch at the idea of counter service, but continued valiantly, 'I'll be in the kitchen mostly, doing the cooking and plating up. If you can keep up with the orders, the service, and keep the tables cleared as they empty, wiping them down with the antibacterial spray and a fresh cloth, then that'll be great.'

'Okay.' Nicola was agreeing at least.

'And in a few moments we'll bring a further selection of the cakes and biscuits through from the kitchen to the counter area. I've made a new menu and price list, there's a copy on every table and one by the till. I take it you already know how to work the till, but maybe you can give me a quick lesson at some point. If it gets busy, I can give you a hand too.'

She was babbling on a bit she knew; it always happened when she was nervous. Doris raised an eyebrow and fixed her with a beady eye at her till comment – as though someone in her position should at least know how to work the till, which was probably true, but the old bat needn't be so pointed about it.

'Any questions?'

'No, seems pretty plain to me. Some of us know what we're doing,' from Doris.

'That's fine,' from Nicola.

Ellie let out a silent sigh. They were ready. Or as ready as they ever would be. The three of them lined up by the counter, prepared for action.

The tearooms looked pretty, she had to admit, and the fire had settled to a pleasant smoke-free glow. Her posies brightened the room and the cakes on the counter top looked damned tasty; Nanna's choffee taking pride of place.

One minute to ten on her watch. The castle opened at ten o'clock. They waited. The air smelled of fresh coffee from the percolator machine, yummy baking aromas and a faint smoky background.

'Well, all we need now are some customers,' a nervous Ellie was stating the obvious.

'Exactly,' Doris chimed.

'Yep.'

After half an hour or so, the shadows of visitors began

to pass by the windows, but no one came in. *Why weren't they coming in?* Was it too early? Would they tour the castle first? Had they no money left for tea and cake? She should have put a sign outside or something. There was a 'teashop' sign on the door, but was that enough? Surely it was labelled on the guide map they got as they came in. Something else to check up on.

By ten-forty she was in mind to make up a board of some kind and send Nicola outside, but didn't want to look too panicky. Instead, she offered to make the three of them a pot of tea. From the kitchen she heard the creaky swing of the tearoom door. Could it be her first customer? She went to take a peek to find Lord Henry chatting to the waitresses, and studying the room to see how things were set up. Ellie offered him some tea and cake, but he politely declined, saying he might pop back later; he had things to do, but he hoped they'd have a successful day. She headed back to the kitchen, where the kettle rumbled to a boil, and she filled the teapot. As she strolled through with it on a tray with three cups, she was thrilled to see a middle-aged couple at the counter ordering tea for two, a scone and a slice of her fruitcake. She could have hugged them – her first-ever customers. But she just grinned, headed back to the kitchen and poured out their three teas, arranged the tray while making up another pot to help Doris with the order.

Then a group of six came in, and another couple. Doris and Nicola were in full swing. Ellie re-filled the kettle and decided to put the big hot-water urn on, then topped up the platter of scones. As she cleared the first table, another group appeared. She hardly had a chance to get a sip of her own tea, but she didn't mind. Soon lunch orders were coming in and she was full-on in the kitchen, trying to keep the order slips in sequence to get them out right, and without too much delay. She was on lunch order four out of six, two jacket potatoes with cheese and beans, a ham and brie panini (oh yes, her much-too-modern paninis that had made Doris frown as surely sandwiches were sufficient, had a sale!) and a soup and roll. But the grated cheese had run out; she'd need to prepare much more in advance for tomorrow, as grating it for each order was taking far too long. Nicola popped her head round the door, shyly stating that the jacket potato and panini order had been waiting for quite some time now and the gentleman was asking when it would be ready.

'Nearly there, Nicola. Sorry, there was a rush of orders all at once.'

She plated the potatoes with their fillings, juggled the panini from the toaster and ladled out the soup. Phew, another order completed. And, next . . .

Doris came marching in, her face like thunder. 'It's not working,' she barked. 'This counter thing. We don't know where the orders are going now there's a few on the go at once. We used to have table numbers, you know, and write them on the chitty. And now you've moved all the tables too, we haven't a clue. We're wandering around like a pair of ninnies, calling out dishes, trying to find the right customers. *Very* unprofessional, if you ask me.' Her scowl said it all.

Oh dear. Deep breath, Ellie, and thinking cap on. 'Just give me a second, Doris.' She finished off plating the order she was on and helped Doris take it out, seeing the confusion for herself. But she really felt the counter service could work, they should sell more that way, and it would be quicker in busier times for those who just wanted coffee and cake to get served.

Ellie took a sheet of A4 paper, drew up a quick table plan just as the room was set out, and labelled the tables one to ten. 'Nicola, can you please nip this to Deana's office and ask for three more copies. I'd go myself, but there are orders waiting.'

'No problem. I'll go right away.'

Doris's attention was distracted by a refill of coffee being requested. Ellie cleared another table and went back to her next lunch order. Nicola was soon back. Ellie took the plan to the counter. 'Right, Doris, Nicola, that's our table plan. Jot the numbers down on your order pads like you used to and we should all know what we're doing then. And, Doris, thank you so much for bringing that to my attention. That was really helpful of you.'

Doris's mouth had dropped open; she didn't know how to counter that. A weak 'Thank you' crossed her lips, and she had the look of someone who'd been outsmarted, but wasn't quite sure how.

Ellie went back to the next order humming. There were a mad couple of hours through the lunchtime, and then things eased a little, giving Ellie the chance to clear the kitchen and check how the waitresses were getting on. Joe was right, the pair of them did work hard, which was more important than anything.

'Do you want to take a break now, ladies? I'll help out here if need be. Doris, Nicola, can I make you up something to eat? What do you fancy? Soup, a sandwich? You go first, Doris, and then when you've had your half hour, Nicola can go. You've both worked hard, anything you take for lunch's on the house.' The least she could do was to provide them with a bite of lunch, and it might just help morale. It would be novel to see a smile on Doris's face, though it wasn't going to happen quite yet by the looks of her deadpan expression.

'Thank you. I'd like the tomato soup. Please.'

'No problems.'

Doris took a seat in the kitchen, silently observing Ellie as she bustled about. Finally she said, 'And are *you* not stopping?'

'No, not just yet, Doris, not while there's still customers to serve. I'm fine.' She'd be knackered for sure tonight, but there were only a couple more hours to go.

Just then, Bossy Nanna's voice cut in her mind with, 'You need to eat.' The same words came from Doris's lips.

That was a bit freaky. 'Yes, okay, I'll make sure I eat something.' Jesus, now there were two of them bossing her around.

Joe popped in a few minutes later, 'Everything okay here? Been busy?'

'Yes, it has been. Bit of a slow start, mind. Would you like anything? I'm getting Doris some soup for her lunch break.'

'No, no, you look busy enough. I had something earlier, anyhow. And I've got loads to do, but if you need anything just give us a shout.'

'Will do, thanks.'

He gave her one of his broad smiles and was off. A silly glow inside warmed her, and yet was a warning too. Yes, he might look okay, well more than okay, to be honest, but he was out of bounds. No work-based relationships allowed. Anyway, she was steering clear of relationships, full stop. She did *not* want to go down that particular road again. Not when she was finally beginning to turn things in her life around.

The long weekend proved hectic. By Monday, three o'clock, her feet were throbbing, the burn on her arm nagging a little, and she felt like she could sleep for a week. She was left with one fruitcake, half a Victoria sponge, three Easter cup-cakes, six scones, two grouchy waitresses and the embers of a fire. Ooh, she'd give anything to slide into a deep, hot (now that would be a miracle) bubbly bath with a glass of fizz. But there were still two hours to go before they closed and unless she wanted to get up at six again, she'd better get a couple of cakes made for tomorrow or they'd run out altogether. She couldn't believe they had sold so much. The stream of customers had kept on coming, their comments were good, and her waitressing duo seemed to be getting on fine and receiving some healthy tips. Her first weekend, though very much a juggling act and a learning on her feet, seemed to have been a success. Wow. She could barely believe it, it was the most amazing feeling!

She'd have to count the takings and work everything out in detail, but she was sure she had more than covered her costs, including the entire week's waitress wages, all the food supplies and some of her lease and setting-up costs. Result! Of course not every weekend could be expected to be as busy as Easter, but it boded well.

Nearly closing time on Easter Monday, Ellie was making the mix for tomorrow's sponge cakes. Doris was busy getting the mop and bucket ready to do the floor when Ellie offered to finish off, saying she'd probably make more mess with her next batch of baking. She thanked them for their hard work over the busy weekend and offered them a couple of scones each to take home. She wouldn't re-use them the next day, preferring to bake them fresh daily. They took them, gave her an end-of-day smile, yes, *even* Doris's lips twitched upwards, probably relief at getting away, to be fair, and set themselves away home.

'See you tomorrow, ladies, and thank you.'

And all was quiet. It was strange, the full-on bustle of the tearooms when they were up and running, and then the lull at the end of the day and early morning when she got on quietly with her baking, prepping, or the last of the clearing up. She quite liked those times, though it took her a few minutes to adjust. Already the days had their pattern, routines were forming. The castle was becoming part of her life, and the people she had met there.

Lord Henry, in worn beige corduroy trousers and a brown-checked shirt, called in just as she was clearing up, to enquire how things were going. It was only the second visit since she had started; Joe's comments that he liked to keep himself to himself seemed to be true.

'How's your first weekend been, then, Ellen. Settling in alright?'

'It's El . . .' She never got chance to correct him.

'Plenty of customers?'

'Yes, it's been busy. I'm really pleased with how it's all gone.' She wanted to sound positive, but she still felt a little on edge with Lord Henry. His manner was so formal, and a coolness exuded from him. It was hard to tell what he was thinking.

'That's good. *But . . .*' he drew a slow breath, 'It *is* early days. The Easter period should be popular. It's an easy time to fill the tearooms . . . Time will tell.' The words hung with gloomy foreboding.

Ellie wondered if he was secretly harbouring hopes of getting the sparkly-topped Cynthia, of the handlebar hips, back in situ.

She needed to prove him wrong.

'Would you like a slice of cake? Cup of tea, Lord Henry?'

'Actually, Ellen, don't mind if I do.'

She cut a slice of her best fruitcake, and sat down with him, feeling a little nervous. She tried to get some conversation going, asking him how long he had lived at the castle, finding out that he'd been there all his life. It was a family property passed down through the generations. She didn't dare mention her little semi back in Heaton. Their lives were worlds apart. Yet here they were, talking over tea and cake. Hopefully he thought the fruitcake was okay, though he didn't say much to confirm that. Just left with a polite thank you. She still had the feeling that he considered her a naïve young snippet, who would soon enough trip herself up.

She had also met Derek and Malcolm, who did the guided tours and kept an eye on the rooms that were open to viewing. They had called in on the Saturday morning just before opening time for a 'most welcome' cup of coffee. And she'd been introduced to Colin, a smiley bald-headed gardener in his mid-fifties, who walked with a slight limp; he seemed to have young James as a helper much of the time.

Deana worked long hours over the weekend, staying on until well after six-thirty. Ellie popped in to see her before heading up to her room, noting the light still on in her office. They had a nice chat. Deana was checking the admissions figures for the castle. She said that Joe had helped her get set up with a new computer system that would record them more easily, and takings were up on the year before for Easter, so she was pleased.

'Been a busy weekend, hasn't it? Goes from nothing to full throttle overnight for Easter. How have you found it, Ellie?'

'Yeah, pretty good. Hectic at times, and I'm shattered, I must admit. My feet are throbbing. But yeah, I've enjoyed it.'

'I'm pleased for you, pet. It's a lot to take on. Especially when catering's not really been your background. But I've been listening to people chatting as they leave and there's been some great comments about the teashop already.'

'Aww, thanks.' That was so lovely to hear. And made her sore feet and aching back worthwhile.

'So, Ellie, I've been wondering about getting a gift shop opened up here. What do you think?'

'Oh, well, that'd be a great idea, I'm sure.'

'What kind of things do you think we should focus on selling?'

It felt nice that her opinion was being sought. 'Well, I suppose the usual – mugs, tea-towels, quality local crafts, jams, honeys . . . Oh, and what about some castle-themed things for the children, books, colouring sets, dressing-up outfits – they always like those, like knights and princesses, that sort of thing.'

'Ooh, that sounds a good idea for the kids. Thanks, Ellie. I'll have a word with Joe to take things forward. But I think a shop will be a good addition to the castle facilities.'

'Yes, definitely. Right, well I think I'll head up for a bath and an early night.'

'Yes, you do that, pet. Put your feet up. See you tomorrow.'

'See you tomorrow, Deana. And thanks, it was nice to chat.'

Ellie felt warm inside, the early stirrings of friendship with Deana giving her a little more confidence in her newfound surroundings.

'Night, pet.'

Back to the tasks in hand for this evening. Ellie would have to think about re-ordering from Breakers tomorrow and might need an early trip to Kirkton to visit the farmers' market and get enough fresh supplies to see her through till Thursday, when they would next deliver. And she'd promised to ring Mum and Kirsty, and Gemma tonight; they were wanting regular updates. She yawned out loud, not able to keep it in as she mounted the spiral staircase.

An hour and a half later she was in the bath, lukewarm thanks to the cranky castle hot-water system, with plenty of bubbles and a bottle of cider. It was the best she was going to get, and bloody lovely, to be honest. Her throbbing toes stuck out at the end of the tub. She might have to find a Clark's shoe store and buy some sensible shoes to work in – now that would please her mother. Her flats were okay, but didn't give any real support, and she'd be on her feet most days. Hah, she hadn't been in a sensible shoe shop since the age of eleven, after which time she'd refused to shop for shoes with her mother, point blank. She couldn't wait to snuggle up in her bed, with the telly on, and drift away. Her alarm would have to be set for seven o'clock, for the morning scone bake-off. But tomorrow was another day. For now she would just lie back and . . .

Thank Christ she hadn't fallen asleep in the bath – it had been a close call, her mobile waking her up, its ringtone droning from the windowsill in the bedroom. It was Jason, seeing how she was. Nearly drowned, she mused drily as she said, 'Fine, it's all going well. How's life with you? Any developments with that Kylie you fancy? Any juicy local gossip I've missed out on?' And as they chatted, she realised she missed him, her little brother, and the comforts of home; she'd do anything for a really hot bath in a centrally heated bathroom, and a big portion of Mum's stew and dumplings right now. But he'd only feed that back to Mum and she'd be fretting, for sure, so Ellie kept the conversation light and fluffy and as positive as possible, enjoying hearing about the trials and tribulations of a teenager in infatuation, and avoiding any talk about her own emotions.

The rest of the week slowed down a little. There was still a steady stream of customers to the teashop, but no one had to wait for a table, and the meal orders came in intermittently, with no pressure to get five done at once, as had been the case over the Easter weekend. It gave Ellie the chance to prep more for the next day, however, and get her baking done, though she'd over-estimated how much to cook for the second half of the week and had far too much left, having to throw three cakes and a whole batch of scones out. Working out what would sell and trying to avoid waste was going to be a minefield, as anything thrown out was just money down the drain.

She did find out from Doris, though, that she could keep the food waste for a local farmer, who'd come and collect every couple of days – at least the pigs were going to be happy, growing fat on Victoria sponge and cherry-and-almond scones.

11

Ellie

Week two, and by the Tuesday the castle was a ghost town. The schools were back, it was still early April and the visitors, bar a few hardy middle-aged ramblers, had disappeared. The weather didn't help either, a steady cold drizzle had set in over the past two days, which settled as a dull, claustrophobic mist over the castle. Once she'd stopped working at a rate of knots, the tiredness flooded Ellie's body, and it gave her time to think, which was never a good thing of late.

Wednesday was a day off, so she didn't need to get up. She snuck back down under the duvet, wondering what she might do with her day. Last Wednesday she'd been that shattered she'd spent most of it in bed and in her room, having a catch-up on iPlayer, and reading all her emails and texts, as well as doing a bit of tearoom prep late afternoon for the next day. She felt she ought to venture a little further afield today, or she was at risk of becoming another of the castle's hermits.

A message popped up on her phone that made her want to stay right there in the safe gloom of her bed: 'We heard about the new venture. Hope all's going well so far. Gavin and Nadine x' Her stomach began to twist. Well, they were a bit late with the good wishes, weren't they? And a kiss, hah, how touching! She pressed delete – didn't want, or need, their kind of luck. But it put her in a sour mood, much as she hated the thought that they might still be able to affect her.

Eleven-fifteen – she'd better get up now. She was hungry for tea and toast. She'd got a little kettle and toaster set up in her room, so she didn't have to traipse all the way to the kitchen if she needed a snack. It was that cold in there the butter kept really well in the chill draught of the windowsill. So she had a quick bite of breakfast.

She needed to get out. She had her car, so zipped off through the lanes to Kirkton; she'd buy a magazine, get herself a coffee – suss out the opposition, and just chill and let someone take care of her for a change. The mists finally lifted and a weak, watery sun filtered through the windscreen. Sitting there in the coffee shop on the small high street twenty minutes later was pleasant, and yet she longed for some company, just to chatter on with Gemma or Kirsty. There was no one much her age at the castle. Nicola was younger, at only nineteen, and had probably seen enough of her new boss all week. Doris, well Doris was a law unto herself – enough said. Deana was really nice, though a different generation, but she had her own life and her husband to think of on their day off.

And then there was Joe. Joe, she thought of him with a little sigh. He must be just a bit older than her, though maybe not that much – he looked late twenties, possibly early thirties, it was hard to tell. Anyway, she didn't feel she could start asking him out for a coffee, or for lunch in the local pub or anything. He might think she was asking him on a date, and that wouldn't do at all. Best to keep her distance there. Lord Henry? She laughed to herself at that one, clutching at straws now. Nah, she couldn't picture herself sat on her day off, having a chat and a coffee with Lord H.

Maybe she could nip home? It wasn't that far, only the hour. Catch up with her family, her mates, but it just seemed *too* soon. It might unsettle her more, and her mother would be on at her with twenty questions, and she wasn't settled enough to come across as happy and convincing yet. She was probably just tired, feeling a little emotional. She'd have a quiet day today, then get back to work tomorrow and get on with everything. That was bound to make her feel better. Maybe she'd visit home in a couple more weeks. She could put some spring flowers on Nanna's grave then and have a little chat, tell her all about it. Yes, that'd be nice, but in a few weeks' time.

Flowers – she ought to get some more for the teashop, the Easter ones had wilted. There were just a few carnations left, which she'd gathered into a vase on the counter. But hey, the way takings were this week she could hardly afford flowers. But she might just nip in and say hello to Wendy while she was here in the town, anyhow, see if there was anything going cheap. She sipped the last of her latte and set off down the street.

'Hello, pet.' Wendy's smile was genuine as Ellie entered the small shop that was fragrant with blooms; tall stems in pinks, creams and purples were bursting from large green pots. 'How's it going at the castle, then? I've been wondering how you've been getting on, been talking about you with Mrs Armitage here earlier. She used to do some cleaning at the castle a while back. *So*, how did it all go?'

'Easter was busy. *Sooo* busy. That was good. Everything went well. No major disasters, even though I felt like I was very much finding my feet. But this week, well it's totally different, it's tailed right off.' She couldn't hold back the disappointment from her voice. Concern was niggling in her mind.

'That's to be expected this time of year, pet. It's the

same here with the flower shop, especially with such an early Easter. There's always a lull.'

'Really?' Ellie perked up a little.

'Oh yes,' Wendy reassured. 'It'll be quiet for a couple of weeks, then steady until May Day and then it gets much busier for the summer season after that.'

'Oh, I see.' She had a lot to learn, obviously.

'Are you in for some more flowers today?'

'Well, yes, but to be honest I can't spend as much as last time.' Ellie hated to disappoint her newfound friend, but needs must, 'It might sound a bit cheeky but do you have anything going cheap? I'm sorry, it's just so quiet this week I can't justify spending a lot. But the flowers looked so pretty last time. In fact, you ought to pop in and see us there at the teashop sometime.'

'Yes, I may well do that. Take a little run out for morning coffee one day. I could bring my mother across. She'd like that.' She smiled, 'Right, for your flowers, hmn – there's two options, I've got some lovely lilies out the back that I can do fairly cheap as they are already open so won't last that long. They're a bit tall for the tables, but might look good on your counter or something. They'll still give you a good week, though. *Or,* now then, there's an idea. See here,' she pointed to some lovely big daisy-looking things, 'Gerberas – come in various shades, and they'll last forever.' Ellie gave her a curious look – *Forever?* 'They'll give instant cheer for your quiet weeks,' Wendy continued,

'And, you won't have to keep shelling out on fresh flowers . . . I don't know why I'm telling you this, I'm doing myself out of business, aren't I?' She was smiling.

'These? They look really lovely, but are they not real?'

'No, not real at all, fake flowers, and just one in a vase will give you instant colour. They come in purple, pink, orange, yellow. Should be £1.50 each, but if you buy the dozen I'll do them for a £1. What do you think? They'll fit in the little posy vases you had the other week, if you just cut the plastic stems down a little. A sharp pair of kitchen scissors will do it, as there's delicate wires through the middle.'

'Wow, they're really pretty. Thank you. It's a deal!' Ellie was ready to snap her hand off. They'd only cost her just over a tenner and they'd never die. 'I *will* still come and get fresh flowers when things pick up again, though.'

'I'm sure you will. They've sat here a couple of months, anyhow, they need moving on.'

Ellie sensed this wasn't quite true, but she was more than grateful for the friendly gesture. 'Thanks, Wendy. I really appreciate it. And your morning-coffee trip with your mum will be on the house, okay?'

'Hmn, sounds a good deal to me. Okay then. Thanks, petal.'

'Oh, and please spread the word, won't you. It's not just tourists who can use the teashop, anyone local can call in, without having to do the whole castle tour.'

Wendy began wrapping the fake gerberas in cerise-pink tissue paper, 'I will do.'

Ellie felt her mood shift: a gesture of friendship, a bouquet of colour, little happy moments to lift a long day.

Thursday was depressingly quiet. Ellie took to reading a history book on the castle to fill in the time, learning that King Edward the First, 'Hammer of the Scots', had stayed there on his way to attack William Wallace (Brave Heart) at Falkirk. *Braveheart,* now that was a classic film she loved, with hunky Mel Gibson in his heyday. However, the real Brave Heart had apparently raided the castle in the prior year and burned all the women and children in a local abbey. Gruesome lot that they were. Thank God all they had to face in the twenty-first century was the tourists.

Nicola and Doris were loitering in the tearooms, with few customers to serve. She sent them home an hour early, after checking with Deana and finding that only three people were touring the castle from two o'clock. The rain hadn't stopped pouring all day. Ellie counted out £20.98 in takings for the day, as she sat there with a half-empty cup of tea in a truly empty tearoom at four o'clock. Now that amount wouldn't cover even *one* of the waitress's wages for the day.

There was a knock on the door and Derek and Malcolm popped in.

'Quiet today?' Malcom asked.

Ellie just looked around her, and it said it all.

'Hmn, thought so. We haven't seen a soul since the last tour at two-thirty.' Derek added.

'Oh, I bet the tours are great. I'd love to know more about the castle. I've been checking out a local history book earlier in fact.'

'No need for history books, young lady, we're the walking-talking history guides. We could give you a tour right now, couldn't we, Malc?'

'Absolutely, there's no visitors left today.'

'Are you sure it'd be alright? I'd have to shut up early.'

'Ellie, there's no one here to serve, flower.'

'Well, I suppose so. I would love to know more about the place.'

'Well, we'd love to tell you. And it is our job, after all.'

'Okay, then. As long as I can repay the favour in tea and cake at the end.'

'Deal.' They both grinned.

'Come on then, Ellie, for our whistle-stop tour of Claverham Castle. Lead the way, Derek.'

They started in the great hall. It was an impressive chamber with leaded-glass windows and French doors that overlooked the large back gardens. Did they call them back gardens in a castle, Ellie mused? Probably not!

'The great hall was used as a location in several films.

The last one being *The Elizabethans*.' Derek set off in polished tour guide tones. 'They set a huge banquet here. It was a-mazing. Even had to build two whole new fire-places to set the scene right. The ones there were the wrong period. Do you remember it, Malc?'

'Oh, yes, and that famous actress, whatever-her-name-was, what a nightmare she was! Talk about diva.'

'This hall looked phenomenal for the film. All set out with pewter plates and cups and a full medieval-style banquet. Roasted a whole pig, didn't they, and the table was *laden* with fruit, breads, the works. Plenty of red wine flowing – meant to be mead, I think. And dancing. Somebody was playing a lute, and there were other instruments. It was all very much in keeping. I suppose they have researchers for those kinds of things.'

'Brought the place to life, didn't it, Derek? Like we'd all been whisked back to the Middle Ages. Anyway, we've kept the table layout similar.'

'With a bit of plastic fruit and fake bread!'

'Yes, they left us the whole dinner set as a gesture. Some visitors still recognise this room from the film. Half expect to see the lead actress waltzing in, and all they get is us pair.'

Ellie smiled along with them. They were good fun.

'Right, onwards and upwards . . . to the drawing room.'

The drawing room looked as though it had been in use more recently. Georgian furniture, maybe? A little threadbare by the looks of it, including a damask-covered chaise longue. Boy, that must have been the life. As long as you weren't one of the servants, Ellie mused. Most of the room was secured behind thick gold ropes that looped from metre-high brass stands.

Ellie spotted some portraits; a row of tall gentleman, dressed in black, with stern faces.

'The Hogarths,' Malcolm announced. 'These are their family portraits. None of that iPhone photo business that we have nowadays, a much more artful way of recording themselves in my opinion. But just imagine having to pose for all those hours. Anyway, there they are all lined up, father, son and so on, on to the next inheritor.'

'That one's Lord Henry's father, another Lord Henry.' Derek added, 'Nice chap, my father always said, though he could be a bit frosty at times. Yes, they used to pass on the family name to the first-born son. There are about fifteen Henrys in all, I think. Well, my father was the butler here, so I've virtually been brought up about the place. We lived in a cottage by the front gates. It was a great childhood, having a castle as a playground. You can imagine.'

'Certainly unusual,' Ellie commented. She could hardly begin to imagine, to be honest, after her childhood in a brick terrace in Newcastle.

Then they headed on up the far spiral staircase to a chamber up near the roof. Derek announced it as 'The

Edward I Room', where the king himself was meant to have stayed with his guards back in 1298. Odd to think that she might really be standing in the same room that a king had. It was all mind-boggling. History really came to life standing there within those cool stone walls, with the relics of hunting horns and swords.

It felt slightly creepy up there, in fact. It seemed chillier than the rest of the castle.

'Is it just me or is it really cool up here?' She pulled her cardigan tighter.

'No, I always feel it's colder here. It is the oldest part of the castle, mind. The original tower.'

'Hmn, is there any history of ghosts about the place?' As she said it, she wished she hadn't asked; that'd be bound to keep her awake at night, for sure.

'Well, there are stories about the Grey Lady. A shifty shadow seen about the place in long grey skirts, with long white hair. But we've never seen anything of her have we, Malc?'

'No, the only thing we've had is the odd thing move about. Like in the drawing room at night all the alarms are on, but still things seem to shift on the coffee table and at the bureau. Bit weird. We've named the mystery mover Trevor. Never seen anything spectre-like at all, though. Just that it seems to move stuff about.'

'Don't worry, Ellie. I think it's Malc, myself. Has a short memory and has been shifting things when he dusts!'

Malcom shook his head. 'Not at all. I even left a cup out once as a test, a Wedgewood one from the dresser display, and that had moved from the bureau across to the coffee table. So, there must be something in it.'

'You've just got a bad memory . . . and a vivid imagination. I've been here all my life, remember, and I've never seen a thing.'

Their banter was amusing and took the chill out of the conversation.

'Right, well, we'll head back down to the tearooms, via the old chapel and the minstrel's gallery. We won't show you the dungeon or that really might scare you.'

'No, we'll leave it at that, guys. But thanks so much. Now I've really got a feel of the old place.'

And they were soon back down at the teashop, drinking tea, chatting away and having slices of her latest lemon drizzle.

On Friday morning Joe dropped by to see how things were going. There was only one couple in the tearooms, the takings were way down, and it was hard to come across positively. Yes, it was nice of him pop in, but then she supposed it was his job, after all, and having him see how quiet it was in there only made Ellie feel worse. She was meant to be attracting customers to the castle with her fabulous food, but she wasn't drawing any crowds, was she? And it felt as if she was letting Joe and the castle down, especially after he'd persuaded Lord Henry to put his faith in her.

Things *really* needed to pick up. She'd saved most of the Easter takings, but there were still food supplies to buy in for next week, and this week's wages to pay. And there were no guarantees that next week would get any better. They had the rest of April to get through before the May Day uplift, if Wendy's predictions were true (and by the looks of last year's visitors' figures, they were). She supposed she could take drastic measures and lay off one of the waitresses or cut their hours, but she didn't want to upset them so soon – they might not be inclined to come back when she needed them.

Well, she'd certainly *not* be drawing a wage herself. At least she could eat the leftovers.

But once Nanna's savings were gone, that was it. What if she really couldn't afford the wages for Doris and Nicola in the coming weeks? They were relying on her salary, no doubt. And then she might have nothing left for the lease payments a couple of months down the line. She'd have wasted all Nanna's hard-earned cash – and she'd put in all those hours working at that care home, bless her. Never complained, even when the arthritis nipped at her fingers; liked looking after the old folks, always baking them extra cakes and taking them in for tea time to cheer them up.

And Ellie's mother, she was already concerned that

Ellie had leaped into something out of her depth and it would all go wrong, that she couldn't do it – run a business, be independent. But she yearned to spread her wings and fly a little on her own. God, she'd love to bloody soar, but a tentative flutter and swoop would be nice.

She couldn't let them all down, as well as herself.

Well, there was a roof over her head – a turreted one at that. She'd just have to ride the storm, but the worry was there, nipping at her insides whenever it got the chance.

What had made her think she could make this work? Too bloody naïve, that was her problem: head in the clouds, clutching at dreams. Lord Henry and her mother were probably right. Had she sat and worked out all the figures, studied the costs, the patterns of last year's takings? No. She just thought she was good at baking cakes and that that would be enough. Or, had she just been running away? What had happened six months ago had been pretty heart-wrenching, after all.

She helped herself to a slice of Victoria sponge that was sitting there waiting for customers who weren't coming, took a big bite, and wondered what the hell she'd got herself into.

12

Ellie

Today should have been her wedding day.

She lay in bed, reluctant to get out into the cold. She didn't really miss him, it had gone way beyond that. She had moved through the gut-wrenching anger, the betrayal, the hurt, to a kind of settled-but-sore sad ground . . . the bastard. Well, perhaps the anger was still there a tad, after all.

Five years of her life she had wasted on that loser Gavin. She'd bought the dress, the shoes, booked the reception, even chosen the bloody reception menu. They'd been engaged for three years, but he hadn't been in a rush to book anything; she'd been the one to organise it all – maybe that should have told her something. In hindsight, it had started to feel too comfy, too settled, too sofa-ready,

143

a boxed set of *Top Gear*, or *Idiot Abroad*. Well, she was the bloody idiot in the end, wasn't she?

Maybe he'd done her a favour, or she'd be swamped in a life of sloth and takeaway dinners by now, working in the same office in the same city for the next twenty years, drowning in a mundane reality. But she *had* loved him – his cheeky grin had swung it, all those years before, at the end of sixth form party. That's why it had hurt so much, still did, she admitted to herself. You couldn't just switch off those feelings, however badly someone betrayed you. She missed having someone to cuddle, to chat with late at night. She missed the feeling of fingertips stroking her back, like butterfly wings, and the contrast of his tense muscled grip that held her to him as they had sex.

But she didn't miss the lies, the betrayal, she reminded herself – the promise of their years to come, all their dreams shattered by an open door, and a broken heart. Her dreams were now embedded here at Claverham Castle, running these tearooms. *She couldn't let it all go wrong.*

So, she'd get up right now, go and make today's batch of scones, maybe even create some new brownie recipes. Yes, a batch of raspberry and white chocolate would be nice, and she could try out some dark-chocolate-and-orange ones. She'd bake a choffee too, to go with the Victoria sponge and fruitcake that were left from yesterday, in honour of the wedding cake she never got. She wondered briefly what it might have been like; she'd fancied something chocolatey instead of traditional, but hadn't had chance to order it. She'd never know now. There was *no way* she was going down that route again, *oh no*. No weddings. No full-on relationships. She hadn't ruled out sex, just the odd fling here and there to keep things oiled, so to speak, but she *was not* going to get emotionally involved. But even the occasional no-strings sex she'd envisaged, had dabbled with once and failed miserably at, had dwindled to nothing these past months. Her friends back in Newcastle had tried to persuade her to get out more, just let herself go and have a one-night stand, but that had lost its appeal. The reality wasn't like *Sex in the City* or *Desperate Housewives*; there were no hunky gardeners lurking about with their pecs on show. Nights out in the Bigg Market began to feel more like a cattle market, and being on her own seemed a better option.

But she'd started to make things change, hadn't she? She was here now in a different life, in her chilly room in Claverham Castle. She was trying to make a go of running her own business. That was something to be proud of, surely? And it was early days. She'd never imagined it would be an overnight success. But it still could be a success, couldn't it?

Right, that was it, no more wallowing in self-pity. There was a long day ahead, hopefully a busier one than the last few. There were brownies to bake, customers to serve. Plenty to keep her mind off the ache in her heart and the what-might-have-beens.

* * *

Joe

The castle would be closing in half an hour. It had been another bloody quiet day; Deana had recorded twelve admissions all day – dire. The hours had dragged. Joe had done some business plans, was working on an idea for getting the castle licensed for weddings, wishing himself luck in persuading Lord Henry to get involved with that, but he was building a strong case . . . and would only present it to his boss once he had all the facts. It seemed pretty straightforward getting a wedding license, but Joe was trying to tie in a full wedding service, the catering, marquees, flowers, the works. If they had everything in place in the next couple of months then they could start taking bookings for next year. They desperately needed to come up with something, the visitor takings hadn't been the same in the past couple of years of recession. 'Another bloody invasion' he could already hear Lord H's grumblings. He held the tourists in the same light as the Vikings or the Border Reivers.

He'd drop by the tearooms, see how Ellie was getting on. It would surely have been a quiet day there too. He might even cadge a slice of chocolate-fudge cake or something if he was lucky. Ellie had seemed a little off yesterday when he had called in, not her usual bubbly self. He didn't think he'd said anything to upset her, but then he never was much good at gauging women's moods. They seemed to work on a different level, and whatever you said didn't seem to be the right thing. He'd learned that from being with Claire those eighteen months, his longest-standing relationship to date. The odd time she was upset, he'd always managed to put his foot in it somehow. Anyway, that was all history – they were never really suited anyhow.

With it being so quiet this week, the tearooms couldn't have taken much. Maybe that was what was worrying Ellie. After all, she had the lease monies to find, bills to pay, and the staff wages, and it was all pretty new to her. But this quiet spell was pretty typical for the time of year, though the dip was bigger than usual. However trade would definitely pick up in the coming weeks. He would mention that, reassure her.

He opened the metal latch of the teashop door, walked in. Ellie was sitting on her own at one of the tables, a half-eaten slice of cake poised before her. She looked up a little guiltily. No one else was there, just the sound of the fire crackling in the grate and the two of them.

'That looks good,' his voice broke the stillness. He smiled as he glanced at the cake.

Her eyes showed her embarrassment, 'Damn, caught in the act. It looked like it might go to waste.' Her glance went across to the counter still laden with scones and cakes.

'That'd be a shame. I know it's been pretty quiet. I should have warned you. Things can get slow for a few weeks this time of year. Don't worry, it'll pick up, always does.'

'It had better do.'

She *was* worried, then, he mused. Of course, she'd have to manage her cash flow. He'd never really thought about it when Mrs Charlton was there, was more worried about making sure the lease payments came in regularly to keep the castle going. He hadn't really got involved – or wanted to.

Ellie seemed quiet, thoughtful. The tone of her voice was different. There was a sadness in her eyes. He wondered if he ought to say something, go and put his foot in it again, no doubt, but took the chance. 'Are you okay, Ellie? Umn, look . . . maybe if cash flow's a bit of an issue this week, I can lower this month's lease payment and add it on to the next, or something.' Lord Henry would give him a bollocking if he found out. He'd just have to make sure he didn't.

'Oh, it's not that,' her voice was faint, 'But thanks.'

Instinctively he laid a hand on her shoulder as she sat there before him. She was wearing a thin black jumper that was really soft beneath his fingertips, her body warm to his touch.

She looked up. There was some kind of connection, which broke with her words, 'Well, I'd better get back to the kitchen to finish tidying up, get ready for tomorrow.' She stood, as if to pass him, then paused. 'Actually . . . a hug would be good.'

'Ah yes . . . of course.' It seemed an unusual request, one he hadn't anticipated, but, yes, he could probably manage a hug.

He put his arms gently around her, a little awkwardly at first. She looked at him with emotions that he couldn't trace, and then nestled her head into his chest. He reached his arms a little tighter, felt her relax against him. She was warm and soft, and smelled of some gorgeous perfume as well as the aroma of baking and cake, which was weirdly sexy. He hadn't had a woman in his arms for a while now, and he had to admit it felt good. A little too good. He felt protective, initially, but then as she snuggled in closer with a small sigh, it happened, oh yes, the dreaded trouser snake was firing up. Shit, shit. This was *so* obviously not meant to be a sexy hug. For whatever reason Ellie needed some comfort, not Mr Snakey making his way toward her hip. Joe shifted his hips back a little, putting a gap between them, desperately trying to think of something else than the gorgeous curves of the woman in his arms. The castle accounts, the tax year-end was coming up, *coming up* – wrong words to choose. Damn, damn. He needed to arrange some new bin collections; try and renegotiate terms. That was working a bit better. Bins, bins, bins. But she was smelling so damned lovely. His arms were around her. He so hoped she hadn't felt him there hard against her hip. Think of something else, man, anything, the bins, the bins . . .

* * *

Ellie

Ellie took a long, slow breath. What on earth had come over her? Yes, it had been a bit of a hard day, but she shouldn't have asked him for a hug – very unprofessional of her. And now this was all very confusing because it felt lovely. Beautiful in fact. To be in a man's arms after so long, *no,* to be in Joe's arms. She knew it was all the shit about the wedding, her emotions had been haywire for the last couple of days, but she shouldn't have involved Joe in it. But now she was here, his arms around her, his hands on her lower back, his breath warm in her hair. She felt a sense of calm. Her soul stilled. She could have stayed just like that for hours. How strange, when she hardly knew this guy. Breathing slowly, letting all those negative thoughts and feelings go. Just the sounds of their rhythmic breathing, the odd crackle from the fire. The light fading outside.

Oooh, she was going to be so embarrassed tomorrow. She pulled back, 'Right . . . Okay, thanks for that.' She tried to sound business-like. 'Sorry about that. It's just been a bit of a bad day, that's all.' She actually dusted herself down, and then felt mortified that he might think she was trying somehow to brush him off her. She felt her cheeks flush. 'Sorry, that wasn't very professional,' she garbled on.

'Do you want to talk?' His eyes were a deep, dark hazel. They looked kind.

'No, I don't think so.' That might tip her over the edge. The last thing she wanted was for Joe to see her crying, and shit-face Gavin was certainly not worth wasting any more tears over. Joe really didn't need to be made aware of her crappy love life, or lack of it. 'But thank you,' she added with a small smile. 'I'll be okay now.'

'Are you sure?'

'Yes.'

* * *

Joe

It was the cue for him to go, but he stood a little longer, watching her as she turned and walked to the kitchen.

What the hell had just happened there? He'd only gone in for a bit of chat and slice of cake. It was like the axis of his world had just shifted and he wasn't sure quite how or why. A 'Kapow' moment, as Batman would have said.

13

Ellie

Well, she was going to make damned sure she didn't let her guard down like that again in a hurry. And it had to be with Joe, her landlord, cringe – what had she been thinking?

That was the problem; she hadn't been thinking, had she? Just feeling – and that was obviously a dangerous pastime. But it was all in control again now. The horrible non-anniversary was over and she could move on with the rest of her life.

It was the weekend. By some miracle the sun was shining, vivid-yellow daffodils were blooming like sentries all along the castle wall and the tearooms had customers – several of them. Doris and Nicola were busy serving, there was money in the till other than the float, and the day had passed in a flurry of soup-pouring, panini-toasting and jacket-potato filling.

Yes, busy was better, not so much time to think. Joe had popped in for the briefest of hellos in the afternoon. That was an awkward moment, but neither of them mentioned a thing about the hug – the best way forward, as far as she was concerned, and a bit of a relief.

But there were still the evenings to handle. She filled them, in the main, with baking for the next day, having a snack for supper while she was still in the kitchen, then back to her room, catching up with texts and emails and watching iPlayer. Lying there on her bed on Sunday evening, she heard the creak of the floorboards above her and wondered how Joe passed his time of a night. Sometimes she heard the tinny treble of his music when he had it on loud or the boom of film sound effects. It was weird to think of him just above her there, in their wing of this centuries-old castle. Who else had lived here? What memories, secrets, loves and lives were held within these walls?

And she remembered the feeling of Joe's arms around her; how very lovely that had been. She supposed there wasn't any harm in just savouring the moment in private. She lay back on the bed with her eyes closed and let herself drift back, almost feeling the warmth, the strength of him around her. The smell of his citrus aftershave and his skin. But it was just a moment in time, a little lapse, pleasant yes, but never to be repeated. He must have thought she was some kind of emotional wreck, coming over all needy like that. Well, he wouldn't see her like that again. She had it all under control.

Deana caught up with her on Monday morning, 'A few of us are going out tomorrow night for my birthday. The Big five-oh, I hate to admit. We're just out for a meal and a couple of drinks down at the pub in Wilmington if you fancy coming along. There's me and Bill, the hubbie that is, Joe, Doris and her husband, Derek and Malcolm, and a couple more friends.'

'Umn, okay that sounds nice. Thanks.' It would be good to go out, do something different.

'We'll be meeting there at about seven. But if you want a lift, my Bill's driving. We could stop by and pick you up here at ten to.'

'Yes, that'd be good. Thanks.' Yes, she'd enjoy some company, have a drink, a bit of supper, let her hair down a bit; she hadn't done that since leaving home. And, being a Tuesday night, no one had to work the next day. Bonus.

The pub was in a pretty village of stone cottages that looked as if it had hardly changed in centuries. The only modern thing there was a pre-fab hut that was being used as a village hall, and even that must had been built in the Second World War. The Swan Inn, like the cottages, was built from the local honey-coloured stone. Inside, it was low-ceilinged with stone walls throughout and flagstone floors. They found a large table in an alcove, it was probably meant for eight, though there were ten of them, so it was a bit cosy along the bench-style seating of the back wall. She shifted in beside Joe, who had Doris and her husband, Clifford, alongside him. Bill went to get a round of drinks in, and they looked at the menus, chatting about their respective days and the nice spell of weather.

After enjoying a hearty supper of beer-battered fish and chips with mushy peas, a welcome change from leftover jacket potatoes and paninis, she sat spooning up the most delicious ice cream, next to Joe, who'd just wolfed down steak and chips.

'This is amazing,' she commented, 'Never tasted anything so creamy. And those little chunks of fudge . . . are to die for.'

'It's from the local dairy.'

'Oh fab! Well, we need to be getting some of this stuff for the teashop. It has to be a hit for the summer season.'

Deana chipped in, 'Oh yes, and have you tried the honey-and-ginger flavour or their chocolate honeycomb? Delicious.'

'I think I've seen little takeaway pots they do, too.' Joe.

'Ideal. Right, that's it. I'm ringing the dairy up first thing in the morning. I'm getting an order in.' She had plenty of room in the kitchen freezer now that the antlered beast had gone, and with the weather hopefully cheering up soon – with any luck it would sell well. Hmn, a trip to the ice-cream dairy might be in order. She might have to test several flavours. What a hardship. The joys of working in catering!

She looked around the group. All bar Derek and Malcolm were couples, she noted (and her vote was still out on them). Everyone had been chatting away; it had been nice easy company. The rest of their party were talking in small clusters, so she fell in with chatting with Joe. She was aware of the flank of Joe's left thigh up close against her right leg, reminding her of his touch. Little electrical pulses seemed to zip between them, which she tried to ignore. She shifted a little, but there was nowhere to go; Doris's ample bottom was filling the seat pad next to Joe, with Clifford, her husband, wedged in next to her. She took a gulp of cider.

'How's the family?' Joe asked.

'Oh fine, I speak to them often. Might even go and visit next week.' That little plan had been forming in her mind. Next Wednesday might be the ideal time.

'Where was it you lived again?'

'Heaton, Newcastle.'

'Yeah, of course, know it well. I was just along at Byker for most of my childhood.'

It had surprised her that he had been brought up there.

It wasn't the poshest end of Newcastle, by any means, and seemed at odds with him being here in a castle in the countryside as estate manager. Mind you, she knew better than to judge a person from where they'd been raised.

'Yeah, my mam still lives there now.' He smiled as he mentioned her, as though he was fond of her.

'Oh, right. Well, ours is a terrace.' Like the many rows and rows of houses in Heaton, brick-built suburbia, everyday life went on; people living, loving, going to work and school. 'The castle seems massive compared to it.'

'Yes.' He wasn't giving much away.

Ellie found herself curious about Joe's background. 'So was it just you and your mum?' The cider was loosening her tongue.

'Yeah, just us two.'

'Oh.' She wondered what had happened to his dad, was afraid to ask in case he'd left them, or something even worse.

'It was fine. She's great.' His eyes twinkled then. 'She worked hard, built up her own cleaning business. Was always busy, but she always tried to be there for me too, well mostly. She'd get back home for when I got in from school, and if she really had to work when I was about she'd take me with her. I'm a dab hand with a duster and a hoover.' He grinned.

'Well that's good to know.'

'Seriously, though, she taught me a lot about work, about running a business.' His tone was full of admiration.

'Do you see her often?'

'Hmn, maybe not as often as I should. It's sometimes difficult to get away from the castle. Maybe once a month or so.'

'Does she come up?'

'No.' His answer was blunt and his tone suddenly flat. It struck Ellie as odd after the warmth in his voice before.

Oh well, maybe his mum didn't drive or something. It was hard place to get to without a car. There wasn't a train station for miles, and the buses were few and far between. She'd looked into it herself for the interview. 'Well, I think I'll visit home next week. I kind of miss them.'

'Uh-huh,' Joe uttered. 'It seems like you get on well?' Joe seemed pleased to shift the conversation back to her.

'Yes, in the main. My mum and I are fairly close, just very different as personalities. I always felt closer to my nanna, really.' Ellie went quiet. Joe looked at her, the past tense hanging like a question. 'She died about eighteen months ago,' Ellie added.

'Oh, I'm sorry.' His hand brushed hers on the tabletop, just the lightest of touches. It was a sympathetic gesture, nothing more, but she didn't know what to do. A bubble of panic filled her, and she shifted her hand away quickly.

'Was she the lady behind the famous choffee cake? I seem to remember you mentioning that at your interview.'

Wow – he'd remembered. 'She is indeed – the very one. I still use her recipe book for it.'

'That's nice. A bit of a legacy, then.'

'Yes, I suppose it is. She used to work at the local old people's home. Made them cakes all the time to take in, to cheer them up. She was an amazing baker. She'd have loved to have her own teashop, I'm sure.'

A flash of light and laughter surrounded them as the landlady brought out a knicker-bocker-glory – Ellie hadn't seen one of those since she was a kid, down on the seafront at Whitley Bay – flaming with an indoor sparkler, and a warbled voice singing 'Happy Birthday', with which they all joined in.

Once the out-of-tune sing-a-long had ceased, Joe offered to get the next round of drinks in for them all, but as he was wedged in along the back seat, he gave Malcolm and Derek a couple of £20 notes to fetch it in for him.

Ellie was on her fifth half of cider now and feeling a tad tipsy. She noticed that Joe had been on Coca-Cola after his initial pint of ale. Malcolm and Derek were standing at the bar. They didn't touch but were standing close, chatting easily, and something in the lean of a head, the warmth of a smile between them made her realise that they probably were a couple. They were in their late fifties, maybe, from a generation where no one really mentioned being homo-sexual. Maybe they had managed to protect their own private world in the shelter of their working lives at the castle and their quiet, rural lives. She knew that they shared a cottage in the castle grounds. Ellie thought they made a great couple. After all, love came in many forms.

They came back with another round of drinks. Malcolm passed across her cider. They did a 'Cheers' for Deana's birthday, and by the time they had emptied their glasses once more, it seemed a good time to be time to be going home. It had been a lovely night.

'I've got my car if you want a lift back?' Joe asked her.

'Ah, alright, yes, thanks.' Other than the hand-brushing moment, it had just been friendly between them, which was fine by Ellie. And a lift would save Deana and Bill having to detour right down the castle driveway and back out again.

There was a mass gathering of coats and kisses, 'Happy Birthdays' and 'Goodbyes'.

The cold air and the dark hit Ellie as she got outside. She felt a little bit wobbly.

'This way,' Joe led her to his car, a little sporty thing in silver. She thought it might be a VW Golf GTI. Gavin was always pointing them out to her back in Newcastle, not that he'd ever have saved enough to get one of his own. The lanes were winding in the dark and she felt a bit giddy, steadying herself by placing her hands on the sides of the seat. He drove fairly fast, obviously familiar with the road, but it seemed safe too. She began to relax and half-closed her eyes, looking forward to her bed and a nice lie-in, no scones to bake at seven in the morning.

'We're here.'

His mellow voice woke her. Crikey! She hadn't fallen asleep, had she? Oh great! She was getting good at embarrassing herself in front of him.

'Ooh, well thanks for the lift,' she smiled softly.

He turned off the car headlights. After a second or two her vision adjusted. She focused on his face in the silvery light of a half moon. He stared back at her. There was the slightest shift of his head towards her. Surely he wasn't going to kiss her? Did she want that or not? She'd done enough daft things lately. But he then leaned back, saying 'You're very welcome. Glad to get you home safe and sound.'

She'd probably just been imagining things. 'Right, well, thanks for the lift,' she muttered as she opened the door and nipped out of his car.

* * *

Joe

He didn't know whether to catch up with her or not. God, he'd *really* wanted to kiss her then. Her lips had looked so damned inviting. He wondered how they would feel against his own, how she would taste? But what the hell was the matter with him? He *never* got involved with staff. It only caused havoc. Best keep things on a professional level. Keep that distance. She was marching away at a rate of knots, anyhow. If she had guessed that he'd wanted to kiss her, it obviously wasn't something she was keen on participating in. 'Goodnight, Ellie,' he called after her, his voice a little hoarse.

She was several metres ahead, digging around in her handbag, approaching the side door they used for their wing of the castle. She looked vulnerable there ahead of him, fumbling for her keys, her back to him, yet there was a strength about her that he admired.

He thought about the other day, when she had asked him to hold her. What had made her so sad? He'd wanted to ask, but tonight hadn't been the right place, too busy there at the pub, and he hadn't wanted to upset her again. Maybe he'd ask another time. Whatever it was, she seemed to want to forget about it. But he hated to think of her feeling down. *Okay, so he couldn't get involved, but if someone had hurt her . . . it had better not be some bloke.* Christ, he'd want to string him up and teach him a lesson. In fact there was an old wooden torture rack down in the dungeon – now that might come in handy.

She was hurrying ahead of him, her shoes clacking over the cobbles. She unlocked the door, stepped through, and wound her way up the stone stairwell. He had trouble keeping up, even with his long strides. As she reached her room, she finally turned to glance at him, 'Night, Joe.' They held eye contact for a second before she looked down, turned the lock and headed in, as though she couldn't get away fast enough.

If she had guessed about the kiss, it was evidently something she didn't want. Jeez, he must be losing his touch with women. Though it was probably for the best all round.

14

Ellie

'Have you taken up residency in here?'

Ellie turned around to see Joe hovering at the kitchen door. Yes, it was meant to be her day off, but she had woken up early and had thought she'd make a head start on the baking for tomorrow – to save such an early start the next day. She wasn't sure what else she was going to do with herself anyhow. The slight cider hangover still clung inside her head, and looking up at him, connecting with those deep-hazel eyes, so did the memory of that nearly-kiss in the car.

'I was just coming down to steal some milk, actually.'

'Ah-hah, caught in the act! Now I know where my supplies keep disappearing to.' She pretended to scowl.

'I don't do it often. It's just a bloody long way to the

shop, and I didn't fancy getting the car out. Can't stand black coffee either.'

'Go on, then,' she laughed, 'Steal away. I'll give you a little jug to take back to your room if you like.'

He stood quietly, watching her for a second.

'Or,' she added in spite of herself, 'You can pop the kettle on here for me. I could do with a cuppa. Just let me pop that tray of cookies in the oven.'

They sat drinking coffee perched on stools at the end of the stainless-steel bench. It was funny how soon this had become her world. What had it been now, three weeks? She liked the bustle of the tearoom's kitchen, the warmth from the big oven that seemed to be permanently on – thank God she didn't have to pay for the gas and electric bills – the buzz of the mixer, the ping of the microwave, the cake and biscuit aromas that surrounded her. She had put Nanna's Be-Ro recipe book up, in pride of place, on the shelf above the work surface at the far end, where she spent most of the day mixing up her cakes or plating out her paninis and jacket potatoes. She was going to expand with some 'specials' next week, perhaps a homemade pie and smoked-salmon-and-cream-cheese bagels, and she had bought herself a chalk board to write them on to display in the teashop.

Joe was watching her as he sipped his coffee. Ooh, she'd been off there in her own little world. Had the castle become his world too, she wondered? Was he happy here? Did it feel like home to him? It was hard to tell. He kept himself pretty much to himself generally – what about Lord Henry being a hermit? For a young man, Joe was a bit of a recluse too. There didn't seem to be any girlfriend lurking about.

'It was a good night last night, wasn't it?' She tried to chat. Their conversation seemed a bit stilted this morning. 'It was nice to get out and about for a change.'

'Yeah, it's a nice little pub there at Wilmington.'

Neither mentioned the getting home bit.

'Good to leave the confines of the castle walls. I feel I'm becoming institutionalised,' she joked.

'Locked up in an ivory tower,' he picked up on the idea.

'Well, a stone one,' she added with a grin.

'Actually, I'm thinking of going for a walk this afternoon. It's a lovely day out there. Do you fancy coming along? Or were you thinking of spending your whole day in here?'

'Umn, okay. Why not?' She wasn't really into walking, but it would be nice to see what was around the castle, tour the gardens. Apparently there was a small lake in the grounds. And she felt herself warm to the thought of spending a little more time with Joe.

'Do you have any boots, like walking boots?'

'Ah, so you mean proper walking. No, the best I've got is these flats.'

He looked down at her feet, shaking his head with a

wry grin. 'You come out to the depths of Northumberland with stilettos – don't deny it, I saw them last night – and plimsolls?'

'Guilty as charged, yes. Served me perfectly well in Newcastle.'

'*Exactly*! Well we're in the wilds now. We'll be hiking across a couple of fields, up through the woods, and up to the top of that hill over there.' He pointed through the small window to a virtual mountainside.

She tried to pull her eyes back in from their stalks, but she'd already said yes. 'O-kay, that's fine,' she replied, not wanting to appear a wuss, but the lilt in her voice gave her away.

'I'll see if Deana's got a spare pair of boots in the office. What size are you? You'll be up to your ankles in mud in those things.'

'Six.'

'Okay, I'll go check. Let me know when you're finished here. Give me a knock at my room.'

'Can't wait.' She didn't try to hide the sarcasm in her tone.

Joe just laughed.

She liked the way his eyes creased at the corners when he grinned like that.

* * *

Joe

Why was he doing this? Digging around in Deana's office looking for a pair of walking boots for her, when he'd actually intended going off for a quiet walk on his own. All he'd gone down to the kitchen for was some milk. But there she was, working away on her day off, and it had brought it back, that near-kiss moment last night, and the earlier memory of her in his arms when she'd asked for the hug. He wasn't quite sure what was going on, and he was damned certain he wasn't going to get into any relationship, especially when they had to work together. But she was good company; last night at the pub had confirmed that.

Maybe he could just keep it as friends, enjoy her company now and again. It could be pretty lonely rattling about here in the castle, especially on those quiet days. And whatever was bugging her, maybe she'd open up if they chatted. He might be able to help somehow. It might be some practical advice she needed, something to do with working here, and he could allay her fears. She worked hard. He'd been impressed by the hours and energy she put in, and the food she cooked was amazing. She might just be overtired. He could cheer her up, crack a few jokes while they walked, bring that gorgeous smile back to her face.

He'd take her out by the lake, he decided, through the

walled garden first, and then into the woods. The rhododendrons were just coming out, with their bold purple flower-heads, and the bluebells should be there, too. They were in bud last time he walked out that way. Then they could carry on up the track. It wasn't too steep that way to reach the top of Claverham hill. She'd surely like the view from up there, even if she was a city girl.

He found a pair of sturdy boots in a corner of Deana's office next to a pair of green wellies. They were brown-leather lace-ups. He turned one over to check the size, six, perfect. He took them, locked the office, and headed upstairs to get himself ready, finding his own walking boots and a waxed Barbour jacket. He wondered if she'd have a decent coat, probably not – she was such a townie. Mind you, he had been once too.

Four and half years he'd worked here now. Worked his way up, started out doing a bit of everything. And his previous experience at the Priory Hotel back at Tynemouth had stood him in good stead. He'd dealt with accounts, staff, stock; started out doing weekend work while at sixth form there as a waiter, and had worked his way up to assistant manager. But here it was very different, it had become a way of life not just a job. The castle kind of grew on you, had a character all of its own. And despite it being quiet at times, almost a little too solitary, he liked the peace, the space, the sense of history. He felt at home here. He wondered if Ellie would get to feel that too. He wanted her to feel settled here, at least for the season. For some reason, he wanted her to be happy.

Why had she needed that hug? It seemed as though coming here was an escape. He wondered what from?

An hour later there was a knock at his door.

'Come on in,' he shouted.

'I'm ready. Well, just about. Do you have the boots?' She was stood there in jeans, jumper, red mac slung over an arm and socked feet. She looked cute.

'Yep, boots are here. Hang on.' He raised the pair into her view, and smiled to himself as she regarded them with disdain. 'Size six, as requested, madam.'

'Who's been wearing them?' Her nose was creased.

'Only Deana, I promise.'

'Alright, I'll put them on then.'

'You don't have to sound so keen. You'd think I'm about to take you mud wrestling or something.'

That made her laugh, though she still looked out of her comfort zone. She came in, sat on a chair in his office. He watched as she laced them up.

'Ready?'

'Ready.'

They took the door out into the walled garden, where the late-spring borders were bursting into life. Colin was evidently doing a good job; the box hedges trimmed and the earth was turned over, chocolate-brown and weed-free.

'I enjoyed last night.' She started up the conversation where they'd left off.

'Yes, the meal was good, wasn't it? And there's always a nice friendly atmosphere there in the Swan.' He wasn't sure if that's what she really meant, but he didn't want to risk reading anything too personal into it. After all, she'd zoomed off at a rate of knots from the car.

They left the walled garden through a wrought-iron gate, following the path that led to the start of the woods and the small ornamental lake. The shade from the trees dappled over them. Leaves, just unfurled and bright lime green, fluttered in a gentle breeze. The undergrowth smelled earthy and dewy. The air was warm down here, but he knew it'd get cooler as they climbed the hill. She'd put her anorak on; it was bright red and contrasted against the honey blonde of her hair, which she tended to wear up. With her green eyes, at least he thought they were green, she was quite striking. A tendril of hair had escaped onto her cheek. He wondered what it would feel like to let the whole lot loose and run his hands through it. Stop. Hold that image right there. Just friends, she works for you, a voice warned in his head. Bloody hell, he was going to have to keep a careful rein on himself here.

'Penny for them?' Her smile pulled him back.

He said nothing. He wasn't going to share that particular thought with her. 'Oh just thinking about something at work,' *or someone*, he bluffed. 'Yeah, I'm still trying to think of the best way to move on with this wedding-venue idea.' He was sure he'd mentioned this last night. They could slip back into work mode. Safe mode. 'I really think it could work for the castle.'

'It's certainly the kind of romantic venue couples would like.'

'Yeah.'

'And I could picture a marquee there on the big lawn.'

'Yes, I'd already considered that. And the great hall would be amazing for receptions for when the weather wasn't as warm. I've already contacted the council about how to get a licence.'

'Is Lord Henry happy with it all?'

'Hmn, that might be the stalling point. He doesn't know yet.'

'Really? Ah, well, that might be a bit of an issue.'

'But if I get all the plans watertight first, and he can see the kind of income it will bring in, I really don't see how he can argue. We can keep it just to Saturdays and Fridays – the rest of the week or when we didn't have wedding bookings we would work as normal. I don't think we could allow our general visitors in on wedding days. You couldn't have tourists gate-crashing the reception and mingling with the guests.'

'Yep, I agree, it would have to be exclusive. But you'd take far more on a wedding booking surely than in admissions. Just booking the place, what would that be? £1,000 plus?' She knew only too well the cost of booking a wedding; that country house near Hexham had cost a mint, and she'd lost all the bloody deposit. 'And you could expect a cut from the catering, the flowers. Were you thinking of providing accommodation too?'

'Well, there's all those spare rooms gathering dust.'

She was definitely on his wavelength here. He liked her business sense. She seemed more relaxed now they were talking work, her step falling into line with his as they strolled through the woods. The birdsong and gentle rustling of spring leaves was a backdrop to their conversation.

* * *

Ellie

She liked his drive, his ambition and energy. He was intelligent without being nerdy. And there was a friendly warmth about him as they chatted that made her relax. But she was still wondering why she was going *rambling* – this was not her thing at all.

Now and again she caught sight of the rise and fall of his thigh muscles under the denim of his jeans. Walking next to him, just inches between them, she remembered the way her head had rested against his collarbone. Ah, and here was the hug moment again, coming back to haunt her. She'd be blushing next, damn.

'Penny for them?' He was coining her own phrase. Actually, it was one of Nanna's sayings too. It sounded odd coming from him.

Now she was blushing. 'Oh . . . nothing.' Only the same image she'd been reliving over the past few nights.

He let it go, striding on purposefully. He was obviously used to walking out here. He was a pace ahead of her, and she now had a good view of his buttocks under the jeans. It was a good image, nice and firm. She averted her gaze. They had reached the lake, the early buds of bluebells carpeted the floor of the woods here and there were also white, star-like flowers. The water was pond-green, and a small black bird with red on its bill paddled gracefully near the reeds at the edge, with the cutest fluffy black chicks in tow. It was pretty and peaceful and felt secluded there, the kind of place you might go skinny-dipping. Okay, so she'd might have been watching and reading a little too much Jane Austen, going all Darcy-comes-shirt-dripping-out-of-the-lake. The buttocks were still marching on ahead.

'Do you swim?' The words came out before she had time to stop them.

He turned and waited for her to catch up, 'What, here?'

'Yeah?' She was curious now.

'What in there? You must be kidding. No chance. It's full of weed and fish, and God knows what. Had a horrid algae all over it last year.'

Oh well, that put paid to any Mr Darcy fantasies. There was obviously no point snooping about in the bushes early morning to get a glimpse of him rising from the waters, all wet torso and dripping hair and . . . She'd just have to use her imagination, as always. It was amazing how creative you could be at times.

'*You* wouldn't swim in there, would you?'

'No, certainly not. It'd have to be Barbados, somewhere exotic *and* hot, to get me swimming in the open water.' Not that she'd ever had the chance. The furthest she'd been was Majorca. Now that had been lovely and warm, but she still stuck with the heated pool of the hotel.

'I used to go surfing down at Tynemouth when I was a teenager. That was pretty damned cold.'

Hmn, she hadn't had him down as the surfer type. But it was nice discovering things about him. Dark hair, all damp, wet-suit clinging to his lean muscles – it wasn't a bad image – *see, told you I was creative*. She smiled at him.

They reached the far end of the lake and the last of the trees. There was a track that led out through a small wooden gate to the open fields. She was a little nervous of the cattle loitering at the far side of the field, but she followed Joe closely up the rise of the hill, keeping near to an old stone wall. She could always leg it over there if they came charging. Her legs began to ache as the bank began to rise steeply, and she was getting out of puff. Joe was marching on ahead, the muscles of his bum still looking rather appealing ahead of her. He turned, realising that she was no longer by his side, 'You okay?'

'Fine.' But she didn't sound fine. It was hard to breathe, walking up this incline, let alone speak. The furthest she'd ever walked in the city was to and from the metro station, going to work and back, usually teetering on high heels and being crushed in the rush of commuter bodies.

'Here.' He strolled back a few paces and offered her a hand. The defined muscles of his lower arm were revealed as the sleeve rode up on his jacket. She felt his strength as he took her weight, and suddenly the uphill climb was a lot easier. His hand felt warm and strong around her own.

'Thanks. So how long have you been here at the castle, then?' She was very aware of his touch, but was trying to sound completely normal.

'Oh, over four years now.'

'What brought you here?'

He looked a little uncomfortable as he answered, 'It was the chance of a different kind of job, a different way of life. I was working for a small hotel back in the Newcastle area. I was doing pretty well, managing the office and the staff, but it was a small family business and there wasn't really any way of getting a promotion.

I'd done various other jobs as a teenager, too, anything I could put my hand to, really.'

She smiled at him. Yes, he seemed the sort that would be a hard worker, and determined to get on.

'And then I came here. The manager had upped and left and Lord Henry, *well* . . .' He smiled, as though he didn't want to run him down, 'Well, let's just say, he doesn't have an awful lot of business sense. He loves this place, but he still can't get his head around the fact that he has to let visitors in to make it viable.'

'Hmn, I can understand that. It's always been his home, I suppose. Was there ever a Lady Hogarth?' Ellie was curious.

'Yes, she died about eight years ago.'

'That must have been tough for him.'

'I'm sure it was.' His tone was a touch curt, as though that was enough said.

They were nearing the brow of the hill now. Joe let go of her hand to open a five-bar gate. He didn't take her hand again, and it seemed wrong for her to reach for his; he'd only been helping her up the steep bit, after all.

'Do you like it out here in the wilds?' she asked.

'Yes, I do.' He looked around at the scenery.

The Cheviot Hills rose majestically in the distance. There was a dusting of snow still lingering over the peaks, which reminded her of icing sugar.

'It's an amazing place,' he continued, 'Very different from Byker.'

'Yeah, and Heaton.'

'It kind of gets into your blood. The countryside. One minute you're moaning about the lack of restaurants, cinemas, bars, but then you go outside and you have all this. And Lord Henry is good to work for – once you get to know his foibles. I love it that I can make a difference. And gradually I've turned things around. We're starting to make a profit. I've got the farm up and running as a business again. It's been a huge learning curve – I knew nothing about farming when I got here. It's not your usual job, but I like it. I like the people, the responsibility, that it's never the same from one day to the next.'

They strolled along the track, starting the climb towards the peak of the hill.

'And *you*, what brings you here, Ellie?' He looked at her with searching dark eyes.

She really didn't want to answer that question, not in any depth. 'Oh . . . just the challenge of something new. I was stuck in a rut at work. Office work, so monotonous. I've always loved baking and cooking, and when I saw the ad, I knew I just had to go for it.' The truth, in a limited version. No point revealing all the personal stuff.

They reached a couple of craggy rocks that marked the top of the hill.

'There you go. Just look around you.' He motioned to the 360-degree view; the hills one side, the sea the other, and their castle down there in the valley below. It was stunning and she had to admit worth the effort of getting up here. 'Right out on the coast, that's Bamburgh Castle and Holy Island.' He stood close behind her as he pointed out the landmarks. The view was amazing. She could smell the warm citrus of his aftershave.

'Wow, it's pretty dramatic. It's also bloody freezing.' The wind was whipping around them on the exposed summit of the hill.

'Come on, let's hunker down below this rock for a minute or two. It'll be out of the wind. I've brought a couple of apples for us.'

'Well that's exciting,' she joked.

'Okay, just because you make gorgeous cakes all day. I don't think a slice of lemon drizzle would have fared too well in my pocket.'

'Maybe not,' she conceded.

They sat in a huddle with their backs against the big stone, munching on crisp Granny Smith apples in companionable silence. He finished his apple and threw the core into the heather. Ellie followed suit, launching hers higher and further.

'You'd have made a great shot-putter,' he grinned.

'Thanks. *I think*.' She gave him a friendly shove.

The ground was beginning to feel cold and there was dampness from the grass soaking into the seat of her jeans. She was wondering about getting up, when Joe turned to her with a serious look on his face.

'Ellie? What upset you so much the other night? When I found you sitting alone in the tearooms? What had happened?'

It took her aback. She'd hoped he'd forget about that little incident. 'Oh, nothing.' She tried to make light of it.

'It can't be nothing to make you that sad . . . But if you don't want to talk about it, that's okay, I understand.'

She took a deep breath. Did she really want to go into this? Something about his tone told her that she could trust him. But, then again, he was her landlord, kind of her boss, did he really need to know the ins and outs and disasters of her love life?

'It was something that *didn't* happen, to be honest . . . But it's all over now. I just had a little blip, that's all. I'm over it now.' But there was a damned tear crowding in her eye.

'You can tell me. It'll not go any further. Mouth zipped and all that.'

'Batman's honour?' She tried to smile.

He laughed, 'Yeah, definitely, Batman's honour.'

She remained silent, weighing up the pros and cons of disclosure, building up the courage.

'Ellie?' He leaned towards her, his gaze on hers. 'It's alright, you don't have to say anything.'

She gave a heavy sigh, 'No, I think I want to.' She leaned in a little further towards him, but looked out across the valley. 'Um, ah, that day . . . the day you found me all

181

upset,' and she was so aware of his warmth next to her, arms and hips touching through their clothes. 'Well, it was meant to be my wedding day.' And the whole story came out, how Gavin had betrayed her with a so-called friend, how she had caught them having sex on the sofa when she'd got away from work early one day, and how, even though she didn't love Gavin any more, the burn of betrayal and the hurt was still there. Tears welled in her eyes and traced a trail of sadness down her face.

Joe put his arm around her and they sat close, 'Oh, Ellie.' He took a strand of hair from across her face, tucked it behind her ear and wiped the tears away with his gentle fingertips.

'Well, there you go, now you know all my jilted, messed-up past.' She tried to make light of it, but the bitterness and hurt was apparent.

'The bastard . . . What an idiot. But, maybe I'm glad too . . .'

She screwed up her face confused. How could he be glad when some pig of a fiancé had let her down? But the look in his eyes gave her a clue and before she could register it, he took her face in his hands and his lips were on hers, gentle at first and then passionate as her mouth accepted and responded. The taste of apples, a tang of salt, and him. Her hands reached into his hair, cupping his head as they kissed. After a while, they pulled away slowly, resting their foreheads together, still huddled against the rock.

What had brought that on?

He looked a little stunned too, as though neither had expected that to happen. And then it began to feel a little awkward. They shifted apart. He stood up first, 'Right, I suppose we'd better head back down, then.'

No more hand-holding. The conversation slightly strained. Striding down the hill, with a space and a sense of confusion between them.

* * *

Joe

So much for a walk as bloody friends – he didn't usually go and kiss people out of the blue. And he was damned well meant to be keeping some air of authority and distance. Well, there was no way he was going to let history repeat itself. Working relationships were a bloody nightmare. *Relationship,* what was he thinking about? There *was* no relationship. It wasn't going to happen. She was just a bit upset, that was all, and he'd taken advantage of the situation, hadn't he? Got her at a low point. Yes, she was a really nice girl. She was probably as taken aback by the whole thing as he was. *Well, that was as far as it would go. Back to professionalism from now on.* Mind you, he'd love to deck that prick of a fiancé for hurting her so much.

15

Ellie

Though the kiss still burned pleasurably in her mind, she tried to carry on as normal over the next few days, back to work at the teashop; baking, cleaning up, trying her best to avoid Joe and that awkward yet oh-so-lovely kiss. Malcolm and Derek had taken to calling in for their morning coffee just before opening time, a welcome diversion. They made her laugh with their stories – of the kid who tried to steal a fake-silver plate and a candelabra from the Great Hall's dining table. It looked rather obvious under his anorak – the parents swearing they knew nothing of it, with guilty expressions on their faces as they clipped him around the ear. Joe had had to become involved, apparently, and the local policeman, just to be seen to be giving out the right message. The kid and his family were let off with a caution. And then there was the story of the old man who sneaked under the security rope for a nap on one of the old chesterfield sofas. They found his wife in the gardens about an hour later, who had 'wondered where he might have got to', but was obviously used to him wandering off, and seemed far more interested in quizzing Colin, the gardener, on the variety of roses in the walled garden.

The weekend was fairly busy, which was good, but still the takings weren't brilliant. After allowing for wages and costs, there was very little left. She began to wonder how on earth she would cover next month's lease payment. At least the days were passing quickly. She realised she hadn't seen Joe except at a distance – perhaps he was avoiding her.

Deana popped in for a slice of cake late on the Sunday afternoon, once the trail of visitors had dissipated. She sat with a mug of tea, perched at the kitchen bench. She had started dropping by more often; Ellie liked her company.

'Don't know what's up with Joe these past few days. Been like a bear with a sore head,' she piped up. 'It's not like him at all.' She sounded genuinely concerned.

Ellie felt herself flush and carried on stacking cups and saucers into the dishwasher. 'Oh,' was all she could muster. It probably had nothing to do with her or the kiss anyhow. Might just be pressure at work, something to do with the castle or the farm.

Doris came through with a tray of empties, her ears pricking up at any sign of gossip. She'd obviously been earwigging, 'Hmn. Yes, something's got into that boy. Hardly managed to raise a smile this morning when I said hello on my way in. I hope the castle's doing okay. Not struggling financially or anything?' She raised her eyebrows at Deana, fishing for information. 'Or maybe there's personal issues.' Doris's eyes lit up, no doubt thinking of all the awful possibilities and scenarios there might be behind Joe's gloom.

Ellie wished the nosy old bat would dump the crockery and get back to wiping the tables out front. 'I'll do that.' She reached across, intercepting the tray. She didn't want the castle staff gossiping about Joe.

'That's enough tittle-tattle now, Doris. I'm sure the castle's doing just fine. And as for Joe, he won't need you meddling in his affairs.' Deana's tone was sharp.

The put-down seemed to work wonders, sending Doris scuttling back to the tearooms with a shrug of her shoulders and a tight furrow of annoyance across her brow.

Ellie felt like high-fiving Deana, but kept her thanks to a smile of gratitude. Deana seemed protective of Joe, she noted. She obviously had a soft spot for him.

Well, if there was something up with Joe, then maybe she should ask him about it privately. After all, he'd been supportive in listening to her troubles. It was the least she could do. And if he was anxious about the kiss, then she could tell him it was all fine – forgotten, a white lie that wouldn't hurt. And hopefully they could get back to being friends and work colleagues again.

She didn't have to wait long to ask him. He was coming down the winding stairway as she was heading back to her room. He had a scowl across his face as he met her.

'Hi.' She tried to sound bright and breezy.

'Hello.' His eyes were low, avoiding contact. Jeez, Doris was right. Mr Grumpy, or what?

'Joe, is everything alright?'

He looked up at her, his eyes dark, brooding, 'Yes, fine.' And he walked on by, as though that was the end of the conversation.

She wouldn't get chance to start asking about the castle or the kiss, that's if she'd even dared. She watched the back of him, three, four, five steps, down and away. Gone. She wasn't sure why but she felt a little tear well up in her eye. They had seemed so close up there on the hilltop, huddled together, just days ago. She'd opened up her heart to him, and now he didn't even want to speak to her. *Bloody men!*

In her room, she decided she would definitely go back home for a visit this week. If she left on Tuesday after work, she'd be back in Heaton by half-six or so, stay the night, catch up with the family, and maybe see Gemma for a bite of lunch on the Wednesday or something. It'd give her chance to see everyone, and have a bit of time out from here too.

*

Heading home, sauntering behind a lorry on the A1 in her little Corsa, everything seemed so different to those four weeks ago. She now lived and worked in a castle – it still made her grin. Doris had actually managed to be nice to her today, offering to finish clearing up so that Ellie could get away. *And*, she was nearly smiling as she offered – was the woman alright? But she gladly took her up on it. It was a kind gesture and one Ellie appreciated, so she was packed and in the car before five o'clock.

She was feeling a little nervous about going back, which was weird. But excited too at the thought of seeing Mum and Dad and Jay, and having someone else to cook for her – bliss. She'd given them a ring yesterday, and Mum had said they'd wait till she got there so they could all eat together, foregoing the habit of a lifetime of eating bang on six o'clock – it must be a special occasion. She was looking forward to some chill-out time tonight with her family, and then tomorrow she'd arranged to meet Gemma in town for some lunch. She dropped the car down a gear and overtook on a good, clear straight, then relaxed her hands on the steering wheel.

City suburbs were soon crowding around her. The

multiple rows of terraced houses cramped around Chillingham Road. She was coming home and yet it felt strange. So many cars and buses, and people everywhere. No sheep . . . no good-looking castle managers who ran hot and cold – *no, she wasn't meant to be thinking about that*. She'd concentrate on the traffic. That was probably wise at this point.

Their street, their house. There was a parking space outside next to Dad's white van. Mum must have been watching out of the bay window as the front door was flung open before she even had chance to get out of the car, Mum and Dad on the threshold grinning. She grabbed her overnight bag, her phone and her purse, and quickly walked towards them, with a big smile on her face that nearly matched theirs. Then she was crushed in a three-way bear hug.

'Oh, how lovely to see you, pet.'

'You're looking good, our lass.' Her dad pulled away to study her, 'Though a little on the skinny side. They been working you hard?'

'A bit . . . but I like it. It's going well.'

'Come on in, pet. The kettle's on. The supper's nearly ready and you can sit down and tell us all about it.'

Jay was there in the hall, his one-arm embrace virtually turning into a headlock.

'Nice to see you, Jay.' She managed to extricate herself from his grip. 'You alright?'

'Sound,' was his reply.

Ah, home sweet home! How nice it was to be back. Though, she was a little worried about what she was going to have to ask her dad about later. A train rattled past, shaking the glass in the window panes. Funny, she never used to notice that when she lived here.

Within a few minutes they were settled in the lounge. Mum had one of her soaps on, Dad was slumped in his armchair, she and Jay sharing the sofa, smells of something homely and stew-like from the kitchen, and everything was as it was before . . . almost. It was she who was different; she felt as if she was changing day by day, but everything here had stayed the same. Yet she'd have hated it if her family had all seemed different and her room had been painted blue or something. *They wouldn't have, would they?*

She nipped upstairs to go to the loo and couldn't resist a peek in at her old bedroom – exactly the same, pale-pink walls, the same old duvet. Her twelve-year-old refuge. It was just tidier than usual, that was all.

They ate a hearty, homely meal with the usual Hall family banter as background.

'Well then, Ellie, how's it *really* going?' Her mum gave her a smile, but Ellie felt she was somehow testing her, 'Is it how you thought?'

'In some ways, yeah.' She'd have to phrase this carefully. 'It's good being able to run the teashop as I like. Being my own boss, as such. Creating the menus, buying in the supplies.'

'And the staff?'

Instinctively, she thought of Joe. 'We're still getting to know each other.' *Some more than others.* 'But the wait-resses are fine. There's two of them work for me, Doris and Nicola. Hard workers.' Keep the answers positive.

'You bringing in enough cash? Are you managing okay for yourself?' Dad was in on the financial and business side.

Ellie felt her face burn. 'Yes.' Little white lies. She didn't want to have to say anything in front of her mum. 'It seems to be working out okay. Not rolling in it or anything, but it's fine. It's obviously early days yet. I'm just building the trade up.' If Mum got wind there was anything wrong, then she'd have her back home and signed up at the job centre in no time, looking for some-thing with a regular salary and a pension scheme.

'No chance of a donation for my new footie boots, then?' Jay looked across at her cheekily.

'Not yet, Bro. Soz.'

'So you're okay there? You're happy, then?' Mum was still trying to whittle her down.

'Yes.' And despite the money worries, dour Doris and the Joe to-be-or-not-to-be relationship issues, she actually felt she was. She'd come a long way in just four weeks, spreading her wings, finding her independence, and her teashop dream was starting to take shape, albeit with several ups and downs. She *so* wanted to make it a success. Coming home had shown her that already she had changed, and that though she missed her family desperately and loved them to bits, tomorrow she'd be fine going back to the castle, to her new life.

* * *

Next morning, she managed to catch up with her dad at his van, just before he had to go off to work.

'Alright, pet?'

'Yes, well not quite.'

'What's up, lass?'

'I-I'm sorry, Dad, I hate to have to ask and I know you'll not have lots to spare, but can I borrow £500 to help with next month's lease on the teashop? I promise I'll pay it back as soon as I can. I'm just turning things around, and I know I can make it work with the summer season now coming up . . . It's just to tide me over.'

'Okay . . . I'll find it for you.' He gave her a wink.

She felt dreadful having to ask. Had always stood on her own two feet. And if her mum found out, well, she'd get a right ear-bashing.

'Give me a couple of days and I'll get it moved across to your account.'

'Thanks, Dad, I really appreciate it. I won't let you down.

I'll pay it back the minute I earn it.' She gave him a big hug. Mum was staring out of the window by now, curious as to why they were taking so long with their goodbyes.

'Right, I'd better get on, got a living to earn. Better crack on, pet. You'll make right, I know you will.'

'Thanks. Love you, Dad.'

A last bear hug in a boiler suit, and he hopped into the driver's seat of his van. 'Take care, pet. See you soon.'

*

It was always peaceful in the graveyard, calming somehow. She knew some people would find it a bit freaky, the thought of all those dead bodies lying just below you, but it never bothered Ellie. And it was the place she'd continued to come these past two years to chat to Nanna.

'I've brought you some flowers. Those nice bright-yellow carnations you always liked.' She had reached the headstone, picked up the glass vase and went off to fill it from the outside tap that was just at the end of their row. She began arranging them and popped the vase back on the grave.

'Sorry I haven't been for a little while, Nanna. It's just been manic busy. I took the job. I really like it, and the castle and the people I've met.' Joe popped up in her head, but she wasn't ready to talk about him yet. Keep it simple for now. She chatted on for a while about the teashop, and Deana and Doris and Nicola. About Lord Henry and his big half-empty castle and the fact he hated all the visitors. She could almost hear Nanna's throaty chuckle at that. Oh, and Kirkton and the flower shop with Wendy. Derek and Malcolm, the tour guides. Nanna was always very open-minded and without prejudice – she saw as she found. Needless to say, she had never actually warmed to Gavin.

The sun was warm on Ellie's back as she sat watching a rabbit nonchalantly chewing grass. He looked over at her, no doubt eyeing up the nice fresh carnations to have a go at later. She was quiet for a while. An old man wandered by, smart in a tweed suit that looked well worn, a small bunch of freesias in his grasp. He tipped his flat cap at Ellie who said 'hello'. She wondered if it was his wife he was visiting, what kind of relationship they might have had, and how he must still miss her. She wondered if anyone would ever love her like that. Like Nanna and her Norman – she was always talking about her Norman, all those years after he'd passed away. If there was a heaven or an afterlife, however it might be, she hoped they'd found each other again. There was a little tight lump in her throat.

'Nanna, there's someone . . . Someone called Joe, at the castle.' It was hard to know how to put this into words, but she found she wanted to try. They hardly had a relationship to speak of, and now he wasn't even talking to her. But something deep inside told her there was something special about him. 'But he's my boss, you see. Well, not quite my boss, but it feels like it. I lease the tearooms from him, well, from the castle I suppose, but he's in charge of it all. And one minute I think he likes me and the next, well, he's really hot and cold, you know . . .'

She could hear Nanna's voice loud and clear in her mind, those lovely warm Geordie tones, 'So you like him, hinnie.'

'Yes, I do', she wasn't sure if she answered in her head or aloud.

'So does he like *you*, lass?'

'I'm not sure, that's the problem.'

'And you say he's blowing hot and cold. Sounds to me that he likes you, then. That's a sure sign.'

Was she really chatting away like this in her head? Was she going crackers or was her brain just making it all up to try and convince herself Joe had actually fallen for her?

Just follow your heart, were the last words that filled her mind. *It'll tell you what to do.*

The old guy was kneeling at a grave a few rows across. Ellie could see his lips moving, too, though she couldn't hear a word. So she wasn't the only one chatting away to the dead. He looked serene and matter of fact, as though this was a regular date. Ellie sighed, happy-sad all at once.

Sad for all the people who had gone and for those left behind, but happy for the love they had had and still had. Her bum was feeling a little damp from the dewy grass. She'd need to go soon and get ready for her lunch out with Gemma – catch up on the office gossip and the social scene she had left behind. No doubt she'd be required to tell all the ins and out of castle life, though she didn't intend being quite so open with Gemma as she had just been with Nanna, not until there was something definite to tell, anyhow. Anyway, it might just all fizzle out and that would have been that. One kiss, one hug, consigned to history.

* * *

Lunch was good. She slipped back into old times with Gemma, tucking into gourmet burgers at a busy American diner in the city centre. Then they had a good mooch about the shops. Boy, did she miss shops, the shoes and fashions. She gazed longingly at a pair of hot-pink stilettos, but knew she'd not get chance to wear them, so picked up a couple of bargains instead; a new pair of black trousers for work, very practical, and a pretty red lace top that took her fancy – she might just get away with it at the village pub on an evening out, teamed with a pair of jeans.

She found out all the goss; who was dating who back at the office, that Moaning Margaret from their call centre claims team had been sideways moved to Sales – much to Gemma's delight, the latest antics of the girls' night out last Friday, which included much vodka, flirting and laughter by the sounds of it.

'So, come on, then, spill the beans. What's it really like up there in your castle pad? And, more to the point, what's it like running your own teashop?'

'Well, it's all going really good . . . overall. Been a few hair-raising moments to start. And Easter weekend I was running around like a blue-arsed fly. But now it's quietened down . . . a little too much.'

Gemma noted the hint of concern in her voice. 'So, is it hard to make much money out of it? We'll not be flying off to New York for a shopping spree anytime soon, then.'

'Not likely, hah. At the moment, yeah, it's a bit of a lean period. I'm inexperienced, I know. And I hadn't realised how much business would dip in April. But I've been told it will pick up soon. It's just a seasonal trade.'

'I'm sure you'll be fine, hun. Just hang on in there. You can do it! Oh, and how's the old bossy bag of a waitress?'

'Ah, Doris, well she still has her moments, but we're getting on okay. I think she'd be like that with anyone she worked for, to be honest. She can be a bit intimidating, mind.'

They laughed.

'And, more importantly . . . anyone hot in the new set-up?'

Phew, now there was a question. The only one hot right at that moment was Ellie, who felt the blush creep up her neck. 'No,' she answered a little too quickly.

Gemma took a sideways look at her, sussing her out, '*There is*, isn't there?'

Damn, she was never any good at lying.

'It's nothing, honest. Early days and all that. And it's probably never going to happen. *Should* never happen. Remember what it was like between you and Mark at the car showroom. Well, I've taken heed. Enough said.'

'Ah. Steer clear, Els. If he's boss material, that's a full-on danger zone.'

And didn't she know it.

'Well, when are you back next? We need a proper night out not just lunch next time.'

'Probably in a few weeks' time. I've missed you all.'

'Well, it's you, me and the girls at Jack's Club, then. And we'll get you sorted with a proper bloke.'

Ellie felt a sense of gloom. Gem was lovely, but her idea of a 'good bloke' was way off Ellie's. But then, she'd failed miserably on the bloke front up to now, hadn't she?

They finished chatting. Gemma was due back at work after a slightly extended lunch hour ('dentist's appointment'). Ellie headed back home to be in time for Jay coming in from sixth form (he even offered to make her a cup of tea, which was a miracle) and her mum and dad coming back from work. She was helping prepare the supper, peeling potatoes for a cottage pie – though her mum protested, wanting to be the one to spoil Ellie before she had to drive back. Mum stood still, stopped peeling her onions. 'Ellie, your dad's told me about the money.' She had a stern look on her face and Ellie felt her stomach sink. She'd hoped Dad might have kept it quiet for a little while, at least.

'We don't have secrets between us.' As if she was reading Ellie's thoughts. 'Your dad's worked really hard for that money, Ellie. There's not an awful lot to spare. I just hope you know what you're doing, that's all.'

'I know, sorry, Mum. I wouldn't have asked unless I felt I had to, but I just have to give it my best shot. The summer months are coming, and I'm just getting there, starting to see more people coming in, building the trade. I promise I'll pay you back, whatever happens.' Even if it meant finding another job, or coming back to the insurance office, then needs must. God, that was such a depressing thought, but she would if it came to it. But she'd give the teashop her absolute all first.

She could feel the disappointment, the uncertainty almost vibrating from her mother.

'I promise,' she repeated.

Her mum didn't reply. Her face said it all. Was she being selfish, chasing some silly dream? Wasting all their money, and Nanna's savings too?

Dad had brought home a big apple pie from the local baker's for them all for pudding. She'd felt a little sick eating her farewell meal. She went upstairs soon after to repack her bag, ready to get back in the car and head north again. She aimed to leave at around seven-thirty.

She was fine about going back to the castle; her life felt almost as much there as here now – it was like she was straddling two worlds. And she was looking forward to getting back into the teashop for the summer season, hopefully the visitors would start flocking in now. She was determined to make it a success. She had to make this work. The next two months were crucial. She had to earn enough to pay her parents back, every single penny, and then to save for the coming months' lease to see her through the rest of the season.

She was going to speak with Joe about advertising, get the teashop mentioned more prominently in any publicity the castle might do, and maybe create a little flyer herself to pop into local shops and the tourist information centre – let people know she was there.

Joe. She pictured his face, his smile, and felt a warm glow within. She couldn't deny that she was looking forward to seeing him again, even if things were a little awkward between them. Yet her heart also felt a little heavy as she drove away from her childhood home, watching her family waving on the step. She waved back out of the open car window and gave a cheery toot, which had a hollow ring to it. No doubt it would always feel strange leaving them behind. She just hoped she wouldn't let them down.

16

Ellie

On the Monday morning, Wendy came into the teashop with her mother. Ellie served them a pot of tea and fresh strawberry scones with jam and cream, on the house. They managed to chat between Ellie serving other customers. Ellie mentioned she'd be back in to Kirkton on Wednesday to buy some fresh flowers again. The takings had been slightly better over the last week, and Ellie also wanted to broach an idea she'd been mulling over about the castle weddings, see if Wendy might be interested in helping out with the flowers – they'd need bouquets, posies for bridesmaids, decorating the hall, or the castle chapel – wherever the weddings would take place – table decorations, button holes, and who better to use than the local friendly florist. It was a gem of an idea, and if Wendy was keen, then Ellie would mention it to Joe. It could help secure the proposal for the castle becoming a wedding venue, and help to convince Lord Henry – they could provide the whole lot, the venue, catering, flowers.

She'd only seen Joe in passing since she had got back from her trip home, but he did come through for a take-away coffee on the Friday morning, which seemed a bit odd as Deana often took him one up to his office. Ellie had been busy with orders at the time, gave him a brief smile, but didn't get a chance to chat. But then, she hadn't seen sight nor sound of him since, other than a creaky floorboard above her of an evening.

Monday night, she stayed on a little later in the kitchens once the waitresses had gone and the castle had closed. She saw the blink of Deana's light going off in the office across the way. She liked the peace, turned the radio on to Classic FM. It was usually set to Radio 1 throughout the day, but she had started tuning in of an evening and liked baking to something a little gentler (and sometimes more rousing, in fact), mixing to Chopin or beating to Bach. There was a knock on the swing door and Joe popped his head around, holding a white china jug before him hopefully.

'Milk?' she guessed. It was nice to see him again. He'd definitely been keeping a low profile, but perhaps he'd just been busy.

'Please. Run out again, sorry.'

How could anyone resist that grin? 'I suppose I might have a little spare.' She filled his jug from the six-litre plastic bottle that she took from the fridge.

He looked a little awkward.

She carried on rolling out the cookie dough she'd been working on before he had come in.

'Umn, well . . . I just wondered . . . would you like to come out for the day with me on Wednesday. Umn, maybe a walk on the beach, some lunch?'

She raised an eyebrow curiously, 'Is this a date?' She needed to know exactly what he was asking – there had been way too many confusing signals of late.

His face reddened. 'Ah, it can be, if you want it to be.'

Did she want it to be? Yes, yes, yes, you bet! Her heart did a double flip. But then, every warning bell and siren was going off in her head too. 'Ah, okay, then.' Her voice sounded amazingly cool, despite her inner antics. What was she doing? But that kiss, whoah, that kiss. And every nerve in her body came alive with him just standing near her. She gave him a wry smile that broke into a grin.

'Great.' He sounded relieved. 'I'll knock on your door about ten on Wednesday morning, then.'

Two o'clock, Wednesday morning, her heart was flipping like a pancake, keeping her awake. What the heck was this guy doing to her? And *she,* who was *never* going to get involved with any man again. And certainly not anyone she worked with. In fact, why was she doing this? Why had she let him get to her? But it had sneaked up on her, hadn't it? Letting her heart rule her bloody head again. That was a very dangerous business.

Eight o'clock – what to wear? Casual for a beach walk, but nice too, like she'd made the effort for the lunch. Smart jeans and the new red top? But it was a bit fancy, and lacy, nah, more for an evening – she didn't want to look overdressed. She frisked the wardrobe, found a pretty floral top with a chiffon effect. Yes that, jeans, a cardie – sorted. Shower time, wash hair. Get ready.

* * *

Joe

He took a slow breath. Ten o'clock on the dot. He was going to take Ellie to Bamburgh for a walk on the beach, and then some lunch. Casual, but hopefully a nice day out – see how they got on.

He knocked. He noticed his palms were slightly sweaty. He still wasn't certain that it was a good idea – taking a member of the castle staff out on a date. It was against all his better judgement, but something inside wouldn't let it go. He'd been feeling miserable and restless since that hug in the kitchen that night a few weeks ago, and even more so after the walk, until he realised he just had to go ahead and ask her. Get it out of his system one way or another. See how things worked out. And that kiss – it had lingered in his mind. It was bloody great and he'd like more of them, hell, yes . . . Right, that was enough of that. He couldn't let his mind go any further or he'd start getting horny.

The door opened. 'Hi.' She was there with a sunny smile just for him, dressed in a cute flowery top and jeans.

Wow, she looked great. 'Hi. You look lovely.'

Her smile broadened. 'I might need to borrow Deana's boots again, if that's okay? If we'll be walking on the beach, that is?' He looked down at her footwear. She was in those black plimsoll things again, not ideal.

'No problem. I'm sure she won't mind. We can pick them up on the way out.'

'I'll just pop on my coat.' Ellie went back into the room, leaving the door opened wide.

He looked in. She'd made it really cosy and rather stylish, all red-and-white bed linen with cushions and nick-nack things that women seemed to love. It looked like a different room altogether from the rather dreary one he'd offered her those few weeks ago. In fact, the castle seemed a different place from what it had been before she had got there.

'Right, I'm ready.' She had put her red mac on. He

liked her in that. It was bright and cheery, just like her.

They were soon off in his VW Golf. He put his foot down, knowing there'd be no tourists hanging around the castle today, and sped off up the driveway. It was great zipping through the country lanes with a gorgeous-looking woman in the passenger seat. He was feeling better about his decision to ask her out. It would be a chance to get to know her a bit more. And then he might be clearer about what next, or if there should be a 'next'.

'Have you been to the beach here before? We're heading to Bamburgh?'

She gave him another smile. He remembered those lips on his, it put him off his driving for a second. He tried hard to focus on the bend ahead.

'I might have done . . . as a little kid. Though we didn't tend to come up this far. I can remember having fish and chips at Amble and ice-skating in Whitley Bay.'

'Was that when you were younger, as a kid, in Newcastle?'

'Yeah, what about you? Did you have days out, trips up the coast?'

'No, not often. There wasn't an awful lot of spare cash for days out. Once or twice we went out to Tynemouth on the bus. I remember having an ice cream down by the castle. And the seagulls going crazy. Mam was usually busy working, though. I'd sometimes go with her, espe-cially when I was younger. Some big posh houses she'd clean, we used to have to take the bus out to those. And then she used to do the cleaning for a couple of factories near our house. They weren't so glamorous, mind.'

* * *

Ellie

His home life sounded very different from hers, even though they hadn't lived that far from each other.

'Oh, I see.' But she couldn't really. Couldn't imagine it being anything but her and her close-knit family. 'Do you have any brothers or sisters?' He had never mentioned anyone.

'No, just me and my mam. It was okay. We always got on fine. And then when I was a bit older I had my mates, we'd play footie when Mam was off on her cleaning jobs on a Saturday. There was a bit of rough grass near our house, mind you it was more gravel than grass. Scuffed your knees to bits if you went down. There wasn't a lot of diving in our matches.' He gave a wry grin, 'Happy days, huh!'

She had a feeling that sometimes they had been far from that.

Majestic on the skyline, a towering, walled castle of salmon-pink stone came into view. Beyond it was the metal blue of the sea, and she got that little thrill she always used to at seeing the coast. She and Jay used to sit in the back of the car, willing that line of deep blue to come into view, and be the first to shout out. She held back from calling out now, in case Joe thought her a total nutter.

'Now, there's a castle for you, Bamburgh.'

It really was impressive, with several layers of walls and lookouts. Even from here she was sure she could see cannons – it must have scared the living daylights out of any potential attackers. She wondered about its history.

'Does anyone live there now?' she asked, thinking about Lord Henry rattling about in their own castle.

'Yes, I believe so, the Armstrong family. Some pad, hey?'

'Hmn, and I bet they have tearooms, or tea palaces in there. We could maybe eye up the opposition?'

'Let's hit the beach first.'

They drove through the village of stone cottages, quaint shops, a pub and hotel, which was set around a grassy, tree-lined green. Joe turned the car into a narrow lane that took them down towards the dunes, where they pulled up. The castle dominated the skyline here too, commandeering the view out across the gunmetal blue-grey of the North Sea. The tide was out and the golden sands of the beach stretched as far as you could see. People looked tiny, like something out of *Gulliver's Travels* on the sands there. As she stepped out of the car, Ellie could hear the 'husshh' of the rolling waves, the cry of a circling gull, the beating of her heart. She was suddenly nervous, being here with Joe. She wanted everything to go well. She wanted him to like her.

She started gabbling on about the lovely view, and that she wasn't sure if she had been here before, she would surely have remembered a view like that. . . . And then he took her hand, held it warm in his, as they made their way down the sandy path between the spiky marram grass. That silenced her.

The early May wind raked through her hair and made her eyes smart as they got on to the beach. It swirled the soft sands around their feet. The pair of them walked, chatting comfortably – about work, her visit home last week.

'My lot are threatening to come up for a day out soon. That'll be fun.' She was playing mock-horror, but was looking forward to it really.

'That'll be nice for you.'

'You reckon?' she joked. 'Does your mum ever come up?' She seemed to remember asking that before, as she was saying it.

He stared ahead, answering, 'No . . . no. I generally go down there.' His tone was blunt, then softened, 'I try and visit fairly often, though maybe not as often as I should.'

'Oh, okay.' Ellie willed him to go on, but didn't want to probe.

They walked across the line of dried seaweed and straggled shells, the debris of the last few tides, and kept to the soft, flat sand, going a good mile or so southwards down the coast. He didn't let her hand go all the while. He seemed so much more relaxed with her today, and that was lovely.

'Ready to turn back?' As they switched direction, they broke hands as they turned, but she felt comfortable enough to loop her arm through the crook of his elbow, and snuggled in a bit closer. It felt good, but then her conscience warned her: this is how it all starts, then you get in too deep. This is how you get hurt. *They leave you, they betray you.* Could she do this all again? But Joe was different; Joe wasn't Gavin. She had to give him a chance and, blimey, it was such early days, they might just realise they weren't really suited and it would all fizzle out anyhow. But with her arm through his and their bodies side by side, it felt that they were meant to be that way. She felt all buzzy inside having a tall, handsome man, with floppy dark hair and a fantastic grin walking alongside her. They looked like any other long-standing couple out for a stroll, and yet this was all so new and exciting it almost hurt.

'So what do you fancy for lunch, then? There's a couple of great pubs, or we could drive along for fish and chips in Seahouses. Or we could try the teashop?'

'No, no teashop, much as I'd like to suss out the

opposition, maybe not today after all. I fancy a total break. A pub sounds fine if they do good food?'

'They do great food. I'll take you to the Cross Keys.'

The Cross Keys was just off the village green in a row of old stone cottages. Despite it being early May, there was a roaring log fire and a cosy feel with tartan-patterned carpets and a dark-wood bar. She eyed up the homemade fishcakes with a side salad on the specials board, or thought she might go for the scampi and chips. They found a small round table and sat on stools. The conversation was easy-going as they joked together about the latest stories of life in the castle – there was always something daft or unusual going on. Last week, they'd had a couple locked in, Joe told her. They'd gone off the tour guide route, probably being nosy. Derek and Malcolm had checked all the main viewing rooms, as per usual, before shutting up for the night. Well, this pair had ignored all the private signs and headed off for a tour of Lord Henry's living quarters so it seemed. Luckily for them, Henry was out or they'd have been met by an aristocratic bear with a very sore head at the invasion of his privacy; though it would have served them right. Joe had found them battering at the inside of the main castle door, shouting for 'Help' at 7 o'clock at night, desperately trying to get out.

Ellie had to laugh.

'So, do you feel you've settled in at the castle? Is it what you expected?' he asked her.

'I wasn't sure what to expect, to be honest. It's all been a steep learning curve. But I love the teashop, and the baking and yeah, well, I have to admit the business side is challenging sometimes, but I'm doing my best.' She felt she could be open with him.

'I think you're doing well, honestly. I know you've had a lot to take on board. But the tearooms are looking great, and the food even better.'

'Thank you.' Wow. She gave a mental air punch and smiled.

She decided to order the fishcakes, which were scrummy. Joe chose the steak-and-ale pie. It looked delicious. His knee moved to rest gently against hers at one point in the meal and she felt her own leg melt like jelly. She tried to ignore it, but it felt quite sexy and a bit naughty – or maybe that was just down to the fact she hadn't actually had any physical contact with a man in months.

People were in and out, eating, drinking, chatting. Then, too soon, it was time to go. Joe settled the bill, even though she offered to halve it, insisting that he pay this time; it had been his suggestion to come out. It was only a short walk to the car, as he'd driven up from the beach to park in the village, no hand-holding this time. She wondered how it would be when they were back at the castle, would they have to go back to appearing all professional? She wondered if he would give her a goodbye kiss as they went back to their rooms, or in the car before they got out. She realised she'd like another kiss, *very much*.

She enjoyed watching him drive on the way back; the way he handled the gearstick, his long fingers, neat nails. He drove well, on the edge of fast, but it still felt safe. He evidently knew the roads. As they entered the tall black wrought-iron gates of the castle, she realised that she didn't want this date, or day, to end. She glanced at her watch – it was only three-thirty, it seemed odd to go back to their own rooms and listen to him wandering about, the faint drone of his telly above her. The castle was quiet, no tourists today, no Deana in the office, no tearoom staff to see them . . . There might be all sorts of possibilities.

There was just Colin pottering about by the main entrance, tidying the border there. They parked up.

'Thanks, that was really lovely – the walk, the lunch, everything.' She was building up the courage to ask him back to her room for a coffee. She wasn't sure if it was *just* coffee herself yet, when there was a rap on the driver's window.

Joe pressed a button for the window to come down.

Colin appeared at the side of the car, 'Lord Henry's been looking for you.' He tipped his cap, then, seeing Ellie there. 'I said I'd thought you'd gone out, what with the car gone, but he seemed quite keen to catch up with you. I said I'd tell you as soon as I saw you come back.'

'Oh, I see. Okay. I'll go and find out what's up.' With that, Joe was up and out of the car, muttering, 'Sorry, Ellie.' But already he seemed distant, as if he was wondering if there might be a problem. She'd barely climbed out of the car when he'd flown up the castle steps, with a brief, 'Catch you later,' shouted over his shoulder.

'Yes, okay, see you later.' Disappointment plummeted through her like a stone.

* * *

Joe

Joe knocked on Lord Henry's door.

'Come in.' The voice was cool, stern. As Joe opened the door, his boss uttered, 'Ah, at last,' grouchily adding, 'Where the devil have you been?'

Joe felt like saying it was his day off and that he was allowed to go out wherever and with whom he liked, his thoughts still lingering with Ellie. It was a bugger he'd been called away like that. Typical. Things had seemed to be going really well with her. But he knew better than to wind Lord Henry up, especially when he was already grumpy. Joe was curious as to what this was all about.

'Is this right, what I've been hearing from Mrs Allan?'

Mrs Allan was the lady who cleaned Lord Hogarth's apartments once a week. 'That you're planning on making us into a wedding venue? Roping in local florists and the like?' His face was stormy. 'And when the hell were you thinking of telling me, seeing as I own the damned place?'

Oh shit. Someone had been talking, and the cat was out of the bag before he'd had the chance to prepare and brief Lord Henry properly. Bloody hell! Who had been gossiping? But hardly anyone else knew. This might jeopardise everything.

'Yes, it's right.' Joe's tone remained calm. He may as well be honest. There was no point beating about the bush now. 'I have been looking into the wedding idea. But there's nothing in place as yet. I wanted to find out as much as I could before I discussed it with you, so I could present you with the full information.'

'Well surely you'd realise I don't want *even more* people traipsing around my home, getting themselves tipsy in the great hall or in some marquee out on my lawn. You'll be turning the castle into a God-damned theme park next.' His cheeks were puffed out and red with indignation.

'No, of course not, Lord Henry. Yes, it would be busy on the wedding-event days, admitted, but it seems a really excellent way of bringing extra income to the castle, *and* looking at the latest accounting figures we certainly need it.'

'Well, yes, I had noticed,' the elder man admitted grudgingly.

'The weddings would just be a few pre-booked dates, probably on a Saturday, or maybe over a weekend if we opened up rooms for the night.'

'Rooms?'

'Maybe, yes, in time. We'd close the castle to general visitors on the wedding dates, so that would mean fewer visitors than now, but ones who were willing to pay a lot more money to have this fantastic castle as a venue. And, yes, they might want to stay overnight. Why not?'

'Christ! We're turning into a hotel now, are we?' His grey brows were knitting together with frustration.

'Look, just let me get all the facts and information together, like I was planning on doing. I'm nearly there, and then we can have a proper meeting and talk everything through with figures to back it up. I'd like the chance to explain fully what I'm proposing and the income opportunities relating to it.' Joe stayed calm, giving it his best shot. 'Letting the rooms out overnight would come much later. It's not something I'd be planning straight away.' Too many costs involved, and they couldn't possibly let out the rooms as they were now. But he didn't mention that to Lord H. It was definitely on a need-to-know basis at this stage. 'So there'd really be minimal disruption, at least to trial the idea initially.'

Lord Henry just raised his eyebrows, his narrowed eyes betraying his scepticism.

'We'd just start by advertising as a wedding venue once

the licence was in place,' Joe continued, 'I've already put feelers out with the local council. It wouldn't be a difficult process.'

'You *have* been busy.' Lord Henry's tone was sarcastic. 'I just don't like being kept in the dark . . . and then to hear it from the God-damned cleaner.'

'Yes, well I apologise for that.' He was going to have to have words with Ellie . . . he was beginning to realise it was the only way it could have got out. 'That shouldn't have happened, I'm sorry. But round here one tiny strand of information gets out and the whole of Northumberland seems to know about it.' Now Ellie was in his mind. 'I was thinking of catering too,' he added, 'Using Ellie from the teashop for buffets and the like. Or we might bring in outside caterers for a sit-down meal, if they wanted silver service.'

'So, you've been discussing all this with that Ellen girl, then?' The words hung heavily, meaning *before he* had been advised of anything himself. 'Just be careful of getting in too thick with the staff.'

What the hell did he mean by that? The cheeky bastard. Joe felt his temper flare. He felt protective about Ellie, even if she might have inadvertently let on about the wedding idea. 'Anyway, she's not staff as such, she's a leaseholder here,' he countered. And Christ! *Henry* was a fine one to talk – the hypocritical old codger. With everything, *everything* that had gone on. Joe felt like decking him, his fist was itching, but he held back enough just to give him a stare of steel. Losing control now wouldn't help his case with the wedding-venue proposals.

'How's the girl getting on, anyway?' Lord Henry seemed to realise he'd overstepped the mark, his tone softened.

'Good. Yes, *Ellie's* doing really well.' Joe emphasised the correct version of her name. 'The teashop takings are up a third on last year already.' It had been a bloody poor year last year, and Ellie was starting to turn things around. 'She's met all her lease payments. And the customers seem very happy. There's been some great feedback on the food and venue on Trip Advisor.'

'Trip-a-Whattie?'

'Trip Advisor. It's a site on the internet.'

'Oh, bloody computer stuff, is it?' Lord Henry was always sceptical about anything to do with a computer.

'Yes, people comment and rate places they have been to: restaurants, hotels and the like.'

'Ah, I suppose people look at that kind of thing, do they?'

'Yes, they do.'

'Hate bloody computers!'

Joe gave a wry smile, 'I know, but it's the way the world's going, Lord Henry. We've got to have a presence there. Our website's looking good.'

'I'll trust you on that.' He pulled a grimace. 'Right, well, back to these damned weddings . . . I suppose it might be a reasonable idea to look into. I'll take a look at your proposals anyhow, no promises or anything. Get all the information together by the end of the week. We'll meet on Friday. That should be time enough for you?'

'Yes, certainly. I'll have it all ready by Friday morning. Thank you.' Joe sounded polite and professional, even though he was still fuming about Lord Henry's personal comments earlier. But inside he also felt a strand of hope for the castle and its future. It wasn't a 'no' and in Lord Henry's book that was a *major* step forward. But he'd still have his work cut out trying to convince him.

What a bloody shame it had all come out this way, though, through hearsay and gossip. It had got Henry's back up before Joe had even had chance to put his case forward.

* * *

Ellie

Ellie heard footsteps coming up the stone stairwell – well, she *had* been listening out for the past hour. She poked her head out of the door, catching Joe on his way up. Result!

'Hi, everything okay?' Her voice was cheery.

'Kind of.' His tone was flat.

'Do you want to come in for a sec?'

'I haven't got long.'

He sounded a bit short. What had happened to the lovely relaxed guy who'd held her hand on the beach?

'Was it to do with work?' She couldn't contain her curiosity and was desperate to recapture some of their intimacy from earlier. Surely if he'd just taken her on a date, he could talk to her if something was up?

'If you must know, Lord Henry was livid when I got to his office. Someone had spilled about the wedding idea. He knew all about Wendy supposedly doing the flowers and everything.'

Oh shite. 'Oh. How was he about it?'

'Annoyed that no one had mentioned it to him first.' He paused, 'Ellie, the only person I can think it could have come from is you. Have you been chatting to anyone else about it?'

Wendy . . . the conversation at the florist's. But, she'd told her to be discreet.

She couldn't work it out. Wendy knew it was all at the planning stage and that she *must* keep things absolutely quiet at this point. Ellie just couldn't understand. Wendy seemed trustworthy; she wouldn't want to risk losing the potential flower business through indiscretion.

'I really don't know how it could have happened. Yes, I had broached the wedding idea to sound out Wendy at the florist's in Kirkton, but she assured me she'd keep quiet on it for now. Are you certain you haven't mentioned it to anyone else? Could someone at the council have let on after you applied for the licence?'

'It came out from Lord Henry's cleaner. Her mum and Wendy's mum are good friends. It's pretty obvious where it's come from.'

Damn, it all fell into place. Wendy's mum had been in the back of the shop that day. She remembered her coming out with a cup of coffee for Wendy just at the very end of their conversation. She'd probably been earwigging all the while. So it *was* her fault. She felt hot and embarrassed, and now Joe was angry with her, but she may as well come clean. 'I think I know what happened . . . I-I did speak to Wendy, yes, and now I remember, her mother was there at the back of the shop. I had no idea at the time. She must have overheard, as I made it clear to Wendy to be discreet. I'm sure Wendy would have been . . . I'm so sorry.'

There was a frown etched across his brow as he uttered, 'Well, Lord Henry's still open-minded about it, thank God. But please be more careful in future. He's not the easiest to deal with at the best of times.'

'I will.' She felt herself going red, but still wanted to spend some time with Joe, to try and recapture a little of that easy togetherness from earlier, 'Umn, look, do you want a coffee or anything?'

'No. I really must get to work on this proposal now.

Henry wants to see the full details, costings, the lot, by Friday, so I've got my work cut out.'

'Oh, okay.' Her idea of a cosy coffee-for-two was knackered now. The magic of their beachside date dissipated. And the worst of it was she'd lost his trust. She felt that she'd let him down.

*

Joe seemed preoccupied the next morning, passing her on the stairwell with a brief 'hello'. He did pop in to chat with her late the next day, once Doris and Nicola had gone, to talk over the catering ideas for the weddings: how many people and what type of buffet she felt she could handle. And at what point did she feel they should bring in outside caterers? He also needed a general idea of costings per head for a buffet menu, with brief menu suggestions. It was a business-like conversation, so far removed from their time holding hands on the beach yesterday that she began to wonder if that had ever really happened.

But she didn't want to go back to just a business relationship. She'd had a taste of something more, of a different, gentler side of Joe that she *really* wanted to get to know. She felt sad that things had shifted. Obviously, he had to focus and was busy getting all the information he needed in place for Friday's discussion with Lord

Henry; maybe he'd be a bit more relaxed thereafter, she conceded hopefully.

It was while she was setting up the tables in the tearooms on Friday morning that it came to her. A table for two – right here. Just for them. She could cook something special, once everyone had gone home. Yes, here in the teashop, that could work. The idea was forming nicely, but would Joe be up for it?

As she wrapped knives and forks in napkins, she wondered what she'd cook. Steak? Yes, steak was always a good option and easy enough to cook for two; she might even make a sauce? Peppercorn or Diane? And something chocolatey for dessert. A starter? She did a mean garlic mushrooms on brioche toast, and it was dead easy to make.

Hmn, she'd catch up with Joe later. See how the proposals had gone with Lord Henry, hopefully well, and then he might be in a better mood. Then she'd ask him. Supper on Sunday – it had a nice casual ring to it. Sunday would be good, the weekend trade over, Monday not so hectic, she might even be able to enjoy a drink or two.

She headed back to the kitchen, feeling optimistic, and found herself humming along to the radio as she scrubbed potatoes ready to bake as jackets for lunchtime. Lunch, as it turned out, was hectic; a coachload of tourists turned up, deciding to all eat at once before they did the castle tour, which was great for the takings but rather manic. But, hey, she wasn't complaining, she needed every penny she could make at the moment, saving what she could to start repaying her dad back. She, Doris and Nicola were on go, go, go, for a full hour and a half, running out of paninis and quiche. They worked well as a team generally, though Doris was tutting heavily as they ran out of quiche – naturally Ellie should be a mind-reader and make an extra six quiches on the offchance that a coachload of hungry tourists should arrive on the doorstep of the teashop. But the two of them did crack on with getting the orders out, which helped immensely. Being hectic also meant that Ellie didn't have time to dwell on whether or not Joe might like her idea of supper.

The man himself popped in later in the day, just as she was mopping the floors, to let her know that the meeting with Lord Henry had gone reasonably well. She shooed him out into the passageway, not wanting him traipsing all over the wet floors, but he seemed happy to chat through the open kitchen door, and seemed in a far better mood than yesterday. Thank heavens. He'd no doubt been under a lot of pressure.

Doris was busy wiping down the tables out in the tearooms, and Nicola had just gone home. It was Ellie's ideal chance. She mopped quickly towards him.

'Joe . . . ?' Now or never, 'I was just wondering . . . well, would you like supper with me on Sunday?'

'Ah . . . yeah. That sounds good. Are you thinking of going out?'

'No, I had something else in mind.'

His eyebrow arched suggestively. She had to giggle, then threw a tea towel at him. 'I mean, I'd like to cook for you . . . here.'

'Oh, I see.' He shrugged his shoulders, as if disappointed, but was sporting his sexy, cheeky grin.

'So, don't you be getting any ideas,' she added, trying to sound affronted.

Doris walked in, barging past Joe with the cloth and disinfectant spray. Ellie *really* didn't want her getting wind of their impending date, and finished the conversation with, 'I'll let you know a time tomorrow, then.'

'Okay.' He got the idea, 'That's fine.'

As he wandered out Doris was straight in like a hawk. 'Time for what?'

'Oh, office meeting, accounts debrief.' Ellie was quick off the mark. Nosy old bat. Surely that sounded boring enough to put her off.

Doris just nodded with a 'Hmph' and put the cleaning materials away, 'That's me done, then.'

Ellie smiled to herself. 'Thanks, Doris.'

She'd have to be extra careful after their supper on Sunday, removing *all* traces of their date before the waitresses were in on Monday morning.

17

Ellie

Date and time confirmed. Teashop closed for the day – well, in their official capacity, anyhow. Her meal for two was organised and ready to finish off later. All that was left was to decide what to wear. Should she dress up, go for the femme fatale? Should she dress down, go for the 'I'm in chef-mode' and this is just a casual supper look? She'd be cooking, anyhow, so whatever she chose would end up having an apron chucked over it.

Had she gone a bit over the top? She didn't want to appear overly romantic. There were candles on the table, which she'd set out with wine glasses and the best tearoom cutlery. She'd even put a small vase of yellow carnations there. Did that already look like a seduction table?

She found a jersey wrap-around dress in the wardrobe.

It was black, looked smart, but with a sultry edge – would show a nice 'V' of cleavage once the apron came off. But, it was comfy and practical too. Boots would go well with it, and that way she wouldn't be teetering in high heels on the uneven floors of the teashop. Tights? Yes tights, stockings would be taking things way too far, and she wasn't sure if she had any, to be honest. Bit of lippie, nice warm-red shade, mascara, eyeliner. Okay, ready to roll, so back down to the teashop to prep the starter. The dessert was already made, a 'special' of raspberry and white-chocolate cheesecake appearing new on the blackboard this afternoon.

A half hour later, radio on, mushrooms chopped, Diane sauce made – she hoped he ate mushrooms. There were still so many things about him she didn't know. She set out tea lights throughout the tearooms, on the windowsills, the counter. It looked rather magical. It also kept the lighting soft and half-dark, so he hopefully wouldn't notice the spot that had managed to erupt on her chin, and was threatening to break out from its cover-up base.

She opened the bottle of Merlot she'd chosen to go with the steaks. She'd told Joe seven-thirty, it was now twenty past. Nerves started jangling about in her stomach. Was she doing the right thing, even thinking of getting involved with another man again? She wondered what other romantic trysts might have taken place here in the castle over the centuries. There were bound to be tales of star-crossed lovers amongst the servants, lords and ladies. Were there love stories sealed between these very walls? Stolen kisses. Nights of passion. The pain of love lost. She poured herself a small glass of the red; it might just help calm those nerves. She tuned the radio station to something classical to serve as background music, and sliced the brioche ready to toast. Bang on cue there was a knock on the kitchen door. She took a long, slow breath.

Joe walked in, dressed smartly in dark jeans and a pale-blue shirt open at the neck, his dark hair in its usual floppy fringe. There was a bottle of something bubbly in his hand, by the looks of it. 'Just something I had in. I thought it might make a good start to the meal.'

Ooh, she spotted a Moët and Chandon label. Bliss. She hadn't had champagne in an age. There hadn't been an awful lot to celebrate lately, to be fair. The last time was probably Nanna's eightieth birthday. Oh, yes, she remembered now, and it set her off giggling.

'What? What's so funny?' Joe quizzed her.

'Sorry, it's just me nanna.'

'And?'

'I'm just remembering something. The last time we had champagne at home, it was for Nanna's birthday. She liked it with orange juice and got her words mixed up, bless her, asking for Fuck's Bizz.' She grinned. It was nice that Nanna was there in her thoughts on her big night with Joe.

Joe was laughing too now.

'She didn't even realise she'd said it wrong. Well, me and Jay, my brother, we were just rolling about on the floor laughing, you can imagine. And my dad was getting all cross, 'cos he didn't want to have to explain to his mother-in-law what she'd just said.'

'Yes, hah, that could be the new cocktail for the castle. We could offer a Fuck's Bizz welcome drink on arrival for the wedding receptions.' A cheeky, sexy grin broke across his face.

Ellie found two flute glasses in a cupboard. 'Plain or Fuck's Bizz?' she asked.

'Just as it is, for me. It's already chilled. I'll go ahead and open it, shall I?'

Well that had broken the ice. The atmosphere between them was warm and relaxed already. 'Yes, please.' And the pop of the cork sounded exciting and extravagant. She had a feeling this was going to be a good night. Hopefully the food would turn out okay.

'Well, if you don't mind watching me cook for a minute, you could grab a stool while I do the starter. Mushrooms okay for you?'

'Love mushrooms.'

Result! 'That's good.'

He passed her a glass of chilled champagne.

'Cheers.'

'Cheers.' They clinked glasses. 'To a good night,' Ellie proposed.

'Yes, thanks for asking me.'

'You're welcome.'

She took a big gulp, then lit the gas flame ready to pan-fry the garlic mushrooms. Her head was spinning already. Giddy with champagne and what might happen next.

By the second glass, the starter was plated and looking good. Time to lead him through to the 'table à deux' and the candlelit tearooms.

'Wow! This doesn't even look like the teashop.'

It did look lovely in there; the glow of the candles setting off the old stone walls. She placed the plates down at the only table lit, and they took their seats opposite each other, Ellie suddenly feeling shy.

'Mmn, this looks good.' He glanced at the food, then up at Ellie. 'Thank you.'

They ate, they chatted. The Wedding Venue Proposal had apparently had a reasonable reception by Lord Henry, and at least Joe was able to move forward now with some of the planning. His eyes were dark, sexy and smiley all at once, as he chatted in the candlelight.

Ellie took a sip of champagne, which bubbled deli- ciously in her mouth then slipped down to join the flutters in her stomach; which was already a mix of excitement and nerves.

'That starter is great, by the way.' He ate the last mushroom and mopped up the sauce with the last of the brioche.

'Good, glad you enjoyed it.'

She stacked their empty plates and said she'd be back soon with the main course. She whizzed about the kitchen cooking the steaks, frying chips and setting out rocket and pan-fried asparagus onto two dinner plates.

Joe popped through. 'Need a hand?'

'No, it's nearly there, but thanks.'

'Wine?'

'There's a bottle of red open here. If you'd take it through that'd be great. I'll join you in five. You said you liked your steak rare, yeah?'

'Yes, that's the way I like it.' He started clicking his fingers, then added, 'Ah-hah, ah-hah,' like the song.

It surprised her that he could be so daft sometimes. She grinned, thinking of the contrast from his sensible Manager-of-the-Castle demeanour.

A few minutes later, they were tucking into steaks and asparagus, 'You're a great cook, Ellie. So, it's not just cakes you're good at.'

'No, I'm a woman of many talents.' She was feeling happy and mellow now.

'I can tell.' He smiled. 'Thanks for going to all this effort this evening, it's really great. And look, I'm sorry if I was a bit sharp with you earlier in the week about the Wendy thing.'

'It's okay. And you were right, I should have been more careful.'

'Yes, but you weren't to know her mother was about. And, with hindsight, perhaps I should have discussed it with Lord Henry before bringing you into the equation. He is warming to the idea, thank heavens. Well, in his own time, that is. God, he can be a hard nut to crack sometimes.'

'I take it it's not always an easy working relationship, then?' She was quite glad she didn't need to work with Lord Henry on a day-to-day basis herself.

'You could say that! No, it's not been an easy relationship.' He was shaking his head, showing the exasperation he sometimes felt. 'But I suppose he's given me this opportunity to be estate manager. And I do love the place. I just want to do my best here.'

'Yeah, me too. Well, after what you said before, it sounds as though it's all worked out alright with Lord Henry in the end. If he's happy to move the idea forward, that's great.'

'Yeah, I'm pleased and relieved. It gives the castle a real future. I'm sure it'll make a great venue for weddings. We can give the happy couples and their families and friends a really fantastic day. Where better than a fairytale castle, hey?'

'Yeah, I think, in time, it'll prove popular. Though there's a lot of hard work ahead to get things in place yet.'

'At least it's a big step in the right direction. You must have done well putting your case across.' Instinctively she reached her hand across the table and brushed his. His skin was warm, soft under her touch. Their eyes locked.

Ooh, something deep inside told her she was falling for this guy. And maybe, just maybe, he was feeling the same way too.

She smiled nervously, then looked down at their hands there together, his long fingers. She had the urge to take them one by one and kiss them, right on the fingertips. How good might it feel to have them brush over her bare skin. Would that ever happen? Should she ever let that happen? Where were her thoughts taking her, for goodness sake?

'Right,' she announced, 'I'd better clear these away and get the pudding sorted.' She got up before she did anything rash, like leaning over to kiss him. She'd only taste of garlic and red wine anyhow.

'I'll help.' He lifted his empty plate and followed her back to the kitchen. 'Can I wash up or anything?'

'Well, I suppose you could rinse off these dishes while I put the cheesecake out.' That'd clear some of the evidence for tomorrow. They'd better not leave *anything* for Doris to find in the dishwasher. 'Are you up for cheese-cake?'

'Sure am. Never been known to refuse food.'

She cut two neat slices, dressing the plate with fresh raspberries and coulis. She had to admit, it looked pretty cool, like something out of *Masterchef*.

'Very impressive.' He was at her shoulder drying a plate with a tea towel. 'Are you sure you're not a Michelin chef or something.'

'Thanks. I just like making it look pretty, that's all.'

They were soon back at their 'table à deux' in the teashop.

'Wow, that is amazing. Hang on,' he put on a food-boffin style voice, his fork poised in the air, 'I'm getting a hint of vanilla, cheese – yes cheese, and that lovely sharpness of raspberries.' He grinned. 'Seriously, Ellie, this is so good. Where did you learn to cook like this?'

'I don't know really. Probably my nanna.'

'Ah, the infamous nanna of the Fuck's Bizz, no less?'

'It is indeed.' She chuckled. 'Now, she *was* an amazing cake-maker. I used to watch her baking on a Saturday morning. She'd make enough cakes and buns for Grandpa for the week. And then a whole load more to take with her to the old people's home where she worked, bless her. And then, if it was a special occasion, she'd do her scrummy choffee cake.'

'Now, *that* cake I remember from your interview day.'

'Yep. It's her own recipe, handwritten in that recipe book I keep on the shelf in the kitchen. Oops, shouldn't have said that – giving away all my trade secrets.'

'Well, I wouldn't worry, there's no chance of me stealing it and branching out into baking. I know my limits.' He grinned. 'You seem very fond of her,' he continued.

'I am . . . I still miss her.'

'Oh, Ellie, I'm sorry.' His hand went over hers.

'It's okay. She was an old lady; she'd had a good life. Not an easy life, but a good life. She was my inspiration.' Ellie's eyes were misty, but she was still smiling.

'Sounds like she was a great role model.'

'She was . . . still is.'

There was a second or two of silence, then Ellie spooned the last of her cheesecake into her mouth.

Joe was staring at her. 'You have the most amazing lips, Ellie.'

'Thanks,' her voice came out as a squeak.

And he reached across and brushed his thumb gently across her lower lip. 'There was a crumb.' He didn't need an excuse to do that, in Ellie's book. Her body felt like it was melting. He leaned across the table and planted a delicate cheesecake-tasting kiss on her lips. Then he sat back down, leaving her wanting more.

Did she want more tonight, her mind was quizzing? What kind of more? And would it put him off if she seemed too keen? Would she be disappointed if it ended up as a one-night stand? Yes, probably. *But a one-night stand at least means that you get some good sex with this hunky man.* Her naughty subconscious was egging her on.

'Joe,' her voice came with a nervous lilt, 'Would you like coffee?'

'Ah, yes.' His gaze was intense.

'Back in my room.' Jesus, she'd said it. She couldn't believe she had been that forward. What the hell was she thinking?

The rest of the washing up was going to have to wait.

'Yes.' His smile widened.

She stood up, swiftly blowing out all the tea lights around the room, until it was just their solitary candle burning, which Joe blew out for her. For a second or two it was pitch black, then her eyes adjusted, and a silvery glimpse of moonlight shafted in through the windows. Joe was on his feet, her hand was in his, and they walked in a calm rush towards the door, tiptoeing across the courtyard. Both trying not to be noisy, not wanting to alert Lord Henry to their moonlight antics.

She couldn't remember if she'd left her room tidy. She hadn't anticipated things moving on as quickly as they had. She unlocked the door, turned on the lamp. It was fairly neat, thank heavens. She grabbed the clothing that was strewn across the bed from her earlier clothes panic, and placed them on the chair. She turned to face Joe. He closed the door behind him. There was a second where they both stared at each other. He then took a step towards her, took her in his arms and kissed her, their bodies pressed together, both edging backwards until she was hard against the wall. It felt powerful, passionate. Her hands through his hair. Tongues entwined. His hands tracing the sides of her body, gripping her hips, reaching around to her buttocks. She pulled away just for a second, the kiss turning into a sigh. Then dived back in to kiss him again.

* * *

Joe

Her soft moan at his ear sent his body crazy. Things were moving so quickly he was having trouble keeping up. Well, his body was doing fantastically well on that front, his mounting erection about to take over all sensible thought. Jesus, was this really happening? Should he *let* this happen?

He didn't want to rush her, though, not after what that prick of an ex had done to her. And he didn't want to get it all wrong. But he had virtually been frog-marched from their supper in the tearooms across here for 'coffee' – there being no sign of coffee as yet, and plenty of snogging like a pair of teenagers.

'Ellie.' He pulled back. Giving himself chance to think. The rest of his body bar his brain shouting out '*What the fuck are you doing, you idiot?*' He ignored it, 'Are you sure about this . . . like absolutely certain?'

She looked back at him, nodding with a nervous smile, 'Yes . . . I'm sure.'

Christ, she was so hot. Her bottom lip was trembling a little, her eyes dark, wanting.

Whoa, he so wanted this gorgeous, sexy woman. What the hell was he waiting for?

He buried his mouth against hers once more. Felt her hands tugging through his hair, in those sexy little pulls. Still kissing, she starting undoing the buttons of his shirt. He felt it loosening till it was flapping open, her hands exploring his chest with butterfly-teasing fingertips.

He pulled back from her to lift the dress she was wearing up and over her head, revealing the most magnificent breasts, cupped in black lace. He couldn't wait until his hands were the only things cupping them.

* * *

Ellie

Oh . . . My . . . God . . . he was undoing her bra. No one had seen her naked in ages. Her boobs always seemed too full, too heavy, were much better trussed in.

But he had a kind of awe on his face as he gazed down

241

at them, then up at her, his eyes intense. 'You're beautiful, Ellie.'

Did he really mean that, or was he just being nice?

He moved even closer, placing a hand tentatively around her bare left breast, then placed a kiss tenderly on her lips, which were already parted in anticipation. Tenderness turned to passion. He was a great kisser, kind of fluid, his tongue sexily probing while his lips moved deliciously with hers, making every nerve ending in her body tingle. As his hand moved expertly to her nipple, it was more than just her nerve endings that were tingling.

She delighted in his touch, in his kiss. Finally, she shifted, only to pull the shirt off his back and move him across to the bed, where he lay facing up at her. His chest was gorgeous, broad, and his stomach slim but toned in just the right places, with a lightly defined six pack, a dark trail of hair leading down to the waistband of his jeans. She kneeled up on the bed beside him in just her panties, leaning over to undo his jeans button and slowly unzip the fly, brushing her hand by accident over the hard shaft that lay ready beneath, its heat so promising beneath the back of her hand. A little of bubble of fear and anticipation rose within her. Oh My God! They were really doing this thing.

She took a slow breath and moved her hand, fingertips trembling slightly, beneath the denim of the jeans, down below the soft jersey cotton of Joe's boxer shorts, heard his oh-so-sexy groan as she touched the hot, smooth hardness of his penis, felt it throb against her palm. She held firmly, without moving her fingertips, lingered there. Then she released her grasp, moving her hands to pull his trousers down over his hips, the boxers coming off with them.

It had been such a long time. Such a long time. But she had a feeling this was going to be worth the wait. He pulled her down to the bed now, kissing her mouth once more. His hand was exploring the soft mound of her stomach. She hope it didn't feel too big and squooshy. She'd never been a flat-stomach kind of girl. He moved down to kiss the skin around her belly button, both of his hands gently stroking her inner thighs. Then, oooh, one hand was under the lace of her panties. Heat and longing soared within her as his fingertips worked tantalisingly and then slid gently, probing within her. Oh, My God! She wanted this man inside her and soon.

Hold on – she wasn't on the pill. They'd all got chucked in the bin the day she'd found Gavin with slutty Nadine. Never bothered with them since.

'Joe,' she sat bolt upright, abruptly interrupting proceedings, 'Joe?'

He lifted his head, his hand stopping its glorious glide.

'Do you have anything?'

'Oh, Christ, yes. Yes. My jeans pocket.'

He scrabbled across the bed to reach over to the floor to grab them. His buttocks were peachy and glorious. Then resurfaced, holding up a silver square packet like a prize and, with a big grin, placed it on the bedside table.

'Okay.' She lay back, ready to resume where they left off. He kissed her, still grinning, then moved back down to pole position. She sighed as his hand slid down once more, moving exquisitely. There was the most gorgeous man now planting delicate kisses along her panty line, his fingers working their magic just below. He slipped off her lacy knickers, his fingers dipping and gliding once more. She could feel the delicious tension building within.

'Joe . . .' she whispered, 'This is so good . . . but just hold fire there a sec.' If she was going to come, she wanted to feel herself around him.

'Okay,' his voice came out a little croaky. He looked up with a sexy smile and shifted back up the bed to face her. Stroked her hair with his fingers, which smelled salty of her and sex, kissed her. Then he moved himself up and over her. Reached for the condom on the bedside table, tore it open and slipped it on as she watched. He shifted back over her, resting his body down against hers for a second or two, pressing her into the bed, nose to nose, chest to chest, breath mingling with hints of red wine and cheesecake. She could feel his erection, hot and hard, against her pubic mound. She reached her hands around his muscular buttocks.

His eyes intense on hers, she nodded, parting her legs wider. But instead of plunging into her, he moved downwards to take her nipples into his mouth, licking them, one by one. Sucking oh-so slowly . . . curling his tongue around them as they hardened, sending electric pulses to her core.

'*Please*,' was all she could utter as she reached to grasp his cock. *Oh My God* . . . 'Joe . . .' her voice was weak, her body desperate to go to a place where speech was no longer possible.

He pulled up from her breasts and suddenly, smoothly and deeply, his shaft was tight within her. She couldn't stop her gasp as he filled her. And then the glide and thrust, setting up a glorious rhythm between them. She was lost to him.

'Ellie, oh God, Ellie.' She heard his half-groaned words at her ear. Felt the tension tighten through him. A deeper thrust. And then, ooooh, the pulsing of pure bliss around him. Yes, *yes*, YES.

His weight dropped slowly down onto her as his body relaxed, spent. His head nestled against hers, his breath slowing at her ear. And the widest smile ever spread across her face. That was just beautiful, *really, overwhelmingly, bloody, beautiful*.

18

Ellie

Seeing him there in the teashop the next day as he popped in for a quick 'hi' and takeaway coffee, she couldn't help but picture his naked body – all that long, lean muscle, and ooh, how it had felt beneath her fingertips. She happened to be chopping cucumber for the salad at the time, and suddenly all she could think of was his erection. She was sure she was flushing bright red.

'You okay?' he asked.

'Yeah.' Her voice came out high-pitched.

'Looks like it's been busy here. I'd better let you get on . . . for now.'

'Yeah, it has been.' As she glanced up, the quirky smile he gave her said it all, along with the lust-tinged look in his eyes. *I just can't wait to be with you again.*

'Catch you later.'

Those words held such promise.

'Okay.' Her voice came out all weak and breathy. *Jeez, she'd got it bad.*

Doris marched in with a tray of dirty crockery, ready to load into the dishwasher.

'Morning, Doris,' Joe's tone was bright, breezy and sexy.

'My, you seem chirpy today.'

Hmn, wonder why? The two of them raised their eyebrows and grinned conspiratorially behind Doris's back.

Ellie had left Joe in her bed at six-thirty, after giving him a very gentle morning kiss. He'd slept through the night like a starfish, while she'd tossed and turned thinking about everything, and despite it being a-m-a-z-i-n-g, she still hoped they were doing the right thing. She'd got up, headed to the teashop to wash up, clear away the many candles and hide every scrap of evidence of the dinner à deux. Then she came back up to have her shower and get ready for the day ahead. As she got back to her room, Joe was just getting up, with bed-head tousled dark hair and the hint of stubble across his chin. He had his boxer shorts on and was scrabbling about for his other clothes.

'Where did you get to? Missed you.'

'Ah, thought I'd better get the tearooms sorted for the day and to hide all the evidence. Don't want Doris gossiping.'

He moved across the room, gave her a lingeringly arousing morning kiss, and she half-wondered about inviting him into the shower with her, but he was already saying he'd better get going and started pulling on his jeans. Oh well, maybe another time.

He grinned as he paused by the door, 'Catch you later, gorgeous.'

As he closed the door she'd felt like cartwheeling around her room. And then she felt weirdly sad that he'd gone. Yes, he was only upstairs. She knew that. She took herself off to the shower, and the prickle of the water on her body made her feel all sexy again. She wondered if he was in his shower up above her . . . lucky shower . . . having him all naked in there.

*

'Two jacket potatoes with cheese and beans, and a cheese-and-ham croissant,' Doris was shrilling across the room. 'Earth to planet, Ellie.'

'Oh, sorry.' Her lovely sexy reverie was broken – God, she was going to have to get a grip. She'd had him mentally in the shower again. Seemed to like that particular daydream. 'Okay, I'm on to it.'

'And two soups, and a quiche with salad.' Nicola popped another white paper slip along the row. 'Thanks.'

Right. Focus. Work. Cooking to do . . . People are

waiting for their lunches. She needed to impress the customers, keep them coming back for more. And the sooner she got through the day at the teashop, the sooner she could see him again.

Now then, did she wait for him to come to her? Play it cool? Or go knocking on his door straight after work with a big smile and a hello, and her best underwear. Or would that seem too forward – *forward?* She'd just had full-on and very lovely sex with the man only last night. But she didn't want to just turn up and get into bed with him again . . . Well, she supposed it wouldn't be *that* bad. She held back a smug grin. But her sensible head kicked in, she felt that she didn't want this to be some casual fling or a one-night stand. She knew now that she wanted more than that. But she didn't want to scare him off, either.

He'd come to the kitchen to see her, hadn't he? That was a good sign. He hadn't done a runner. How could he do a bloody runner, stupid cow? He lives here. Ooh, this could get really awkward. It was worse than an office affair. Not only did she work for him, they had to live in the same building too. What had she got herself into?

All this was frazzling through her head as she was going up the sixteen stone steps to her room . . . She could just make it twenty-four, make a decision and head straight to his? *Hussy.*

Nah, she was in too much of a dither and would come across all ditsy. She'd cool off in her own room. Chill out for a while after the hectic day she'd had in the tearooms, which had been busy again, thank God.

She turned the lock, entered her room. The sunlight streamed across the bed. She lay down on it. It smelled gorgeous, the scent of him still lingering there, his musky cool aftershave, stirring up all kind of warm, sexy memories, and she closed her eyes and let herself think about him. Wow – what a night! It had been like Christmas and birthdays all at once – with a big ice cream sundae on the top, plus a couple of chocolate brownies.

Hmn, and she *did* rather want to experience that all over again.

Tap. Rap.

She opened her eyes with a start.

Tap. Rap. Rap. Again.

Who the heck was that? She flew up off the bed, flattening her hair down just in case. Of course, it might not be him.

Through the crack of the door, she saw hazel-brown eyes with dark, dark pupils like melted toffee you could sink and wallow in. A slow, steady, oh-so-sexy smile. His floppy, nearly black, fringe.

'Hi, Joe,' she smiled, trying her best to keep calm, though she could feel her heart pounding away in her chest.

'I just wanted to thank you for last night.' As she

opened the door to him, he brought out from behind him a gorgeous bouquet in pinks and creams tied in pink satin ribbon. She recognised roses and carnations, but there were other, more unusual, flowers. 'Thanks for the meal,' he continued, 'the evening, well, for everything.'

'Wow! Thank you. That is *so* pretty.' Her smile broadened, 'Yeah, it was a good night.' And she felt herself blush.

She let him in, took the flowers and popped them in her bathroom sink, wondering if she had a vase anywhere. Then they perched rather primly on the end of her bed. The few inches between them was like static.

'Busy today?'

'Yep, must have had about thirty tables through.'

'That's good.'

'Yeah, things are really picking up.' In more ways than one, she mused.

They were being awfully polite and proper, and yet just last night on this very bed there wasn't a shred of clothing between them.

'Anyway, after last night . . .'

Ooh was this it? Did he not feel the same? Was it just an awkward one-night stand, and the flowers were to say sorry, it should never have happened. She felt her throat tighten. She wouldn't cry, she was a grown-up, these one-night stands happened all the time. Keep it professional.

'Well, I wondered if I could return the favour.' Her

mind wandered deliciously for a second. 'Cook for you, I mean,' he blurted out, it was his turn to blush now. 'Well, I'm no cook, really,' he gabbled on. 'Don't get too excited or anything. But after your busy day, you might like someone to cook your supper for a change. Just something casual. My repertoire just about extends to chilli con carne or a spaghetti bolognese. I hazarded a guess and went for the chilli. It's all made.'

She grinned. *It wasn't a one-off, quick shag, love 'em and leave 'em, after all.* 'Yes, that would be lovely. Thank you.'

'Just up in my room, if that's okay.'

She nodded, taking a deep breath. Hmn, were there some ulterior motives going on here? Jeez, it wasn't like she was some demure damsel. Yes, that was okay.

'Sure and thanks. What kind of time? I need a quick shower.' *Some hasty grooming preparations. Wash out the cooking smells from her hair.*

'That's fine. Any time really. Seven-ish? Something like that?'

'Great. See you soon.'

He rose from the bed. 'See you later, then.'

They shared an expectant grin.

His room was *rooms*. In fact, a suite, taking up a whole corner of the castle. After the office, which she had seen, he led her through into the living area, closing the door behind her.

Caroline Roberts

The room was panelled with dark wood. It smelled of
that gorgeous aftershave (she'd have to sneak into his
bathroom and find out what he used at some point this
evening), red wine, and a hint of musty castle – well, that
pervaded everywhere in this place. Through another
doorway off the living area she spotted his bedroom, a
massive four-poster bed dominated the space. Ellie's
throat tightened a little, her mouth drying, yet it wasn't
fear, more anticipation.

He had laid out a small table with cutlery and napkins,
a bottle of red wine, and two cut-glass goblets; it looked
rather like a hotel room. She wondered fleetingly if he
regularly 'entertained' here; it seemed very cosy all set
out for two, but she hadn't heard any gossip, hadn't seen
him with anyone. She put the thought out of her mind.

'Would you like a coffee or a tea?' his tone was nervous,
which after last night seemed laughable, and yet . . . She
was feeling it too, like this really mattered. 'Or wine?' he
continued.

She looked at him. Didn't answer. She *so* wanted to
touch him, her fingertips tingling at the thought of it. To
know his skin, every inch of it. She wondered where this
sensual goddess in her head had come from? It certainly
hadn't been there when Gavin was on the scene – she
could see that now.

Joe's eyes held hers as he walked slowly across the room
to where she stood. Close enough now for her to feel his

warmth. She touched his cheek, felt his breath against her skin, traced a finger over the slight stubble on his chin, wanted to kiss there, so she did. It was rough against her lips. She could smell the scent of his aftershave and the saltiness of his skin.

As she drew away, he stared at her.

'Is everything alright?' her voice came out huskier than usual.

'More than alright,' his lip twisted with amusement.

So she thought she'd plant a kiss there too.

He responded, from his groin as well as his lips. His erection was nudging hard against her hip. Her newfound sensual goddess punched the air.

The kiss became more intense and they stumbled back towards a chair. Still standing, she began to unbutton his white cotton shirt . . . *slowly* undoing the buttons . . . one by one . . . from the neck down. He seemed to unleash some sexual instinct within her. She had him pinned between her, the chair and the panelled wall. He sighed, well, something between a sigh and a moan.

They never got as far as the chilli . . .

The sex was hot, tempestuous. Bodies pressed sweatily against the wall, their kisses licking like flames. Then she pushed him down by the shoulders, down onto the velvet padded chair, taking his shirt off, then her dress off in one swift move, his jeans, her bra, his boxers, her panties. Until, after carefully placing a condom on his hot and ready shaft, she slid down deliciously over him, taking him within her. Slowing down her moves to a delectable glide that filled her. Part of her wondered what the hell had come over her. This wasn't the woman she used to be – the missionary queen. But it was this man, this gorgeous man beneath her, Joe. Just being with him filled her with such sensual delight, and opened up all sorts of possibilities. Such sweet, hot, horny sex.

'Wow' was all he could utter. As he sat sated beneath her.

She had shifted carefully on to his lap. After a minute or so, he grinned at her like the cat who had got the cream. 'And we never even made it to the bed.'

She grinned back, 'Oh well, we can save that for later.' And she had a look in her eye that told him she was not joking. She moved off of him. Her limbs ached a little. The sexual athletics finding muscles she hadn't used in a while. He popped his boxers back on, while she put on his shirt and her panties, and they moved across to lounge on the bed, where it was more comfy.

'Wine, some supper . . . or more sex? Now we've actu-ally made it to the bed.' He smiled cheekily.

'Can I have all three?'

'Now that's just plain greedy . . . all at once?'

She grinned back. 'Actually, can I have a breather? Just some wine – and then we'll see.'

'We'll see indeed, you little vixen. And there was me thinking you were a quiet girl, more on the shy side.'

'The quiet ones are always the worst. That's what my nanna used to say.'

'Well, I think your nanna was most definitely right.'

She was, mused Ellie. And she knew instinctively that she would have liked Joe. It was such a shame they would never get the chance to meet.

He fetched the bottle of Merlot and the two glasses, and poured while Ellie held them tight, afraid of spilling the plummy liquid over his velvet covers. Then he walked across and opened a big dark-wood cupboard. Out popped a very modern flat-screen television. She laughed, twenty-first century technology hits seventeenth-century furniture; it seemed so incongruous with the room, and yet so very Joe – a real mix of traditional and modern.

'Rom-com? Thriller? Something scary, then I get an excuse to hold you close on the scary bits?'

'It's a bit late for that,' Ellie smirked.

'Hmn, true.'

They watched a nice, easy rom-com featuring Jennifer Aniston. It was light and fun, and they chatted and sipped wine. It was strange and yet lovely that after being so intimate they could just lie back and chat – it felt so natural being there with him.

'So, how do you like spending your downtime? Any hobbies?' Joe asked.

'Well, obviously I've always enjoyed baking. That's what I loved to do outside of work. But now, since I've been baking all day, hmn, been watching some films, reading books. I always have a stack of novels ready by the bed.'

'Okay then, favourite film?'

'Ah, that's got to be *The Notebook*. I'm just a soppy romantic at heart. It was just so beautiful. Have you seen it?'

'No, not that one, though I don't mind the odd rom-com. Me, well has to be a *Batman* film, obviously.'

'Which was the best version, then?'

'*The Dark Knight*, no doubt about it. Heath Ledger played such an amazing role as the Joker in that film.'

'Yeah, I watched that one – it was pretty gripping.'

'So, which lucky books are by your bed, then?' He quirked an eyebrow.

'The latest Jojo Moyes, love her relationship dramas. And I also like a historical novel. You know, like Philippa Gregory, that type of thing. God those Tudors were a right brutal bunch.'

The bed was big and bouncy, and by the end of the movie she was testing it out like a kid. It was like something out of a medieval film; big wooden posts carved with decorative flowers and fruit, drapes of plush plum velvet. His plain grey duvet was more twenty-first century, but the throw was velvet plum too. Hah, she could be his Guinevere or something. Or maybe he was like Henry VIII. Ooh dear, all those wives he'd got through, that was a scary thought. She obviously had been reading too many historical novels. 'Off with her head!' she spoke the words aloud as the credits rolled. He eyed her quizzically.

'This bed, it's like something out of the Middle Ages!' She bounced harder.

'Hmn, suppose so. Maybe not off with her head, but *down?*' He gestured cheekily towards his crotch. Oooh, she couldn't possibly. But then, he was opening her up to a world of new possibilities.

'Now any bad behaviour or thoughts of non-compliance, *well* . . . The axe just might have to come out . . .'

She felt a bit uneasy. Did he really want her to? Could she really do that? It had always been a no-no with Gavin. She began to think she'd been a bit of a prude.

Joe burst out laughing. He'd been teasing – well, there may have been a hint of longing in his eyes.

'You horror!' *Well, maybe one day, sensual goddess chipped in.* She wasn't that much of a prude. She hit him with a pillow and they were rolling about the bed like a pair of teenagers. He trapped her under him, then caught her hands above her head, grasping her wrists as if he could do anything he liked with her. God there was no one around, no one on this level of the castle, and Lord Henry was safely tucked away in his third-floor suite of rooms in the other wing. The tension was palpable between them. But something in her knew he would never hurt her, or force her. He released his grip as if in recognition of that.

She raised her head up off the bed to meet his lips. He lay, his weight upon her, kissing her as though he never wanted to stop. And she didn't want it to stop either. But then it got harder to breath, with his body crushing down on hers. She wriggled a little, their lips still clasped together, and then it got *really* hard to breathe and she began to make little suffocating sounds. He pulled up quickly.

'Coming up for air,' she gasped.

'Aah, sorry,' he smiled, his eyes smouldering, 'Well, I'm going down to do some real suffocating.'

'*What . . . ?*' He amazed her as he moved down over her tummy, pushed up his shirt that she was wearing, slid off her panties and then nestled his head between her legs. OH MY GOD! He started licking her slowly down there, flicking with the point of his tongue, tasting, lingering there. She gulped back a knot in her throat, tried to concentrate on breathing, tried to relax, but that was a virtual impossibility.

He lifted his face to grin up at her. 'Ladies first, of course.'

Gavin had tried this once, and it had all gone horribly wrong. He'd lapped like a cat at a saucer of milk and made this funny noise, expecting her to writhe in ecstasy and come within seconds. What seemed like minutes later her ex had finally given up, giving her a look as though he'd just tasted something awful. It hadn't inspired them to try it again.

But this, *this* was something else. She could see the dark silky hair of Joe's head, down there, his face buried into her. Those gentle tickling licks, and then *his* groan of pleasure as though he were loving it. Shit, she may as well give in to it. She was tightening, tense, quivering, and then, then she couldn't think any more. Feeling had taken over everything, drawing herself tight to the core. His tongue dipped inside her, then out, teasing again. Ah, sweet Jesus, she was going to come. Her hands were through his hair, tugging at it, yet not pulling him away, no way José.

'Jesus, Joe,' her voice rose to a crisis. Then she couldn't speak. Drawn into a core of pulsing orgasm, like light and quivering flame through her. Her back arched up to him and the softest scream escaped from her lips.

They never did have the chilli. She lay in his arms all night, feeling sexed-up, protected and loved. Wondering when life had become so sweet. Sensing that something wonderful was starting to happen.

She thought it strange that she hadn't seen him all day. She'd hoped he might pop in to the kitchens for a quick hello, and a glimpse of that gorgeous smile of his. It was now four in the afternoon and still no sign.

Oh well, he must be busy. He did have his own work to do, of course. She stopped herself from asking Doris or Nicola if they'd seen him about that day. She didn't want anyone alerted to the fact that *something was going on between them.*

Anyway, it was merely hours since she'd stolen away from his big four poster and nipped off to freshen up and shower back in her own room. She remembered waking that morning, lying there and staring at him, mesmerised at the groove of his cheek bones, the tousle of his hair on the pillow as he lay asleep, afraid to touch him in case it all melted away and she realised it was just a dream . . . one hot dream!

Okay, then, just get on with prepping the last order, a soup and two cheese toasties. And there were cakes to bake for tomorrow. Hmn, she might just celebrate by baking a choffee special, he'd liked that at the interview, she'd save him a slice. She found herself humming a few minutes later as she mixed in the cocoa and espresso. Life was good, hum, hum. In fact, her whole body seemed to be humming happily, as if every nerve had been woken up last night and was still in a state of bliss.

So, he must be busy. She could always pop by and see him later. Or would that seem a bit full-on, as if she was expecting another hot session? Mind you the sex was A-MAZ-ING! Hum, hum. But she didn't want it all to be about sex. Could she now rewind and turn up for just a cuddle and a bit of TV and a chat? Blimey, it had all moved on rather fast. What did he really think of her?

Maybe she shouldn't give a hoot, just keep turning up at his door and enjoy the ride, so to speak. Oh dear, why was life, even when it was good, always complicated?

The choffee was smelling delicious, with just ten minutes baking time to go. Doris popped her head around the door.

'We're off now, Ellie, unless there's anything . . . ?'

'Oh no, thanks, ladies, that's fine. See you in the morning.'

'Bye, then.'

'Bye.'

They had settled together as a rather incongruous, yet happy, team. Yes, Doris was still a bit of a busy-body. She certainly wasn't going to change now. And she still had her moments, making clipped comments about new additions to the menu, 'It'll never sell.' And getting het up if some kid demanded a choice of flavours in the crisps that came with the packed-lunch box. And often Ellie spotted her taking far too long clearing a table next to some locals she knew, keeping an ear out for any juicy gossip. They didn't need to buy the local broadsheet, not with Doris around. God knows what she'd think, or *say*, if she ever got wind of her and Joe being at it like rabbits.

And Nicola, well she was hardworking and a real sweetie, if still slightly timid, though Ellie had noted she had started making conversation more with the customers lately. The day before, they had even shared a conspiratorial eyebrow raise and smirk over one of Doris's comments. Ellie had learned from Nicola's silent resolve that often the best way to deal with Doris's barbed comments was to ignore them, then they could only fall like misplaced arrows.

The four sponge sections of the cake were cooling on the side; she'd already made the frosting. She'd pop back down to the kitchen later to sandwich it together. Walking up the stairs to her room, she felt a strange yearning in her stomach, a kind of longing. How could she miss him after just a few hours, silly moo? Maybe she could suggest a walk in the woods or the castle grounds? Some time to talk, be together. Ooh, it might even lead to open-air sex, another new experience . . . all sorts of possibilities.

Or, she could just go back to her room and stay cool, not pester him? Let him come to her.

She texted her mum, sent a brief message to Gemma, and Facebooked Jason, omitting any details of what was *really* going on in her life at the moment. It was all just a bit too soon. But, equally, she knew she sounded happy, was letting them know life was fine. She looked at Joe's flowers there on the side in a jug she'd found. They'd wilted a little; she'd have to add some more water.

Then she soaked in the bath, soothing herself in the warm water, letting the bubbles foam over her. Her feet always ached after a day standing in the kitchens – it was bliss to let them soak. Ten minutes later she got out and dressed in her best knickers-and-bra set, just in case, popping a lacy vest top and jeans over. Well, he might just knock at any time.

19

Ellie

He never came.

Ellie had ended up taking a stroll around the walled gardens – that just happened to be beneath his windows. It was a warm night and she didn't feel like being cooped up in her room.

In bed later she listened for a creak of the floorboards above her, evidence that he was still there in the castle, but couldn't tell if it was the usual creaks and groans of the castle pipework or his footsteps. Yes, she knew she was being paranoid, and no, he hadn't sworn to love her for ever, or even arranged to see her again in any personal way, but she'd just *hoped*, hadn't she?

Hope – it lifted you up, made anything seem possible. It was a dangerous thing.

Joe

He put his foot down hard on the accelerator and revved away along the driveway, gravel flying out behind his wheels, leaving the castle behind him. He just needed some time out and a bit of space. Things had moved on *way too fast.* And, he had to admit, that scared him a little.

Henry's words, the other week, about not getting too involved, mocked him. He'd always vowed never to get into any personal relationships with anyone at the castle – not that he'd ever felt the want, or need, to before. . . . Well, he'd gone and done it now.

And the best and the worst of it was she'd been great, really lovely, and somewhat surprisingly hot as hell – like something had let loose in her within those bedroom walls. A more-than-pleasant discovery. But this was all getting out of hand. She was a really nice girl, and this was going to be so hard – having to come back and tell her that it couldn't carry on.

Just thinking about it made him feel crap. Why the hell had he let himself get drawn in? Let it happen? All these years he'd sworn he'd never be the same. *Never* to do that to anyone. That he was different. And here he was. History repeating its bloody self. He'd get out quick, while he could.

He swerved out of the huge stone gateposts onto the lanes.

But, then again, could they make a go of it? Why did he have to be so fearful? Something was niggling inside. But he couldn't risk it, couldn't let it all go wrong, let her get attached, end up hurting her even more than he'd have to now. Better this way. He knew that well enough.

He took a bend too sharp – there'd been a cyclist coming. Shit. That was way too close. He received a one-fingered salute, which he well deserved. Mouthed 'Sorry'. Right, slow down, take it steady . . . *Steady*, you should have thought of that three days ago, instead of letting yourself get caught up in all this, his mind mocked. Stupid twat.

Bugger. Bugger. Bugger.

But she was so damned lovely.

Now, that got him thinking again, reminding him of her skin against his, her lips pressed tight to his. The way she'd had him up against that wall. Sweet Jesus. *And you're going to put a stop to it? Are you mad?*

But it had gone beyond sex already. Don't get involved. Don't let it get to where something goes wrong. Which it inevitably always does.

Watch the road! A pheasant – brainless bird – strutted into the road as the car approached. He slowed, there was no telling what those birds would do, and if you collided, well, they could make one hell of a mess of themselves and the front end of your car, as he'd learned to his peril some years ago. He was glad when he reached the junction at the A1, away from all the dangers of the countryside.

He'd decided to give himself a bit of time out and spend a couple of days back at home. Visit his mam. She was so pleased when he called last night, he could hear the smile in her voice. It had been a while – he usually got home every month or so. She wouldn't visit him at the castle. He could picture her, there in her kitchen, busy preparing one of his favourite meals. They had a bigger house now, semi-detached, still on the edge of Byker. She loved being near the river for a wander along the Tyne, watching the boats come in and out, the tourists and the hen nights, the hustle and bustle of the quayside. And her friends were all there, she'd reassured Joe when he'd left to work at the castle. Joe found himself smiling, calming, just thinking about her. She'd been his inspiration, even if she had got herself in a bit of a mess in those early years. 'No one ever got anywhere by sitting on their backside, Joseph,' she'd comment, in her sing-song Geordie accent.

Maybe he could have a chat with her about Ellie while he was home. He hadn't ever spoken in any depth about his personal relationships with his mam before, but felt himself floundering with this one, like he might need some advice. She'd had relationships, not always good ones, for sure, but she'd seen a lot of life.

He was still feeling shit about having to tell Ellie that it couldn't go on; he remembered that day when she opened up to him about her ex-fiancé, her broken wedding date. Well, he was hardly much better himself, was he? Though he hadn't betrayed her, or gone off with anyone else, he'd still abused her heart. Maybe his mam could give some advice on how to say the right thing, put it gently to her. Damage limitation.

While he was there in Newcastle, he was also going to tie in a visit to the Wedding Fayre at the Hilton on the quayside, pick up some tips, and see who was advertising wedding venues locally, what the competition would be like, and get some ideas on how they could promote the castle for next year. The license had finally been agreed by the council, so they needed a final push to persuade Lord Henry it was the way to go, get themselves organised, get everything tip-top and make Claverham Castle *the* place to get hitched. And he'd need Ellie's help, enthusiasm and professionalism to do that – why, oh why, had he messed things up between them? Weddings, huh – yes, he could get the venue looking great, serve amazing food, set up a marquee, but after that, *really*, when did marriages ever work out? Mam had always said she was better off on her own. He knew only too well that life wasn't always sunshine and roses.

* * *

Ellie

Every time the kitchen door swung open, she hoped it might be him. But no, just Doris or Nicola ferrying cups and saucers for the dishwasher, and Colin, the gardener, for a sneaky coffee refill to take out with him. Ellie handed him a homemade cookie for good measure.

Derek and Malcolm appeared at lunchtime to buy a couple of sandwiches.

'How are things going, Ellie? Looks busy out front. Have you got time to make us up a couple of ham and mustards on brown, petal?' Malcolm popped his head round the swing door of the kitchen.

'Oh, and you'd better pop in a slice of your Lemon D. I just love that stuff.' Derek added, at his shoulder now.

'Remember your waistline now, Derek,' Malcolm quipped.

'It'll keep me going on the tourist trail this afternoon.'

'Well, it's looking like business is building here, Ellie. Nearly a full house in there. We keep sending them your way. It's become part of the tour now. We finish at the teashop door by some odd chance, and then tell them how marvellous the lemon drizzle and your choffee cake is. They just can't resist.'

So that was where a lot of her new trade was coming from. How lovely of them! No need for billboards when she had walking, talking tour guides to promote her.

'Thanks, gents, that's brilliant of you.' And she added an extra slice of lemon drizzle to the package. 'Enjoy.'

'We always do.' Malcom gave her a cheeky wink, and they were off.

But even with their chatty banter, it was getting to her. There was someone else she really wanted to see. Where the hell was he? Even before they'd got it together she saw him just about every day, even if it was a quick 'hi' and a wave across the courtyard. He must be avoiding her, but why?

After the lunchtime rush, Ellie nipped off to find Deana, on the pretence of going to the loo. Maybe she'd know something. There was some archery event to be held in the castle grounds for the August bank holiday that Joe had mentioned to Ellie. She might need to cater for it at the end of the month. She'd say she needed a word with him about that.

Deana's office was cool and dim, even in high summer. She sat huddled in a thick cardie.

'Hi, Ellie.' She gave her a warm smile nonetheless.

'Deana, you haven't seen Joe about, have you?'

'No, he's not in today, lovey.'

Ellie's heart plummeted. He must be taking an extra day off or something. And he hadn't thought to tell her, even after everything – the closeness she thought they had shared. *Had he just used her?* 'Oh.'

'Yes, he called in yesterday, said he was going to take

273

a couple of days off. I got the impression he might be going home to his mum's. But he wasn't in a chatty mood. Didn't seem himself. So I didn't press for details.'

'Oh.'

'Are you alright, Ellie?'

She must have gone pale or something.

'Oh, yes, fine. No worries,' Ellie rallied, masking the feelings of rejection. 'I'll catch him later when he's back, then.' She tried to capture a blasé tone.

'Nothing I can help with?' Deana ventured.

Ellie just shook her head, biting the inside of her mouth to stop the tears that were starting to well. She didn't think Deana would have any magic potions to heal fractured hearts.

'No, it's fine. I was just wondering about the archery thing coming up, that's all. It can wait.'

There was a second of silence. Deana looked kindly at Ellie. 'He can be quite deep sometimes, can Joe.'

Was Deana hinting that she knew there might be something going on between them? Did she know something? Had he talked to her? Ellie was curious, but didn't want to look an idiot. 'Oh no, it's nothing personal.' Lies, lies, little white lies. Falling like dust to smother her feelings. She'd better get out of here before she gave anything away. 'Okay, then, thanks. That's fine, Deana. I'd better be getting back to the teashop.'

'Well, you know where I am, if you ever need a chat.'

Ellie left the offer hanging in the air. Deana gave her a kind, yet quizzical, look as she dashed out.

*

The news of his departure ate away at Ellie. And the fact he hadn't even thought to tell her. She'd been waiting for him for the past day and a half like some lovelorn pup. *Why, why, why* had she let herself get involved again? Why did her stupid feelings have to get in the way? Why couldn't she have normal one-night stand sex like other people – have a bit of fun, stay detached – like Joe obviously had. *But how did you do that?* How did you stay detached, when you were already in way too deep?

'Well, then, what's up with you, lassie?' Doris dropped her tray down with a clatter on the kitchen side and folded her arms under her ample bosom. 'You've had a face on like a wet weekend these past two days.'

Crikey, was it that obvious? But the last person she wanted to confide in was Doris – the castle broadsheet.

'Oh, I'm okay.'

Doris just stood shaking her head slowly, 'I know when someone's okay and when they're not . . .' her tone softened, 'Look, it's quietened down out there. Nicola can keep an eye on the last two tables while I make you a good strong cup of tea.'

There was no arguing about it. And a cup of tea did actually sound good.

'Alright, then, thank you.' But she still wasn't going to tell her anything.

Doris was filling the kettle. 'There's something up with you and Joe, isn't there?'

Jesus Christ, she didn't miss a trick, did she? Ellie said nothing, just watched Doris busying herself with a teapot and two mugs.

'One minute he's high as a kite,' Doris prattled on, 'Big grin on his face, the works. The next he's heading off to his car. Well, looking very much like you are now. I don't suppose that's connected in any way . . .'

She had Ellie's full attention now. 'When was that, Doris? When did he go?'

'Yesterday afternoon. Soon as he'd finished work, he was heading off the same time as me. I was waiting outside for Clifford to fetch me.'

'Oh.' Ellie tried to smile, but it just wasn't working right.

Doris poured the hot water in the teapot, 'Look, I know I can come across as a nosy old bat sometimes.' *She knew that?* 'But when people are close to me, when it's something I knows is a bit serious, well, believe it or not, I can keep things close to my chest.' She gave a broad, caring smile. Then handed Ellie a steaming cup of tea; she'd popped in a teaspoon of sugar for good measure.

Ellie let out a long sigh, 'When you saw him go, did he say anything to you? Like where or why he was off?'

'Wasn't my place to ask, hinnie. But I got the feeling he had some thinking to do.'

'Deana said she thought he'd gone home. Back to Newcastle for a couple of nights.'

'Sounds likely. His mam's down that way.'

Ellie sipped the sweet tea. Wondering if she really could trust Doris. There was something in the way the middle-aged woman was looking at her, with genuine concern. 'We . . . Well, we kind of got it together,' Ellie wasn't about to go into any details, 'But now he's just upped and left. He could at least have told me if he was going to go home.'

'I doubt he'll be away long. He never takes much leave at this time in the summer season, pet. He'll probably be back tomorrow.'

Hmn, he might soon be back at the castle, but not with her, by the looks of things. She'd be lucky if he was even speaking to her. He'd been in some rush to get away, hadn't he?

'Don't fret too much, pet. These things have a way of working themselves out.'

Ellie couldn't sleep that night. The teashop finances, which were better but not brilliant, and this latest episode with Joe, was all spinning around in her mind. She checked her watch again, 3.15 a.m. She'd been awake at least an hour now.

She could just get up, get some baking done, a batch of brownies or something, down in the teashop kitchen – at least she'd be doing something useful with her time. It seemed a lot better than lying here tossing and turning.

Right, that was it, she was getting up. She pulled on her dressing gown over her pyjamas, found her slippers. Grabbed the little torch her dad had given her as she had moved into the castle, just in case – being unsure if they lit the castle at night, or where all the switches would be en route to the tearooms.

As she got to the bottom of the stone stairs, she saw that it was teeming with rain outside; she'd be drenched before she got across the courtyard. There was another way through to the tearooms, Derek and Malcolm had shown her on their tour that day. Across the castle on the first floor via the Georgian drawing room. It was worth a try. She was up and ready now. Back up the stairs, she found the right door. It wasn't locked. She headed on through in the half light, guided by the beam of her torch. She stepped out tentatively into the drawing room, wondering if it might be alarmed, and then she'd have the whole of the castle up. Well, Lord Henry, anyhow, and perhaps an alert to the Northumbrian police force. That'd make her popular.

No flashing lights or sirens, so she carried on. She

realised she was in the room that Malcolm had mentioned objects had moved around in, and felt a sense of chill. What if there was any truth in it . . . ? Right, Ellie, stop being a scaredy-cat and just get on with it and walk on through. She scanned the room. There was a shadowy figure sitting on the chesterfield sofa.

Oh my God – that was not her imagination. There really was something there!

She crept along the walkway, keeping an eye on it. Nearly at the door now, when it moved, taking a sip from what looked like a cup in its hand.

'Whah!' the shriek escaped her lips before she could stop it.

The figure stood up, 'What the devil . . . ?'

Ellie jumped out of her skin. 'Shit!'

Was this some ancient ancestor ghost, maybe? It looked like it was dressed in a long stripy dressing gown, but the light was dim, the spectre of a half-moon glowed silver-grey at the window. In her panic she'd dropped the torch.

'Ellen?' It knew her name. Weird. 'What the devil are you doing up at this hour of the night? Where on earth are you going? You're not sleep-walking, are you?'

The voice coming out of the blackness sounded just like Lord Henry.

'Lord Henry? Jeez, you frightened the life out of me.' She found the torch and beamed it across at him. 'Oh, it *is* you, Lord Henry. I thought I'd seen a ghost.' She managed a nervous laugh, the fear, now unfounded, still flitting inside her.

He chuckled. 'No, only an old man who can't sleep sitting in his living room. Sometimes there's rather a lot on my mind . . . I've always liked this room. Can't make use of it in the daytime now, with all the bloody tourists wandering about.'

'Yes, it is a lovely room.'

'Get fed up cooped up in my living quarters, same bloody four walls. If I can't sleep I have a wander sometimes, have a cup of tea.'

She remembered Malcolm's story of the teacups left on the side, the furniture of the drawing room mysteriously being moved, smiled to herself. So, Trevor – the Drawing Room Ghost – was revealed. Mind you, it seemed a shame to tell. She'd keep this between herself and Lord Henry – leave Malcolm with his theories.

'So, Ellen, what are you doing up here at this time of the night, anyhow?'

'Well, I wasn't sleeping well either, so I thought I'd get up and do a bit of baking for tomorrow. I'd have gone the courtyard way, but it was tipping with rain . . . sorry to have disturbed you.'

'I see, well then, I suppose I'd better not stop you.'

'Night then, Lord Henry. Can I make you another cup of tea or anything, pop it up to you?'

'No thanks, Ellen. I might just try and head back to my bed in a while. Goodnight.'

'Night.' So, in the half light of the moon, with not a ghost in sight, she headed for the tearooms and left him in peace. This place really was a little crazy sometimes.

So she made it through the tearoom day on three hours' sleep. Heading back up the stone stairwell to her room, Ellie couldn't help but look out through each portcullis window, just in case. The long, thin rectangles gave a snapshot of the avenue of trees that lined the driveway, and . . . a shifting vehicle . . . an outline of a tall, dark-haired driver. Her nerves stretched like elastic the nearer it came. A VW Silver Golf. She recognised a couple of letters in the registration plate.

So, Joe was back.

And nothing. All night she'd waited for that knock on her door, her guts churning with a sense of expectation. Okay, yes, she'd been a coward and retreated to her room rather than wait to face him on the stairs. She'd heard his footsteps coming up . . . and go past. Of course, he'd have to set down his bags, maybe take a shower. So she watched TV, pushed pasta that she'd microwaved for her supper around a plate. Imagined some sexy reunion, or maybe just a few kind words, a smile, a 'sorry, I had to go away for a couple of days, Mum was ill. . . I forgot to mention. . . already had it planned', even the inevitable heart-sinking 'thanks but no thanks, it was great but just a bit of a fling'. But nothing. A whole horrid, wretched evening of wondering, hoping and dreading, that came to nothing. What did that mean, then?

Up at seven, then down to the teashop to make today's batch of scones and chocolate cookies. Kneading the dough rather roughly today, but it felt therapeutic. Well, if *they* didn't have a future, at least she'd give everything to making the tearooms the best they could possibly be. She didn't need Joe-bloody-Ward in her life. She was going to flyer-drop for the school summer holidays, get details in the local papers, leaflets in the tourist information, do a 'Tea for Two' special on a weekday afternoon, 'Senior Citizens' Monday Lunch'. She was going to give Ellie's Teashop her all. And she had plenty of ideas to take forward the wedding buffet menus, whenever Joe decided to show up and start speaking with her again.

It was early August now, only three months left until the end of the season, the end of October. But then what? Foolishly, she hadn't really considered the coming winter months. Unless the weddings got up and running quickly and they had a booking or two, then there was nothing to keep her here. She'd managed to save £400 towards paying her dad back, but she hadn't managed to save enough from the teashop takings to keep her going financially over the winter. In fact, nearly all of Nanna's savings had gone too. What would she do when the castle closed? She'd have to go back home to Newcastle, take on some casual work.

And would she come back next spring, if the position was held for her? Could she face it after all this palaver with Joe?

It was all starting to feel overwhelming – she'd just have to take one day at a time. The first batch of scones was ready to come out of the oven. The next, sultana-and-orange ones, were ready to go in. She slid the tray onto the oven shelf, took out the others. They smelled gorgeous, hot, buttery and doughy.

And then, what she'd hoped for every minute of the past two days happened – the swing door of the kitchen opened and there was Joe. She didn't know whether to melt or freeze.

'Ellie, would you mind popping up to my office for a quick chat?' His tone was awfully formal and his usual smile was strained.

Oh, Jeez, had she done something wrong? Was there something besides the personal stuff going on? Some trouble with the castle, the teashop?

* * *

Joe

Well, he might as well get this over with. Be as professional as possible. And call things on a personal level to a halt.

He'd had time to mull things over, and it seemed the only way forward. Mam hadn't been as helpful as he'd hoped on the advice front. She'd actually told him to follow his heart – that if he felt he might be falling for Ellie, then why not give it a try? That he shouldn't miss out on love. What the hell was love anyway? He liked her *a lot*, was that the same, was it enough? No, if he had any doubt then he had to stop things now. And '*follow your heart*'? Look where that had left his mother, left high and dry as a single parent to a life of grind. He hadn't even met his damned father till six years ago. No, he never wanted to go down that route. He couldn't risk ending up like *him*, getting it wrong, getting some girl pregnant, breaking her heart.

There was a knock. The door swung open and she was there, hair pulled up in a ponytail, her face tense. He saw the rise of her bosom under a casual white T-shirt, the curve of her hips in black trousers, and he felt his heart lodge somewhere in his throat.

'Ah-hem,' he coughed. He could do this. Had to do this. 'Thanks for popping up, Ellie.' This was going to be harder than he had imagined. Get to the point, man. Get it over with. Put the both of you out of your misery.

She looked so lovely there, and yet so damned sad, as though she knew what was coming. He felt such a shit. She'd already had one dickhead of an ex-fiancé mess up her life.

She stayed quiet, facing him, waiting.

'Please, take a seat. Ellie . . . look, what happened, these past few days. Well, I don't think it should happen again. You and me, I mean. I'm sorry.' There, it was said. Done.

'Oh, I see.' Her eyes had totally lost their sparkle. She looked hurt.

Damn. Damn. Damn. But it was inevitable – better now than if they'd got more attached.

Yet he didn't want her to think he hadn't liked her, that he was just using her. 'Umn, it was good . . . nice.' Feeble words. He couldn't possibly let her know just how good. 'But we still need to work together. I just don't think it's a good idea. I'm sorry. I shouldn't have let it happen in the first place. It wasn't very professional of me.'

'Oh, okay.' *Not okay, not okay.* But, she wasn't giving anything away. Her voice sounded cool.

'Anyway, I think we need to put things back on a professional basis. I wouldn't want it to affect the way we work together. The teashop has been doing well, and there's been some great feedback. I wouldn't want to jeopardise that in any way.'

'No, I totally agree.'

'Well, I hope we can still be friends.' God, he sounded

so clichéd, even to himself. He had been doing well until now, but his voice squeaked a bit on that last phrase – he hoped she hadn't noticed. And his throat was parchment-dry, and clogged up. Okay, it was said. And it hadn't made him feel any better at all. As for clearing the air, it felt like there was static between them. She sat there, calm and quiet, however. Why didn't she shout and tell him what a twat he was? Being professional to the last, no doubt. Dammit, isn't that what he'd just asked for? He saw her make a move to stand. She was going to go.

He stood up as well. Just the desk between them. His gaze landed on those luscious lips he had so enjoyed kissing. You'll never be able to kiss them again or hold her in your arms. What are you doing, you idiot?

She turned away, her words reaching him, 'Yes, I understand, Joe. I'd better get back to work now.'

He could still stop her. Hold her close, like every cell of his body was yearning to do.

He let her go.

* * *

Ellie

So, she was just a big mistake, then. And just how were they meant to work together as though nothing had happened? When every damned second she could picture him naked, feel his touch, smell him. She kneaded cookie dough with a fist.

Oh well, she'd show him. She'd make the teashop the very best it could be. The figures were starting to creep up on last year's, and she had her plans to put a flyer out before the weekend, and an advert in the local press. Yes, she had lots of ideas to put into place: she'd do proper afternoon teas, kids-eat-half-price for the school holidays, and once the schools were back, a mid-week lunch offer for pensioners. Even Lord Henry seemed to be warming to her, or to her homemade quiche, to be precise. He'd taken to dropping by a couple of times a week at closing time, to pick up a takeaway supper of quiche, new potatoes and salad. He insisted on paying, but Ellie would slip an extra slice of cake in with the order. He'd chat briefly, then head off to his quarters. He still remained resolutely private, but the coolness had thawed and in his snippets of conversation she got the feeling that he was pleased with how the teashop was going.

So Joe couldn't contemplate giving the lease to someone else, not if she had Lord Henry on-side. Or could he? And next year, would she want to come back? Put herself in this situation again, where every time she looked at him, she'd remember. And it would hurt all over again. The selfish, user, loser, bastard, twat! Twat. Twat. Twat. He wasn't worth it.

But how did she get it so very wrong *again*? How did she let someone in, past her defences, just to hurt her? When it had seemed like he really cared, had felt something for her too? She must be such a crap judge of character . . . Or was it just that all men were like that?

20

Ellie

She didn't mean to, but she folded when she was speaking to Gemma that night. She'd phoned her, wanting to hear a friendly voice, chit-chat about girlie things. She wasn't going to tell her about Joe, how things had moved on so fantastically, but then been crushed by his absence and his damning decision. Like she was some minion beneath him, needing to be kept at a distance. No need to mingle with the staff. Not once you've given them a good shagging, anyhow. Had he just used her all along?

And it all poured out, along with the tears.

'Right, that's it. I'm coming up to have words with this Joe bloke. Who the hell does he think he is?'

'You can't.'

'Why not?'

'He's my landlord. I still have to work with him.'

'He can't get away with treating you like that, Ellie.'

'Please, just leave it.'

'The little shit.'

'It's okay. I'm alright.'

'You don't sound it . . . I know you, Ellie, putting a brave face on things. Well, if I can't come up and kick his backside, can I come up and see you, then? Cheer you up? It's about time I saw where you are, and the teashop and everything.'

'I suppose. Okay.'

'Don't sound so bloody keen.'

And then they both laughed.

'It's just I have to work. And my head's a mess.'

'Me too, and my head's always a mess, but I'll get the afternoon off. Spin some yarn. I'll come see you tomorrow, okay? I need to try out some of this choffee cake you keep going on about. And see for myself what kind of back-of-beyond place you're living in, too.'

'Okay, then. Tomorrow, that'll be good. Thanks, Gemma.'

'We can crash out, after you finish tearoom-ing, with a DVD and a bottle or two of rosé. Be like old times.'

Ellie realised how much she missed their easy friendship. Having someone to share her hopes and fears with.

*

'So this is it, then?' Gemma charged through the swing door, 'Hi, hun. You okay?', and grasped her friend in a bear hug.

'Ah-huh.' Ellie was so pleased to see her friend's smiling face, share a hug.

'The tearooms look okay out there. Bit old-fashioned and chintzy, but I suppose that's the idea around here. The food looks pretty good, mind.' And with that she picked up a cookie from a tray Ellie had just taken out of the oven and took a big bite.

'Hey . . . hands off, you!' But Ellie was laughing.

'God, I miss you in the office, and on the doughnut run. No one can be bothered to go now. It's dire, I'm withering away.'

'Ooh yes, and how is life at North East Mutual?'

'Much the same. Except they never replaced you, did they? So we all have to work even harder. Long hours, low pay . . . you know the score.'

'Pretty much the same here . . .' Ellie smiled wryly, then paused. 'But I love it,' she added earnestly.

'Except for the bloody management,' Gemma chipped in.

'Well, the less said about that the better.' Damn, Ellie could feel prickles of tears coming behind her eyes.

Gemma got all ballsy on her behalf. 'Well, if he can drop you like that, he's not worth it. The tosser.' And with that she took another big bite of the cookie.

'I'll make us a cup of tea, then, and when I get five minutes, I'll show you up to my room and you can make yourself at home.'

'Tea? I've something much better than that in my rucksack.' With that she pulled out a bottle of vodka.

'Jeez, Gemma. Not now. I've still a couple of hours to go here.' Mind you, she might be glad of a shot or two later.

'I've brought some Diet Coke for it too.' Gemma was beaming wickedly.

'Later, okay?'

'Look forward to it. Suppose tea'll have to do then, thanks.'

They were going to be in for a boozy night, by the sounds of it. Oh well, it might do her good. Take her mind off things.

Doris and Nicola were introduced to Gemma as they popped into the kitchen.

'Nice hairdo,' Gemma chuckled as Doris headed back out with a fresh plate of the cookies. Doris had just had it cut and it did have a rather bowl-like effect.

'Shush,' Ellie pleaded, but ended up in a fit of the giggles.

Ellie had packed up the teashop for the night and could hear the music pounding from her room as she mounted her stairwell – some indie band Gemma was into. Oh shit, that'd disturb Joe above her. Oh well, serve him right. Hopefully the noise wouldn't reach as far across as Lord Henry's rooms.

She opened her door to find Gemma dancing in the space by the bed, glass of rosé in hand.

On the bed was laid out a DVD of *Dirty Dancing*, a half-empty litre of rosé, a bottle of vodka and some cans of Diet Coke, plus a family-sized pack of toffee popcorn and a huge bar of Dairy Milk.

'Remedies for sore hearts. Tosser-resistant.' Gemma reached for the other glass, picked up the bottle of rosé, and poured. 'Cheers, me dears. To us.'

'To good friends.' Ellie was feeling emotional already. Must be her unsettled mood.

'And sod all the miserable bastards who don't know a good thing when they see it.'

'Yes, sod the bastards.' Ellie raised her glass towards the roof meaningfully.

DVD on, they were soon engrossed in the film, sipping vodka and Coke and munching popcorn. Then, they were singing along as the credits rolled and Ellie found herself in tears. Even gorgeous Patrick Swayze was dead. It was all too much. Bloody Joe. Bloody cancer. Bloody men. It must be all the alcohol breaking down her defences.

They were both on Ellie's bed. Gemma turned to her. 'It's alright, hun. Let it all out.' And they lay in a hug on the double duvet. Tipsy and tearful.

'I love you, Ellie. Don't you worry about him.'

'Love you too, Gems. Thanks for coming to cheer me up.' The tears were still dripping down her cheeks.

'Did a bloody good job, didn't I?' And they laughed and cried together.

They finished another glass of vodka and Coke and drifted into an unexpectedly sound sleep.

*

The alarm buzzed offensively.

'What the hell's that?' Gemma groaned, shoving her head back under a pillow. 'What the hell time is it, anyhow?'

'Seven. Got to get up. Make scones.' Ellie fumbled a hand to the bedside table, trying to locate and stop the damn thing. Her head was being hammered from the inside.

'UGHH!'

Ellie managed to stop the buzzing. 'I'll be back soon. Or if you like, pop down for some breakfast.'

'Bleugh!' was the response from under the pillow, which pretty much matched her own. On autopilot, she dressed in yesterday's clothes and made her way down to the kitchen. Somehow she managed to make two batches of scones and a quiche, sipped half a cup of tea, which sunk heavily in her stomach, making her feel even more queasy, and got back to find that Gemma hadn't moved. Ellie lay down on the bed beside her, this time on top of the duvet, until she *really* had to get up and get to work in the teashop, cutting it more than fine, finding Doris already bustling about. She tried her best to act normally but could only creep about at snail pace.

Five minutes later, Doris set down a glass of water and two paracetamol on the worktop next to her. 'You might need these,' was all she said.

Ellie mouthed a 'Thanks'.

Gemma turned up an hour and a half later, her face pale, eyes bloodshot, 'I think I'd better head back down the road. I'm meant to be back in the office this afternoon.'

'Take it steady, then. Are you sure you'll be okay? Here, have a big glass of water before you go.'

'Cheers,' it was said in a very different tone than last night. Gemma glugged back the water.

'It was a good night, though. Thanks for coming up.' Ellie managed a smile.

'You're going to be alright, Ellie.'

'I know. Thanks.' Her words sounded more sure than she felt.

Ellie kept her head down, got on with work, and tried her best to be as professional as she could when inevitably she and Joe met, either by chance, or when they had to discuss some work project. They had taken the event planning for the weddings a stage further; Joe was to place adverts in *Brides* magazine and set up a small stand at a couple of wedding fayres in Edinburgh and Newcastle. The accommodation wouldn't be ready till next year, at least, but they could book out the hall and catering, and flowers – care of Wendy. Conversations were cool but polite and business-like.

The teashop was busy most days now, thank heavens, which was good: for business, the bank account, and for keeping her mind occupied. Well, most of the time. Her mind still had its moments and strayed right back into his arms and his bed every now and then, but she kept it in check as best she could. But her room seemed awfully lonely at nights, and her heart felt pared down, as if she'd given away too much.

*

There was a fiftieth birthday party event coming up, the husband had come in and booked it a while back. Ellie needed to coordinate flowers – he'd mentioned roses as his wife's favourite, and there was the buffet menu to plan. The husband had asked to hire the great hall as it featured in a film version of Robin Hood that his wife had always loved, apparently. How thoughtful of him. Ellie wondered how long they'd been married. Maybe all men weren't bad, after all. It was just the small matter of finding the right one. A needle in a haystack came to mind. And Ellie had met too many pricks to bother to keep looking.

'What on earth is the matter with you two?' Doris was standing in the middle of the tearoom's kitchen with her arms folded.

Joe had just popped in to say they'd need to meet up to discuss the fiftieth birthday bash soon, as he had to feed back ideas and final prices to Mr Fiftieth in the next couple of days. He mentioned that they'd need Wendy from the flower shop at the meeting too, as there were the table decorations and a couple of pedestals to organise. Then he'd dashed off out.

'Honestly, you've both been going around with faces like a wet weekend for the past two weeks.' Doris droned on, 'The atmosphere in this place is awful. You need your heads smacking together. Make you see some sense. What's to be done about it, hey?'

'There's nothing to be *done* about it, Doris,' Ellie's tone was surprisingly sharp, 'He's already made it quite clear that he wants nothing to do with me . . . not on a personal level, anyhow.'

Please just let it be, Doris. She didn't want to hear, or think, any more about it, or him. She wished she hadn't said anything to Doris now. She hoped she might be feeling a bit better about things, but the hurt hadn't eased, and he crept back into her mind when she heard the creak of his floorboards above her in her room, or the metallic clunk and patter of the water pipes when he showered. Bringing back into focus the muscle and tone of his naked body, remembering how it felt beneath her fingertips. Damn him.

'Well, something's got to be done about it.' Doris muttered as she waltzed off to fetch milk to fill the little porcelain jugs that went with the teas.

The meeting was scheduled for three-thirty. Doris and Ellie were to be there to discuss the catering arrangements, Wendy to talk flowers, and Joe to coordinate it all and feed back to Mr Fiftieth. Doris had bustled off five minutes earlier, so Ellie presumed she'd meet her in the great hall, seeing as she hadn't come back. 'We'll be about twenty minutes, I would think, Nicola. Are you sure you'll be alright?'

'Yes, fine. It's quietened down now – nothing I can't handle.'

'Well, nip up and get us or ring Joe's mobile if it gets busy or anything.'

'Will do, but I'll be fine.'

'Yes, I'm sure you will. Thanks, Nicola.' The girl had grown in confidence over the past few months, it was obvious from the way she laughed and joked with the customers, even becoming friendly with some of the regulars. She was blossoming into a lovely young lady.

Ellie had a proposed menu printed out; a full-on after-noon tea – mini sandwiches, homemade pastries and quiches, a collection of cakes and shortbread, including cupcakes with crystallised rose petals on to go with the 'rose' flower theme, champagne or sparkling wine, depending on budgets, jugs of iced water for the tables, and plenty of tea and coffee.

Ellie walked into the great hall – they'd arranged to meet there as that was where the event was to take place. It was three-twenty-five. She was the first there. Doris still hadn't appeared – maybe she'd had to visit the ladies or something. Wendy was probably parking up. And Joe, well, he was usually pretty good on time-keeping.

She noticed that someone had set coffee out, which was nice of them; perhaps Joe had had Deana organise it. She walked along the hall, looking out of the tall windows at the rear gardens, a few late-in-the-day visitors were strolling the pathways admiring the herbaceous borders. There were several roses, which were in full splendid bloom, hollyhocks and flowering shrubs tall behind; the overall effect was rather stunning.

She wandered back to the long dark-wood table that was polished to a conker-like glow. Wondered about pouring herself a coffee. There was a silver coffee pot, steam curling invitingly from the spout and two cups and saucers. Someone had also put out a couple of brownies and squares of homemade shortbread that looked suspiciously like the ones she made for the teashop.

Two cups.

And where was Doris?

Joe walked in, tall, lean and oh-so-bloody-handsome it hurt.

No Doris. No Wendy.

Coffee for two – that was odd. Surely Deana would have been made aware that there were four of them meeting up. She was always on the ball. Joe loitered a few feet from the table, said an awkward 'Hello'. Then paced the floor, not looking at Ellie.

'Have you seen anything of Wendy?' she asked, just as he started with, 'I thought Doris was coming along with you?'

And then she had the feeling that this might well have been engineered. 'Hmn, I wonder . . . She glanced down at the *two* cups and her watch – it was nearly twenty to.

'Two cups?' His anxious glance turned into a wry smile. 'A set-up?'

'I think it might well be.' She couldn't help but give a half-smile too. She'd kill Doris when she caught up with her, the meddling woman. 'Coffee?'

'Seems a shame to waste it.'

She poured. He finally seemed to relax and drew out a chair opposite her.

Well, they may as well get started. God knows what

the other two were up to. 'Right, well, I've got the buffet suggestions all sorted.' Ellie said, 'I could do it for £14.95 per head with a glass of sparkly. Have to be a bit more if they want real champagne. And if they want a birthday cake, that would be additional too.' She passed Joe the A4 sheet she'd printed out, with everything listed.

'That looks great.' He seemed impressed. 'And you've even thought about the roses theme. I'm sure they'll love it.'

'Over the phone, Wendy had mentioned a country garden floral theme for the tables. It'll work well. Give us a taster for the wedding dos as well – on a smaller scale.'

'Yes, yes . . . Where the hell is Wendy, anyhow?'

'She might be held up in traffic, I suppose.' Ellie was still giving her the benefit of the doubt.

'And Doris?'

They waited a while in a silence that became more awkward as the time ticked on.

Too many recent memories were crowding in. He was so close, just there across the table. She didn't want to look him in the eye. Anger was fizzing up within her too. How dare he use her like that for sex and then just cast her off like she was nothing. It was so hard to remain damned professional.

He looked at her, then slowly reached across the table. His hand slid over hers, making her skin tingle. Oh my, how she had missed his touch. Her eyes locked with his intense gaze. What the hell was going on?

'How dare you.' She pulled her hand away brusquely.

'I–I'm sorry, Ellie.' His look was sincere, serious, 'I never meant to hurt you.'

'Well, you did a damned good job of it.' She paused. 'Those few days, I thought it meant something. More fool me! Then you just upped and left, not saying a word, waltzed back, telling me it meant nothing, and now this?'

Silence then. Too many feelings churning inside. And saying sorry wasn't bloody enough. Was it just to make *him* feel a bit better?

His eyes were on hers. 'I've missed you.'

Talk about Jekyll and Hyde. Where was this going? What did it mean?

She heard his long, slow sigh. He moved his hand up to her face, stroked her cheek so delicately.

She had missed him too, of course she had. But, could she be honest? Make herself vulnerable again?

'Look, can we talk? Later on, properly. There's . . . there's some stuff you should know.'

Curiosity nipped at her. But she was still hurting. Should she give him that chance? The chance to hurt her more? He seemed to still care for her. But what on earth did all this mean? That they might get back together? Or was he about to explain why it had to be no? And what if they tried again, lasted a few weeks, months, and then it all went wrong again?

The touch on her cheek, the look in his eyes. His words. 'I thought it would be easier, keeping you distant, but it's not . . .' And before she could think any more, he leaned across the table and pressed his lips, oh so tenderly, against hers. He tasted of chocolate brownie and coffee and Joe. So good. He still wanted her. His body couldn't lie. His lips told her so as they kissed, deeper now, his hand gentle on the back of her head. She just wanted to climb across the damned table and feel the whole of him against her. Now that might look interesting should any visitors take a peek in through the windows from the garden.

Finally, they pulled away.

A kiss like that deserved a second chance, how could she resist? 'Okay, we'll talk.'

'Do you think the damned pair of them are spying somewhere?' His cheeky smile was back, like sunshine lighting his face. She realised she hadn't seen that for weeks.

'Wouldn't put it past them. In that big antique cabinet or something.' She laughed, pointing at the chest at the far end of the hall.

'I'd better track down Wendy, anyhow, finalise these details and ring the chap back.'

'I don't think those two will be far away, somehow.'

'We'll meet later, yeah? I'll come and knock your door after work. We'll go for a walk or something.'

'Yes, I'll be finished about six.' She wondered exactly what it was he needed to explain.

Doris and Wendy looked extremely suspicious as Ellie walked back into the tearoom kitchens. They both raised their eyebrows, Doris quipping, 'Oh, did we get the wrong room? Where did you two get to?'

'What exactly was all that about?' Ellie pretended to be annoyed.

The two ladies grinned conspiratorially.

'Did he turn up?'

'Did you kiss and make up?'

Ellie remembered the burn of his lips and found herself blushing.

'Well somebody had to get the pair of you together.' Doris was indignant. 'And . . . ?' she was pressing for details.

'O-kay,' Ellie caved in, 'Yes, we talked.' She was saying nothing about the kiss. 'And we're seeing each other tonight, if you must know . . . But that's all. I'm not quite sure which way things are going as yet.'

Two sets of eyebrows were raised at her.

'But it looks promising.' Ellie added, to try and stop the twenty questions that were about to be launched.

'Promising?' quizzed Doris.

'Anyway, it was very unprofessional of you both, not turning up for the meeting.'

'Huh, we *did*, we just had our own down here. Wendy's going to catch Joe in a sec. Deana was in on it too, so she'll let him know that we were here all along, and I already know all the catering arrangements. I've given a copy of your menu to Wendy. She loves the rose petal cup-cake idea.'

'Yes, the buffet sounds gorgeous. So,' added Wendy, 'It's all sorted, then.'

The function was indeed, pending Mr Fiftieth's agreement. But Ellie still wasn't so sure about her relationship with Joe. What exactly was he intending to tell her tonight?

21

Ellie

The knock on her door couldn't come soon enough.

She really didn't know what to think any more. The highs of their lovemaking two weeks ago, the sinking low of his rejection, and all the mixed-up emotions in between. And today's apology, and now this 'We need to talk' business – what was that all about? He hadn't said he wanted to be with her. There was more to this yet, she sensed. It could still be a big, fat no. But maybe he needed to say that he had felt something too, even if it could go no further. Would that be any better to know, or just make her feel more miserable?

'Hey.' He was standing on the threshold to her door dressed in a pair of dark jeans, and a pale-blue open-neck shirt. His trademark look that she'd grown to love.

Smart-casual, but somehow with the shirtsleeves rolled up and the top buttons undone, revealing a little patch of his dark chest hair, it made him look sexily dishevelled.

'Hi,' she replied. There was an awkward tension between them. She had changed into jeans, too, with a pretty chiffon-style top and her canvas pumps. She had also tied a cardigan around her waist. The evenings could get cool here, even though it was early August; the earlier nights already starting to draw in.

'Let's walk.' He sounded a little nervous.

She followed him down the winding staircase and kept a safe distance as they walked into the courtyard.

'Quite some set-up today, wasn't it? Wendy came to see me afterwards.'

'Ah-huh,' Ellie smiled.

He stopped, smiled back. 'I'm glad. I was wondering how on earth I was going to get to speak to you . . . after being such an idiot shutting you off like that . . .' He rubbed a hand through his hair. They were in the square of light in the centre of the courtyard, a pigeon cooing from the battlements, all the visitors gone home. Doris, Nicola, Deana away too – only Lord Henry up there somewhere loitering in his rooms within the castle. Joe took her to him, pulled her oh-so-close and just held her there so her head nestled in against his chest until their breathing slowed and they relaxed together. He didn't try to kiss her, just held her tight, and whispered 'I missed you', into her hair.

She tensed, still unsure of where this was going. But his arms felt so wonderful around her. 'I know,' she answered, because she'd felt it too, missed every cell of him, missed him to her bones.

Please, please don't let this be a 'goodbye' walk. But who the hell knew? I miss you, *but* . . . Always the *but* ready to catch you out, toss your heart in the air and let it splat back down on the flagstones.

He pulled away slightly, 'Come on, let's get out of here.'

Out through the castle keep, through the arch of the heavy wooden door, escaping the grounds into the woods. Their conversation roamed non-committedly around work, the view, the weather. Joe seemed to relax the further they got from the castle, as the green of the hills enclosed them. Boy, he seemed to love those hills. As she began to run out of steam from the uphill climb, he was just getting going, his long legs striding out. Bloody hell, if they did get back together, she might have to take up bloody rambling and buy herself a pair of walking boots. No more stilettos or kitten heels. Was she sure she was doing the right thing here? She might even end up wearing a cagoule at this rate.

But she was smiling as she took his hand. He helped her up the steep bank, and then, that view again – it made it all worthwhile. He certainly had a way of taking her breath away. The rolling hills of Northumberland, an expanse of browns, golds and greens, crops and grass, sheep and cattle, a tractor, and in the distance the majestic rise of the Cheviots, the heather just starting to turn them mauve. They walked a little further on, fat fronds of fern caressed their path, and birds darted in and out of the prickly gorse, whose flowers had died back to a burned bronze.

They reached a slab of sandstone sunk into the hillside, making a perfect bench. They sat, taking in the panorama before them.

Joe knew this was the time to open his heart, to try and explain. 'Ellie, I'm so sorry . . .' He shifted to face her, 'I thought I was doing the right thing. Trying to call a halt, trying to keep it strictly professional between us.'

'I think it was a bit late for that.'

'Hah, yeah, idiot, wasn't I? But I wished to God I hadn't hurt you, Ellie. You must have wondered what the hell was going on? I–I just got scared, back-tracked. Needed some headspace. I couldn't get into something if I didn't mean it, if it wasn't going to last, especially with us working together. I just needed some time to think . . .'

She watched him intently – this wasn't easy for him, she could tell.

'I couldn't risk you falling for me,' he continued, 'And then having to let you down. And what if I'd got you pregnant or something . . . it happens? I was thinking

310

about my mam, about her being a single parent. I grew up without a dad around. It wasn't easy . . .'

'Do you think it was easy for me, Joe? Trusting someone again . . . and then you just disappeared, as though I meant absolutely nothing.'

'I'm sorry, Ellie.'

'So, you've been doing some thinking.' She needed to know where this was going.

'Yeah, well, it wasn't the thinking that made me see. The thinking told me to break it off. But I just felt rotten . . . bloody miserable. And then I knew I'd got it all wrong. But I didn't know if you'd even want me back.'

How could she not want him? Even though she wanted to kick him extremely hard up the butt at this very moment.

'Can you give me a second chance, Ellie? Give *us* a second chance?' He paused, fixing his gaze on hers. 'I want to be with you – be there for you. Everything.'

The wind curled around them, blowing her hair across her face. He gently pulled a strand from her lips. He looked anxious.

Her answer was easy, inevitable. Worth all the risk.

'Yes.' Her voice was sure.

His arms reached around her shoulders as the smile spread across his face, and he leaned in to kiss her, oh so tenderly. Longing and relief bonding them. Afterwards, they sat close, she leaning into him, his arm around her, feeling the warmth of their bodies united against the cool of the breeze. She could smell his aftershave, feel the crisp cotton of his shirt. She placed her hand gently on his thigh. Just to be able to touch him again was a joy.

'Oh, Ellie.' His voice was soft in her hair.

In a strange way she felt so overwhelmed that she wanted to cry. She wanted to be there for him from now on too, with him, loving him, always. 'Joe,' she whispered his name. It made her feel vulnerable and beautiful.

The wind whipped up around them as they sat there a long while. The cool evening air began to nip, as the peachy colours of dusk began to paint the sky. They walked slowly down the hill, hands tight together, back to the castle.

Up the stone stairwell, two sets of footsteps echoing in time.

They stayed clothed, lay down on his bed, caressing, bodies curled together, her hand tracing his palm with delicate fingertips. They didn't make love, not yet – just lay there together. It was as though they knew they now had time, didn't want to rush things, or get it wrong this time.

She felt so very tired, as the emotions of the past weeks caught up with her, and she relaxed in his arms. Found that she had napped and when she woke, he was watching her, a gentle smile on his lips.

'Hi, sleepy.'

'Hello, you.'

'Hungry?'

She found she was. 'Ah-hm.' She hadn't even thought about supper. But it must be, what, nine, ten o'clock by now?

'I haven't got much in. Some local cheeses, bread. Sure I can find a bottle of red lurking about somewhere.'

'Sounds good.' She sat herself up on the bed. His bed. So it hadn't all just been wishful thinking, a lovely dream.

'How does a picnic on the roof sound?' he grinned at her.

'Scary . . . Joe, it's nearly dark. Roofs are dangerous. Especially great big castle ones.'

'Well, then, that's where you're wrong. There's a door at the top of this tower and it leads to a flat roof. It's okay – it has walls around the edges and you can look out over the whole estate.'

'Oh, well, I suppose I could give it a try. Though I am nervous of heights.'

'I'll keep you safe.'

He went to his kitchen – she heard him gathering food from the fridge, a clink of cutlery, clatter of plates. He returned with a laden supermarket carrier bag, no wicker picnic hamper – who said romance was dead?

'Okay, ready to roll.' As they passed the coat rack, he grabbed a fleece, then reached again for another for her. 'You might need this up there, at this time of night.'

She wrapped it around her shoulders, revelling in the aftershave smell of him on it, and followed him out and up the winding staircase.

'You haven't got any other secrets you're keeping, have you?' she quipped, 'No mad Mrs Rochester hidden up here, or something?'

He glanced back at her with a quirky, uneasy smile.

On the last twist of the stairs, they reached a heavy wooden door. He had a key ready in his pocket, and held the carrier bag and a blanket over his arm. Ellie stepped out first onto the tower roof. The stone wall was high enough to feel safe, with rectangular cut-outs, the medieval crenellations, but it still made her feel giddy up there. Twilight spread inkily across the sky, she could see the walled gardens, the grey sweep of the drive, the woods now murky and secretive, the grand hills rising in the distance, their heather-mauve dipped in indigo. He was there next to her.

'Wow, that's one cool view. Though, I don't think I can stand near the edge too long.'

'Here.' He motioned to the blanket, he'd placed it where they could sit with their backs resting against the wall. He set out a selection of cheeses, some grapes, a small baguette, a pack of butter, two wine glasses, corkscrew and a bottle of Merlot.

'Supper is served, madam,' he made a sweeping gesture with his arm.

They sat down and tucked in, breaking off bread and slicing chunks of cheese, nibbling at grapes. Night crept cosily around them. The fleeces kept off the chill. Stars began to appear in the clear night sky above, turning on one by one. Ellie rested her head against the wall, staring up. It made her feel small – like a speck in the universe.

'Stunning, isn't it?' Joe said, 'I come up here sometimes just to look at the stars. Chill out a bit. Forget about life. No problem ever seems big up here. Should have come up here instead of running off down to Newcastle. Might have seen sense quicker that way.' He pressed an arm around her. 'Ellie, there's something else I need to tell you.'

She froze inside. Was this the big *but*?

He seemed tense, took a slow breath, 'Right, well . . . it's just . . . I did find out who my father was.'

'Oh.'

'Eventually . . . once I'd turned eighteen. My mother never mentioned him up till then, not once. I'd kept pestering her, but she'd never say. Wanted to protect him. She worked here at the castle. Got pregnant. He was married at the time.' He paused, looking out at the night sky. Ellie let him have the space he needed, kept quiet. 'His wife was ill, confined to a wheelchair. And my mam said she felt dreadful. She shouldn't have let it happen, that she never meant to hurt her. They shouldn't have let the affair go so far. It was best they didn't know that she was pregnant, then it couldn't destroy them, their marriage. So she just upped and left. Never told him. But she couldn't bear to have an abortion either. So she got herself a job and looked after us, on her own.'

'Oh.' She thought of her own dad, his broad smile, strong arms, the man who'd do anything for her. Joe had never had that. So who was this man who had never been there for him?

'Ellie, Lord Henry is my father.'

'Woah . . . Lord Henry is your father?' She was trying to process this information, 'But you don't seem close . . . I'd never have thought.'

'No, we're not close. He never even knew I existed until I was eighteen. And then, he was still married, he wanted to keep it quiet here at the castle. He only agreed to meet me after his wife, Lady Pamela, had died. And even then, our relationship was never disclosed publicly. So no one knows at work, only Deana. She knew my mam from her working here, all those years before. She arranged the initial meetings. So please, I'd like to keep it that way. I don't want the other staff knowing.'

'Of course.'

'It was a few years later when he asked me to come and work for him here. I wasn't sure initially, but I was good at business, had a feeling I could turn things around here. And when I came up to see him that first time, I just loved the place. We both felt happier keeping it as a business arrangement. He's never really felt like my dad. Yes, he's my father, a biological thing, but he's never been a dad to me. You have to earn the right to be a dad, and I know it wasn't really his fault, but he'd already missed all my childhood.' There was a touch of bitterness in his tone.

Ellie could understand that. She'd been lucky to have such a secure childhood, had taken her close-knit family for granted. How sad to have missed all that. She found herself thinking of the mannerisms between Joe and Lord Henry: looks, the height was roughly the same, both tall, fairly lean. And, yes, they did both do that rubbing-the-chin thing when they were thoughtful. There weren't many more similarities, though. Lord Henry's hair had thinned and was grey, but yes, maybe years ago, a younger man with darker, thicker hair. There might be something there.

There was so much for Ellie to get her head around. No wonder his mother didn't feel comfortable visiting the castle. Other thoughts and implications were flooding Ellie's mind.

She placed her hand over his.

'I can't blame my mam too much. She did what she thought she had to, and then she just got on with it. Got her own cleaning company up and running. Looked after me . . . It doesn't change anything, does it?' Joe continued, 'With you and me? I don't want there to be any more secrets. I don't want to keep anything from you.'

'No, I don't think so. It's just a lot to take in, that's all . . . Blimey, does this mean you'll inherit this place? The castle, the estate?' Would Joe become a lord or something? How crazy!

'Yeah, that's a bit crazy, isn't it?' He was stealing her thoughts. 'Well at least, I think so. That's unless he's got any other children hidden anywhere. Wouldn't put it past him.' The irony was bitter in his tone.

'Hmn, now there's a thought. Wonder if they'd be better looking than this one?' Ellie tried to lighten the mood. She gave Joe a playful dig in the ribs.

He poked her back, tickling her ribs until she squirmed and giggled, pushing her down until he lay above her on the blanket. And they stopped, stared at each other, then kissed fervently, provocatively. Mouths, tongues, bodies, pressed hard. Hot and sexy and wanting. The stars a canopy above. And he made love to her slowly and intensely, pulling down her jeans, her panties, tugging his own trousers and boxers aside, fleeces and tops still on, a strange sexy mix of nakedness and clothing. And the feeling of him inside her, which filled her with pleasure and awe and love, arching her body to him until they pulsed together. His low groan and her crying out a sensual echo around the castle walls.

22

Ellie

Life was good. So amazingly good, she often felt like pinching herself. Ellie hummed away in the kitchen, mixing up choffee cake, the old recipe book to hand, thinking how much her nanna would have liked Joe. Doris kept saying how lovely it was to see them both smiling again, and loudly crediting herself for her splendid matchmaking abilities. But even Doris harping on couldn't upset Ellie. She was truly happy for the first time in years.

Joe hadn't backtracked about their relationship or turned into a sloppy kisser. They had a full-on, loving and very sexual relationship. But it wasn't just about the sex, they could chat for hours, or they could as easily sit in companionable silence. They ate out, they ate in, strolled the beach, walked the countryside. They talked, they loved, they laughed.

Even the father–son thing didn't seem as daunting now. At first she found it awkward speaking with Lord Henry, knowing the truth and having to keep it secret. She even found herself checking them both out for similarities. There was something across the eyes, the shape of the brows, that was alike, but other than that and their height, there seemed very little in common; nurture must have won out over nature, not surprisingly, really, seeing as the young Joe had had nothing to do with his father. And Joe explained a bit more about the inheritance side of things, with Lord Henry fit and healthy – he seemed to be as strong as an ox, and as bullish as one – the prospect was likely to be years away. In reality, Joe explained how there would be huge inheritance tax to pay, though Lord Henry had mentioned some small investments, and it wasn't even a given that he had decided to make his son sole heir (knowing the quirky ways of Lord Henry there might be something else up his sleeve – give it all to some charity or something). But if so, by the time tax and repairs were taken into account, unless he sold up, Joe would hardly be wealthy – he'd still have to work hard to keep the castle going as a viable entity, the farming side of the estate was only making a small profit, so the wedding bookings, the teashop lease and day-to-day takings were as important as ever.

Ellie's parents and Jason had popped up for a day visit one Sunday, and Joe had been more than happy to be introduced as 'the boyfriend'. Watching Joe chat with them over a cup of tea in the teashop, about fishing with her dad, complimenting her mother on her new high-lighted hairdo, and talking football with Jay – Ellie was impressed. His easy manner ensured smiles all round, though he admitted later in the warmth of her bed that he'd felt pretty nervous, not wanting to mess it up at the first hurdle with her family.

The fiftieth birthday tea went off exceptionally well. The room, with English country-style flowers, cakes, including the prettiest cup-cakes with sugar rose buds on the top, and buffet, looked amazing. Mrs Birthday Girl was so pleased with it all, there were tears all round at the speeches. Life really was coming up roses.

Ellie was happy, but also wary of her happiness. It was almost *too* good. She was still expecting the big *but*, waiting for the fall, for life to trip her up once more.

*

Leaves of red and gold drifted down to the castle driveway, morning mists cooled the late September air, and the days were beginning to shorten.

Less than six weeks now until the end of the season, when the castle would close its doors to visitors and become Lord Henry's quiet home for a few months once more. Joe stayed on in the winter months, keeping an eye on the estate and the farm; there was plenty for him to do, he'd said. But Ellie couldn't help but feel anxious. She didn't want to leave now that things were going so well with Joe, but the two wedding functions they had booked (yes, they had *two* now) were hardly going to see her through the closed season. She'd finally managed to save a few hundred pounds from the teashop takings over the summer as well as paying back her dad, but with all the costs and paying Doris and Nicola, there was really very little left in her bank account. She might just last a couple of weeks on it, certainly not months. The likely thing was that she'd have to go home – minimal rent back at Heaton, and find some casual work in Newcastle, temping or something. She had been keeping her eye out for something up here in Kirkton, but there was very little in the job centre or local papers, unless she could drive a tractor or had a teaching qualification. She'd be happy to work in a supermarket or a bar if need be. If she could find something, maybe Lord Henry would allow her to stay. But jobs seemed thin on the ground this time of year, the end of the summer season meant less work available, not more.

There was one last event planned for the castle in a month's time, for the end of the season: a fireworks and Halloween do, on the last Friday of the October school half term. It had gone well in previous years, apparently, and they hoped to make it even bigger and better, with a professional fireworks display, fancy dress for the children and a pumpkin-carving competition. Ellie was in charge of organising soup, hotdogs and burgers.

But for now, the teashop was slowing down. Visitor numbers were tailing off – with all the schools back, there were fewer families in for lunches, and more middle-aged couples coming in for just a cup of tea and slice of cake.

While it was quiet, Joe and Ellie decided to do a 'meet the parents' away visit; he'd been wanting her to meet his mum, Sue. And though he had met her parents briefly when they had visited the castle, it would be nice to stay over a night and for him to get to know them properly.

Doris was going to oversee the teashop: 'It'll be fine, honestly. Get away while it's quiet here and have a nice time. Me and Nicola will be in control.'

'Yes, we'll have it sussed, Ellie. You go and enjoy yourself. Don't worry, I'll keep Doris in order,' Nicola laughed cheekily, as Doris flicked a tea towel at her. It was lovely to see the new dynamic between them as Nicola was growing in confidence.

So they set off in his Golf down the A1. First stop was his mum's house. It was mid-afternoon by the time they got there, as Joe had had some farm business to settle before they could leave. They pulled up outside a neat red-brick semi-detached house on a suburban street on the outskirts of Byker. Just down the hill you could see the smart apartment blocks that marked the more exclusive quayside area. As they got out of the car, Ellie took in the view across the River Tyne. She could make out the tall red-brick industrial building that was now the Baltic Art Gallery and half of the sweep of the Millennium Bridge.

'Great view,' Ellie commented, as she followed Joe through a small wrought-iron gate, up the paving-stone path to the front door. 'Did you live here?'

'Just for a while when I was a teenager. But before then we were in a council place in Byker. Bit of a dive.'

'Hello, bonny lad.' Sue was at the door, giving Joe a big hug. Then turned to Ellie, 'And you must be Ellie. I've heard *so* much about you . . . You must be the one he was all in a fret over the other week.'

Joe grimaced with embarrassment.

'Come on in then, the pair of you. Oh, what a lovely dress, Ellie, very pretty. You'll have to excuse me, I'm still in my work slacks. Had a job this morning.'

Sue was dressed in smart black trousers and a white blouse that had a soft frill trailing the front. Her hair was dark, nearly black, most likely dyed, but it suited her. It was to her shoulders with a stylish wave. She wore a lot of mascara and eyeliner, a touch too much, but it kind of suited her bubbly character and highlighted her attractive eyes; they were very like Joe's in their almond shape but a lighter shade than his, more green than brown. Yes, you could tell they were related. She was talkative and easy-going. Ushering them in to the house with a, 'Well, what can I get you then, tea, coffee? I've made an attempt at a Victoria sponge, though I doubt it's anything like as good as yours, Ellie. Joe says you're making a smashing job of the teashop there at the castle.'

'Thanks, and I'm sure your cake will be lovely. It's kind of you to go to the effort, especially if you've been working today too.'

'Oh, it's no problem. You okay, Joey?'

It sounded funny to Ellie, hearing her call him 'Joey', but it rang with affection too. Actually Ellie hoped her dad wouldn't come up with *her* good old nicknames later on: 'Titch' (from Dad) and 'Ells-bells' and 'Lardy Arse' (both from Jason) were better kept under wraps at this stage in their relationship.

'Good thanks, Mam,' Joe replied, 'Everything's going well, really well,' and with that he gave Ellie a wink.

They sat in the lounge, on a modern beige sofa set with comfy red cushions, and chatted away while filling up on sponge cake and chocolate-dipped flapjack. They heard all about Sue's latest holiday to Bulgaria with her best friend, Marge. Ellie, in turn, had to tell her all about the tearooms, and what she'd been doing before that, and how she found the castle.

'H alright these days?' Sue turned to Joe.

Ellie twigged – Lord Henry – and was a little surprised that Sue had mentioned him, but there seemed no ill will in her tone.

'Yes, he's fine. Much the same as ever.' Joe gave a wry smile. 'He'll be glad to get shot of the guests for another winter. How we're supposed to make money to keep the place going without them, though, I'll never know!'

'Well, send him my regards.' She seemed comfortable talking about him but, Ellie supposed, it was all a long time ago, and there must have been some affection there. It was still weird to think he was Joe's father. But, then, how would anyone have guessed without him publically acknowledging it?

Sue had a little dog, Bertie, a pug-terrier cross who was extremely cute. He was allowed in to the lounge once the cake and biscuits had been put away. He made friends with Ellie instantly and ended up snuggled against her on the sofa, making little contented grunts as she stroked him.

An hour or so later it was time to get going. 'We'd better get ourselves away, Mam. Ellie's parents are expecting us there too. Sorry it has to be so short and sweet this time. Once the castle's closed, we'll pop back for longer, maybe stay for a couple of days if that's okay?'

'Yes, of course you can. Any time. And make sure you bring Ellie too. We could go out for supper or something.

Me and Marge have found a lovely little Italian place down on the quayside.'

There were goodbye hugs and kisses. Sue stood waving from the step, with a big smile. 'Lovely to meet you, Ellie. Bye, Joey love. By-ye.'

Soon they were drawing up outside Ellie's terrace in Heaton.

The Hall Welcoming Committee were there, grinning on the front step at Fifth Avenue.

Dad was first to welcome Ellie with a big bear hug, and then virtually took Joe out with an over-effusive pat on the back worthy of a grizzly bear, which nearly floored him. Mum flourished kisses all round, and Jason honoured them with his presence at the door, appearing miraculously without the addition of headphones or phone. 'Hi.'

'Hello, pet, journey okay? Did you say you were going to see Joe's mum first?'

'Yes, Mum. She was really nice.' Joe and Ellie smiled across at each other. They really were playing happy families and it felt good. It was great to be welcomed home and with Joe with her too. It made it feel all the more special.

'Well, I've made your favourite dinner, mince and dumplings, and plenty of it.' Sarah's tone had a competitive edge to it. As though she were out to impress and indulge, for Joe in particular.

Ellie's stomach protested. They were still pretty full

from all the cake and flapjack. But Ellie knew that they'd have to make a good go of it.

'Now then.' Sarah turned to Joe, 'I've made a camp bed up in Ellie's room for you. I hope that's okay. Or you could always have the sofa, if you prefer.'

'The camp bed sounds fine, Mrs Hall.'

'Just call me Sarah – none of that Mrs Hall formality.' Wow, Ellie noticed that she was actually fluttering her eyelashes. Jeez. Thank God she hadn't told them of his lineage. The camp bed would never have done. Her mother would have been all of a flurry. Jason would have been hoisted out of his room and the silver service would be out at supper.

They dropped their overnight bags in Ellie's room. It seemed tiny after the high ceilings and expanses of the castle rooms.

Ten minutes later, they were sitting down to mega-portions of mince and dumplings, potatoes and vegetables, to be followed by apple crumble and custard. Joe had had to accept second helpings. Sarah was having none of it when he said that he'd had plenty, commenting that he was very slim, needed looking after, and needed more meat on those bones. Parents could be *so* embarrassing sometimes. Joe just laughed it off. Ellie thought, in his defence, but didn't like to say aloud for fear of giving her mother palpitations, that underneath the clothes there was actually plenty of taut meat on those bones. He was pretty tall and gave the impression of being slim, that was all.

Mum had even stretched to a bottle of red wine – thought *Joe* might like it. They rarely drank alcohol themselves in the house. Dad might push the boundaries with a bottle of lager in the summer months after work, though he did like the occasional pint down the pub with his mates the odd Friday night. And there was always a bottle of Baileys at Christmas.

They ate, chatted, Mum asking about life at the castle, Dad saying that his plumbing business was keeping him fairly busy. The noise levels rose and life was pretty much as normal in the Hall household. Ellie made a choffee cake that evening, wanting to leave some for her family and she also had a plan up her sleeve for the next morning. A visit she felt she had to make.

They lay side by side, Joe virtually at floor level – the camp bed was extremely low, and pretty damned precarious. If you sat at one end the other flew up in the air – like something off *Total Wipe-out*. In the half-light, Ellie could see his bare feet sticking out the end. They had started out trying to share the single bed, managed a quick kiss and a cuddle, anything more was out of the question with Jason on one side of the wall, and her parents the other. The creaking of her childhood bed from the sneaky kiss would have given them away for sure as it was. It was weird but wonderful having Joe here in her little room with her. In the bed where she used to daydream about Gavin. How life had changed. But she didn't miss Gavin at all. Felt so relieved she hadn't walked down that aisle with him.

'Joe . . .' Her whispers sought him out in the grey light. 'Your mam was lovely.'

'Thanks. I'm glad you got on well.'

She sensed that had been really important to him.

'You're very close, aren't you?'

'Yeah, probably comes from being just the two of us all the time I was growing up.'

'Uh-huh.'

'Your family are great too. Although it's hard getting a word in edgeways most of the time.' She could tell he was smiling as he spoke. 'It's like who can speak loudest at the dinner table? Reminded me of the Royle family.' He was laughing now. She chucked a cushion from the bed down at him. 'It's great, though. They made me feel really welcome. Mind you, if I ate any more I think I'd burst.' He'd dutifully finished off the second portion.

'Hah, yes, Mum thinks you need feeding up.'

'Ah-hah, well little does she know that beneath this slim exterior, there lurks a body of steel – sleek and toned.'

'Hmn, *I* know that, though.' She reached down for his hand. 'Can't wait for tomorrow night,' she said suggestively. He grasped her hand with a squeeze, anything more and she'd be likely to tumble out down on to the camp bed with him and they'd both be flipped to the ceiling. Maybe her mother had planned it on purpose. Stop any pre-marital antics.

Hmn, Ellie mused, roll on tomorrow night when she could get intimately re-acquainted with that body of steel – though he'd been joking he wasn't *too* far off. He was definitely on the right side of muscled, and she loved exploring every inch – all six foot two of him.

'Thanks for putting up with the camp bed, Joe.'

'My pleasure, m'lady,' adding, 'Anything for you.'

She hoped he wouldn't mind what she had in store for him in the morning.

23

Joe

'Hi, Nanna. I'm Joe.' He refrained from adding 'Nice to meet you', as it wasn't strictly true. What on earth was he doing speaking to a bloody headstone? But it only seemed polite to join in, seeing as Ellie had been chatting away for the last five minutes, as though Nanna was standing right next to her. He had glowed inside when Ellie had said she'd brought someone special to meet her, and had somehow felt it appropriate to say hello himself.

'Joe, would you mind going to fill up the vase with fresh water? There's a tap in the stone wall just over there. Oh, and there's a compost heap just along from it, where you can put these old flowers. Thanks.'

The last offerings were indeed looking worse for wear:

ropey brown stems poked out of the vase. The water was a slimy green. How come he always got the best jobs?

'I've bought you some fresh carnations and those freesias you always liked.' She was off talking to the headstone again. So he thought he'd go and get on as asked, at least it'd give him something practical to do. Ellie had even brought along a picnic: choffee cake and a flask of coffee. He'd never had a picnic in a graveyard before, nor spoken to a grave, come to think of it. This girl was full of firsts and amazing experiences, if sometimes they were a little weird. But hey, just being with her was pretty amazing.

He still couldn't quite believe the way things were working out and was still kicking himself that he'd nearly given her up. How had he thought he could just leave it as friends? He'd never felt more comfortable or at ease with a woman, and yet it didn't feel boring or too settled. Every day she surprised him, like picnics in graveyards, for example, and sleeping on five-foot-long camp beds. And every day he grew to love her body more, the curve of her hips, fantastic breasts, the way she smiled, the sexy sighs she made when they made love. Right, that was enough! Very inappropriate thoughts for a graveyard – sorry, Nanna!

He headed towards the stone wall, still musing. Unlike previous girlfriends she didn't nag on for expensive gifts or trips out. He enjoyed their walks together on the beach and in the countryside, even though it wasn't particularly her thing – though lately he'd got a sneaky feeling that she was starting to enjoy them too. She'd even mentioned buying a pair of walking boots. He found the compost heap, poured out the sludgy water and refreshed the vase at the tap.

Walking back towards Ellie, he could see her lit by sunlight, her hair golden, loose around her shoulders. She looked happy, simply chatting away to thin air. She was alive and vivid against this backdrop of death, and yet somehow it didn't seem morbid here.

'Here you go.' He handed her the vase.

'Thank you.' She filled it with the new flowers, putting away the cellophane wrap in her shoulder bag. Then she sat down, pouring out coffee and putting slices of choffee onto paper napkins.

'You obviously thought, *think*,' he re-phrased, 'The world of your nanna.' Love didn't stop after death, did it?

'Yeah, I do. She was the one who gave me the courage to go for my dreams. She was the one who inspired me to try for the teashop.'

Ellie was looking thoughtful, beautiful to Joe. He nodded, letting her carry on.

'I told you how I used to cook with her. Well, I say cook, it was more licking the mixture off the spoons and the bowl . . . I remember vividly being on a stool on tiptoes in her kitchen. Mum was often working so I'd go back there for an hour or so after primary school . . . the gorgeous smell of scones and cake. Heavenly . . . The choffee recipe – that's hers.' Ellie took a bite of cake, 'That's her book I keep in the teashop. I know the recipes virtually off by heart now, but I like that it's in her hand-writing. I feel closer to her when I use it, like she's there with me, supporting me. I know she wouldn't have wanted me to settle for a boring desk job that I didn't enjoy.'

'What about your grandad? Was he about?'

'Norman, my granda, I don't remember him much, sadly. He died when I was about four. It was always just Nanna as I was growing up. She must have adored him, though, was always chatting on about him. And she never looked to remarry.'

They shared a poignant look. Sometimes that one person was all you wanted, needed.

'What about you, anyhow? I've been going on long enough. What are your dreams? Any big plans?'

'Me, well, I'd love to make a real success of the castle. Turn things around for Lord Henry's sake, and to see the place thrive again. I know it can't just be a grand country home, not with the way it's falling apart; it needs an income and I really think the wedding events could do that – give it a future. And I like to think people can enjoy it even as visitors, that they can love the place as much as I do, even if it's just for a day trip. Or have the best wedding day ever there. It's such an amazing place.'

He took a sip of coffee from the plastic cup. 'It has a character all of its own, don't you think?'

'Yeah, I can see that. It would be awful to let it go to wrack and ruin.'

'It was dreadful when I started there. We had to get the roof sorted; there were pigeons living in the eaves in some of the upstairs bedrooms.'

'Oh, my God! So you've done a lot already, then. Turned things around.'

'Well, I try. It sometimes seems like just as I put something right, something else happens, though. The chimney stacks are starting to crack now and there's a load of repointing to do. I've got someone booked to do that in the autumn, once we're closed.'

He went quiet then, thoughtful.

'You okay?' Her tone was gentle.

He wondered whether to open up or not. He'd kept all this so private for so long. Thought he'd accepted it, but there it was, nagging away.

'I'd always wished,' he started, 'That I'd had a dad about. That was one of my dreams . . . Seeing your dad, your family, and noisy and chaotic as it is, it's great. Oh, don't get me wrong, I love Mam to bits, and I admire her so much. She brought me up really well. But I'd see other kids when I was little, and want my own dad to kick a ball with, go off fishing or something . . .'

'Yeah, I bet that was hard,' Ellie lay a hand over his.

He went quiet for a moment, memories flooding back, that sense of being different, being vulnerable. 'One time . . . it was at that patch of ground we used to play football on and skinned our knees. I was maybe eight, something like that. Well, they'd put up metal barriers around it, moved in the diggers and started working. It got turned into a housing estate. We would watch the building work going on from the top of a bank of grass across the way. But there was this one guy, one of the builders . . .' Joe paused, the image of the sandy-haired, solid-built man fresh even now. 'He'd always wave. Then one break time, he came out and chatted with us. Showed us some little boat thing he'd carved out of some spare wood. Then he made us one. It was really good. By the end of two weeks we'd got one each – all four of us. Played for hours floating them on puddles . . . He said he used to make them for his own kids. And I had this rising feeling, full of want and jealousy. I wanted that. Wanted that chatty, clever, working man for my dad, not one that I never saw.'

Ellie didn't speak, let Joe continue.

'Then one day we heard the ice-cream van's tinkly music, was no point getting excited, we didn't have any money, as usual. The guy came out, said it was his last day, told us to go and choose what we liked. Mine was a 99 Flake, should have been yummy, but I could hardly taste it. I just felt so sad. Had this ache right through me. Managed to keep it in in front of my mates. We watched the workers all afternoon till they packed up to go. And then I went home, up to my room, and cried my eyes out. And there was always that sense of missing something, even more after that, cos I'd had a glimpse of what I'd never had.'

'Oh, Joe.' Her look was tender, her tone understanding.

It made it easier for Joe to carry on. 'Then I found him. I found my father. Yes, in the end he gave me a job, supported me in that way, I suppose. But . . . we just feel miles apart. It's more like a business relationship. And I've always found it hard, thinking how he could have had an affair in the first place. And then he never tried to discover what had happened to her. When I first found out, I wanted to hunt him down and punch him. It's not the ideal father–son relationship is it? And he's never told anyone about me, even now, even with his wife dead; only Deana knows at the castle. It's like he's ashamed . . . like *I* should never have happened.' Joe went quiet, the words drying up. He'd never shared that with anyone before, not even his mam. Hadn't wanted to make things any more difficult for her. And, jeez, it was hard to make sense of his feelings, even to himself.

Ellie's hand stroked his softly. 'Maybe he feels embarrassed . . . by his actions back then. And then the shock of finding out – when you were already grown up. He'd missed out on all that time too. I'm sure he must think an awful lot of you, in his own way.'

'Maybe . . . But he's never really shown it.'

'He's a very private man, I suppose. But yes, as his son, that must be tough. You'd have wanted so much more.'

'One day, when I'm a dad,' Joe's voice lifted, 'I'm going to be there, at sports days and parents' evenings, and whatever else my kids are into. I'll support them. I want to be a good dad, Ellie, the best.'

'I think you'll make a great dad, Joe.' She smiled. Her hand still warm on his.

'Thanks.' And he pulled his arms about her in a loving hug. Planted a tender kiss briefly on her cheek; after all, they were in a graveyard.

'Well, Nanna, we'd better get going.' Ellie was off chatting to thin air again, 'Said we'd see Mum and Dad before we set off.'

'Bye, Nanna,' Joe added, feeling slightly easier about talking to a headstone now.

* * *

Ellie

They made their farewells; Sarah was delighted with the bouquet Joe had bought for her, as a thank-you for having him. Kisses and bear hugs all round once more. Ellie noticed that Joe planted his feet firmly before accepting the mammoth pat on the back from her dad. She waved out of the car window all the way along Fifth Avenue, but she didn't feel sad leaving this time, just happy to be going back to the castle with Joe, which gave her a very warm, lovely glow. Both places felt like home now . . . Or maybe, home was wherever Joe was from now on. Things had moved on so very fast. She still felt that little niggling fear of something going wrong. Life wasn't meant to be this good, this happy.

Back at the castle, at five o'clock, she knew she had to get straight back to work in the kitchen; with being off a couple of days she needed to make a fresh supply of cookies, cakes and quiches.

They were carrying their overnight bags back up to their prospective rooms.

'Do you really have to work right now? I was just hoping . . .' Joe paused at her door.

'Yes,' she said firmly, then laughed, 'How can I run a teashop without any cake?'

'But . . .' He had a hang-dog look on his face.

'I know, look, I'll just be a couple of hours. I'll come and see you as soon as I'm done cooking. Promise.'

He looked disappointed and damned sexy. 'If you really have to. Can I not sit and watch you? Chat a bit, while you cook?'

'Ah, I suppose.' He did look cute. 'Can you just give

me an hour or so to crack on, make some headway with a couple of sponges, and then pop down and we'll have a cup of tea or something.'

'I like the sound of the *"or something"*,' he grinned mischievously.

'I mean a biscuit . . . nothing else . . . so don't go getting any ideas . . . or you'll be banned from the kitchen altogether.' She had to laugh – he really did have a wicked look on his face.

'Argh, you're torturing me, Ellie.'

'You just need to exercise some self-control, Mr Ward. And anyway, how did you manage until I came along?'

He raised his eyebrows with a wicked smile.

'No, stop. Don't go there. I *really* don't want to know. Enough.'

'See you later then.' He spoke like a grudging youth and started walking the last flight of steps.

'Later. An hour at least.'

'I can't wait,' came a sunnier voice echoing down the stairwell.

She dumped her bag in her room, which looked cosy and welcoming. It was nice to be back. Then she headed straight back down to the kitchen to crack on. She was also looking forward to a little free time later with Joe.

She made a mix for a Victoria sponge, which would also double up for some cup-cakes. And she decided to make cookies with chocolate chips and some chocolate orange brownies. That was all smelling gorgeous by the time the hour was up, some still in the oven, and some cooling on metal racks. She'd better think of something savoury too, so mixed up some shortcrust pastry in her Magimix and began rolling it out on the stainless-steel surface, sprinkling it liberally with flour. She'd bake them blind while the oven was still hot and then fill them for quiches in the morning. She'd have to be up early to make a fresh batch of scones anyhow. So she might be able to make a quick getaway and catch up with Joe. Hmn, his room or hers? Didn't matter one iota, just being together without a flip-up camp bed and parents the other side of the wall would be great.

Okay, then, focus back on the baking, girl. She cut the dough into three and rolled out the first, carefully filling the flan dish, making sure all the fluted edges were neat to the sides. She had the radio set to the Classics channel and hummed along to some chilled piano music. She was just rolling out the second sheet of pastry when Joe appeared with a wide grin.

'Hi, sexy.' Nothing like being subtle.

'Hello, you.' She glanced at the wall clock. He had made the hour, just.

'I've just got to finish these pastry cases,' she nodded her head at the rolled-out dough, 'But I'll not be too long. You can make yourself useful and make us a cup of tea if you like.'

'Yes, m'lady.' He smiled as he went to fill the kettle, finding mugs and tea bags.

He was great, willing to help, though she'd never let him loose on the actual cooking. She smiled watching him. She was rolling out quiche number three when he passed her a mug of steaming tea. 'Thanks.' They'd take about fifteen minutes to get a golden bake. She set the timer and popped them in the big oven, taking out the last of the brownies.

'Hmn, what *can* we do while we wait for those to cook?' He had that naughty look plastered on his face again. 'Do you want a hand clearing up?' He came close, dabbed a hand into the flour on the surface and wiped it across the bridge of her nose.

Hmn, two could play at that game. She took a big swipe along the same surface and smudged two streaks across his sexy stubbled cheeks. He looked a little like an American Indian from cowboy films; he had the dark hair, just needed it a bit longer.

'Right then.' He swiped his two forefingers along a deep ridge of flour and smudged her nose again and added some across her lips.

'This means war.' Her hand dug into the flour bag. She took a fistful and threw it smack into his face.

His eyes blinked free, and a dust cloud of flour drifted down his face, his neck, covering his shirt as he shook his face – oops, that was a little more flour than she had intended.

'Right then, madam. That's just taking things too far.' He grabbed her wrists playfully, yet she could feel his underlying strength. He was smiling wickedly, leaned in against her, pressing her bottom into the work surface and began to rub his face against hers, until their lips met and parted, tasting of dusty flour and then each other. She lingered a few seconds, letting her tongue find his, then pulled back. 'I've still got quiche bases in the oven.'

'Too late for back-tracking . . . You've pushed the boundaries here, and for that you must be severely repri-manded.' His grin was extremely naughty.

Oh, jeez. His erection was digging hard and hungry against her pelvis. Her crotch responding with an aching warmth. Surely he wasn't suggesting . . .

She'd never done anything like that before in her life. No dinner-table sex, no food games nor hoisting up on the work surface like *Nine and a Half Weeks*, no outside *excursions*. No, she and Gavin had always been very straightforward with sex . . . and, yeah, she hated to admit it – probably downright boring.

'Joe . . . you're not thinking . . .'

With that he angled her legs apart with an expert knee and a wicked gleam in his eye.

Her legs felt a bit wobbly.

'There's no one around, Ellie.'

Well, Lord Henry might be about, she mentally

345

corrected him, but she'd never seen him in the kitchen of an evening, ever.

'It's just the two of us . . .' he confirmed.

His dark hazel-brown eyes were so damned gorgeous. Ooh and his hand was snaking its way up her inner thigh. The other hand was firm on her hip. She was wearing a flimsy skirt. It would be so easy.

'But . . . what about health and safety? The hygiene angle? It's the kitchen . . .'

He laughed out loud as he raised a gentle hand from her hip to close her mouth. 'I'll scrub the surface afterwards, disinfectant, the works,' he promised. Then he moved his palm to place his lips there against hers, hot and hungry. His hand moving back firm on her hip, the other having found the line of her panties, reaching inside, his thumb finding her in just the very best spot, gliding to and fro.

OH MY GOD.

Her mind was off into spin now. No more arguments. SHE DID NOT WANT THIS TO STOP.

'Ellie, I want you so much.' His voice was husky, melting away the last shreds of her inhibitions.

'Okay, okay . . . *yes*.' Oh yes, do not stop what you are doing you sexy son-of-a-bitch.

He took hold of both her hips, placed her spread-eagled on the floured work surface, dust puffing up around them as he undid the fly on his trousers, then pulled them down, his boxers soon straddling his knees. She watched in awe and anticipation, and stayed watching as he sheathed himself and then thrust into her deeply, filling her, feeling herself tight around him. Soon finding a rhythm there was no going back from.

'Joe!' she gasped.

It was all he needed to send him over the edge. He thrust deeply again, filling her, taking her to places she'd never been, with his love, his passion.

'Ellie . . .' He came hot and hard inside her.

The timer went off loud and clear just as he was beginning to wilt within her. They started giggling, sweatily straddled across the work surface, dusted in flour.

'Just in time,' he said, deadpan.

'I'd better go get them out, then.'

He eased out of her. 'Shame to spoil them.'

'Absolutely.'

24

Ellie

Life was good and sweet and sexy. September shifted into October. Leaves were falling steadily, the driveway thick with mushy piles of bronze and ochre, the bones of the trees above beginning to show. The log fire was well stocked up in the tearooms, and sales of soup and hot chocolate had soared.

There was a real sense of the seasons here at the castle, so much more than in the city, and the sense of time passing, of change.

Her relationship with Joe was everything she had hoped for, and so much more. She couldn't remember *ever* being so happy, though there were still the concerns about how she would make a living over the coming months until the tearooms re-opened in the spring. Hopefully her staying on at the teashop for next year was a foregone conclusion, but she needed to reconfirm that with Lord Henry and Joe and renegotiate the lease. Joe didn't seem to think there would be a problem, as she'd done so well turning things around.

She felt so pleased that she'd managed to make the teashop a reasonable success. The customers were saying how much they were enjoying her food, and she was getting on so much better with her staff; she really felt as if she was running a good business. And it would only get better next year. She had that experience now, she could build on it. But, she needed to spend some time looking for work, *anything*, in the local area, and hopefully they might then also let her keep on her room in the castle.

For now, she had to focus on organising the Halloween and fireworks event for the end of the month. They would be catering for at least 250, if last year's figures were anything to go by. Ellie had already put in an order for sausages and burgers at the local butcher's in Kirkton, and for several fat orange pumpkins from Wendy – Ellie was going to carve them out, and have tea lights in them to make the tearooms suitably spooky. She needed bread rolls by the hundreds and masses of veggies for soups, but she could get those nearer the time, plenty of napkins, polystyrene soup cups . . . her mind was spinning, so she made a long list.

The days rolled on.

* * *

350

It was the night before the Halloween extravaganza. Deana had, earlier in the week, come up with the idea of fancy dress for the staff, to make it more fun. Ellie was trying on the all-in-one black cat outfit she'd managed to get online. It did look fairly cute, though a little too clingy in parts. Tomorrow, she'd add a flick of eyeliner at the corner of her eyes to give her a cat-like look and draw on some whiskers across her cheeks.

There was a knock at her door . . . ooh, bum! She hoped it wasn't someone official or Lord Henry. It was Joe, with a very daft grin on his face as he looked her up and down, 'Oh . . . I *like* . . . very sexy.'

'Joe, you'd think I look sexy in a carrier bag at the moment.' She raised her eyebrows.

'True . . . very true. I can't help that I'm going out with the sexiest woman in Northumberland . . . no, make that England . . . the world.'

She was having none of it, 'Well, don't you go getting any ideas. I'm not having this costume manhandled or sullied.'

'Sullied . . . What do you take me for?' He gave a wicked smile. 'You make me sound like some kind of perve . . . But God, "*sullied*" – what a lovely word. I might have to turn up in a rain mac tomorrow. Actually,' his grin got wider, 'I have something even better up my sleeve.'

'Get away with you.' She gave him a playful shove. What the heck was he planning now?

351

'Anyway, what are you here for?'

'Well, that's a nice welcome. Just came to see you, if that's alright.'

'I suppose,' she joked, 'Got any supper lined up? I'm sick of the sight of sausages.' She'd been prepping sausages, burgers, and dipping bloody toffee apples – what a gloopy mess that was, all afternoon, she'd never even thought about her own supper tonight.

'*Shame that.*' He gave her another dirty grin. Then gave up as she gave him a stony stare. Little did he know that she was laughing inside. 'Could stretch to a pizza from the freezer,' he said. 'Might even have oven chips.'

'Sounds okay to me. Your place or mine?'

'Well, I'm the one with the oven in my room, unless you really want to be trekking back down to the tearoom kitchen.'

'Okay. Deal.'

'You can keep your cat suit on, if you like.' The mischievous look was back in his eye.

'Enough. No. In fact, it's coming off right now.' And with that she started to peel the black lycra down over her shoulders.

'Even better,' he grinned.

'Stop it. I can't keep having sex.'

'Why not?'

Why not indeed?

They managed to keep their hands off each other until

later in the evening, after their pizza supper and a scary movie – very in keeping with the Halloween theme, ending up snuggled together, sated, in the four-poster ready for a good night's sleep.

Tomorrow was going to be a busy day.

*

Pumpkins, hot dogs, burgers. The kitchens stank of fried onions and Ellie reckoned her hair must do too – such a glamorous scent. Oh well, she didn't have time to go and wash it. The castle doors opened in half an hour and there was still loads to do. They were serving food upstairs in the great hall (being nearer to the gardens and the fireworks display) as well as down in the tearooms. So they had to lug warming tables up the narrow stairs and get set up there too.

The teashop was looking great, she had to admit; she'd put out church candles and tea lights up high on the windowsills and behind the counter area, giving a soft, eerie glow. A couple of spooky pumpkin faces welcomed the customers at the doors. It had taken her ages to scrape them out and carve them.

Huge pots of pumpkin and sweet potato soup were simmering on the stove, and she and Doris had just split and buttered two hundred rolls, and there were more out back just in case.

She'd hardly seen Joe all day; he'd been busy with the fireworks team organising the grounds and safe spectator areas. Deana had popped in for a 'proper' coffee and to announce that they had now sold a hundred and ninety tickets before making any sales on the door. It had been advertised in the local press and posters in Kirkton and the area's tourist information offices. The weather forecast was good; it was meant to be staying dry. It was going to be a busy night.

The cat suit was on, if now smelling of onions, her whiskers were drawn on and there was a smudge of pink lipstick on her nose. Doris looked fabulous dressed in a big orange pumpkin ball with green stalk hat – though Ellie realised she was going to have trouble serving and clearing the tables, the amount of space she was taking up. She'd be bouncing off the customers, and small children could well be flattened! She was grumbling on already about finding it hot in there and was looking very flushed. Nicola was in a devil's outfit, which only just reached below her bottom. It was certainly on the sexy end of devil rather than scary.

They were just about set to go when Batman waltzed in. Tall, dark, and in a very *snug* suit – he obviously hadn't bought the version for over six-foot males – revealing those all-important parts. Oh, good lord, they looked as if they'd been clingfilm-wrapped. So here was Joe. Of course, it had to be Batman, yep.

354

'Thought I'd get in the spirit of the occasion.' He grinned.

Ellie giggled, 'I should have guessed . . . any chance to dress up as Batman!'

'Of course. And I've been *so* waiting to catch up with Catwoman.'

She ignored the comment, had way too much to do. 'All organised with the fireworks?'

'Think so. Just about there. Got all the safety cordons in place. Are you coming up to watch?'

'Be too busy, I think. Though I'd like to. I love fireworks. Kind of magical, aren't they?'

'We could have our own later.' He moved in for a quick kiss.

'Don't you smudge my whiskers.'

'I'll keep firmly to your lips, then.'

Blimey, Doris was about and Nicola, 'I've got loads to do . . .'

His eyes were on hers, then he leaned in against her. All the snug bits pressed close, and gave her the most tender, sexy, slow kiss.

As he pulled away, he lifted a handful of her hair, 'God, what's that smell?'

'Ah, onions, I think. Sorry, I've been slow-frying the buggers for hours.'

'Hmn, the delectable scent of fried onions. Right, well I suppose I'd better crack on up yonder.'

And, then, to her amazement, Dracula, in full black cloak, walked in rather breathless. 'Joe, need you back at the fireworks area. They need a powerful torch – one of theirs has broken. Do we have one somewhere?' The corners of his mouth were oozing red blood. 'Evening, Ellen, how's it going, all okay here?' The plummy voice gave him away.

'Lord Henry?' Ellie felt her jaw drop.

He seemed oblivious to the fact that he was dressed in a Dracula outfit.

Joe nodded. 'Yes, I'm sure there'll be one in Deana's office.' And with that they both dashed off like action heroes. Bizarre.

Ellie and Doris just looked at each other and laughed. Ellie could never imagine anything like this happening at the insurance offices back in Newcastle. And just those few months ago, she could never have imagined falling in love with a manager of a huge castle, who also happened to be a lord's son.

Nicola was organised and ready to serve upstairs at the makeshift counter/trestle-table in the great hall. Malcolm and Derek were primed to help as 'runners' between the serving zones if she ran short of anything, as well as helping out generally with the event. Doris and Ellie were ready for the off in the teashop. The burgers and sausages were all cooked and keeping warm. Paper plates and napkins were stacked. Huge squeezy tubs of ketchup, mustard and brown sauce were lined up ready for battle of the burger buns. James, the young lad who helped at the castle, popped in for a mug of soup to take with him back to the gardens, where he was helping Joe. He gave her the brightest, wonky-toothed smile when she said he could have it for free.

Ellie hoped she'd make a decent profit tonight. It was the last big event until the first wedding, which was booked in the run-up to Christmas. She'd agreed to do a couple of shifts on the till at the local petrol station, just to keep some funds flowing, but the winter months were going to be tough. At least Joe had arranged, with Lord Henry's permission, to let her stay on in her room until the wedding booking, at least. He'd said Lord Henry was fond of her and that he'd admitted he'd been impressed with her work at the tearooms – high praise from the reticent man himself. They'd have to work on getting a few more events booked, however. The winter months were definitely a work in progress.

A few customers started trailing in, and then within half an hour there seemed to be a mass invasion. The queue was never-ending. It was damned hot in her all-in-one cat suit, standing there ladling out soup and serving hotdogs, but it was all extra money in the till. She wished she hadn't stoked the fire up so much before they'd opened now, though.

Her feet were throbbing by nine-thirty. The fireworks were over. The tearooms were emptying out. There had been a real buzz as the spectators had swarmed back in: 'That was *brilliant*, Dad.' 'Very professional. What a great display.' And a little girl sobbing 'cos it had all been *'too noisy'* – a sticky sweet toffee apple had cheered her up, though.

It seemed to have been a great success. Ellie hadn't had a chance to add up the takings, but from the sheer volume of customers, her sore feet and the fact they had run out of burgers and only had a couple of hotdogs left, it seemed likely they had done really well. She'd give Doris and Nicola a bit of a bonus in their pay packet this week. They'd worked really hard for her. Her unlikely team at the start of the season had really come together. She felt proud of them.

Right, time to start the major clear-up. At least the food had been served on paper plates, so she armed herself with a couple of black sacks and set to work. Doris was upstairs, still helping Nicola sort out in the great hall.

Ellie wiped down all the tables, blowing out all the tea lights as she went – she must remember to check all the church candles on the windowsills too. The fire was still crackling in the grate, taking the chill off the high-ceilinged ancient room, they usually left it lit, adding a big log as they left of a night – then it only needed stoking up in the morning again.

The kitchen was all clear and she gave the floor a mop over. There'd be no teas to serve tomorrow, anyhow. The teashop would be closed. She stopped in her tracks. The thought made her feel a little odd. She'd arranged to come in with Doris and Nicola and give it a thorough disinfect for the end of the season. *Actually* . . . Doris and Nicola seemed to be taking a while; she'd go up and see if they needed help up there. She nearly collided with James on the stairs who was dashing down them.

'Sorry, James, everything okay?'

'Need a pan and brush.' The words came out staccato. 'Glass broken.'

'Oh, okay. Don't worry, I'll fetch one – is it needed in the great hall?'

'Yes.'

'That's fine. I'll take one up.'

'Thanks.' He turned and was off, dashing back up the stairwell.

Probably just a minor breakage. Inevitable on a busy night like this. She hoped it was just a drinking glass, not some antique relic, but anything valuable was usually kept out the way of the guests and cordoned off.

She headed back in to the kitchens for the dustpan and brush, noting the tea lights were still burning softly in the two carved-out pumpkins by the door; she'd make sure to blow them out as she came back down, better get the dustpan upstairs first in case the broken glass was dangerous.

'Thanks, Ellie.' Doris said as she spotted her, 'It's just a juice glass someone brought up from the teashop. I'll clear it up, pet.' She took the brush and started cleaning up.

'Been busy up here, Nicola?'

'Yep, manic. Sold out of just about everything. Bloody feet are killing me.'

'Mine too. And thanks, ladies, you've worked really hard.'

'That's okay.'

Ellie was knackered, couldn't wait to lie down on a cosy bed, *with* Batman would be nice, just to snuggle up . . . If he thought Catwoman was up for anything other than a cuddle tonight, unfortunately he would be disappointed.

She was helping Nicola fold up the white tablecloths and pack down the benches when there was a weird whirring noise and then the lights all went out. Typical.

'Don't worry, it's just the resident ghost,' chipped in Lord Henry, who'd just come back in from the garden. 'It'll probably come back on in a minute.'

To be fair, it was nothing too unusual for the castle; the electrics were ancient like the rest of the place. Joe had been on about getting a proper overhaul done of the electrics during the winter months – more expense.

'Anyone got a torch?' Ellie ventured.

'Where's Joe? He had one. Got the one from Deana's office earlier,' Lord Henry stated.

'Probably outside somewhere checking the grounds and finishing off with the display team,' Colin's voice announced in the dark; he'd been helping outside too, 'I'll go and take a look at the main fuse box. Something might have tripped.'

There was a thin beam of light; James, carrying a small torch. And with that, he and Colin walked off. The great hall returned to darkness.

'We might as well go outside,' suggested Ellie.

There was a beam of moonlight illuminating the French doors that led to the garden.

'Okay, can't do much in here for now,' Doris agreed, heading for the doors. 'What's that dreadful smell?' Doris was the first out.

There was a strong tang of smoke in the air, perhaps just the leftover acridity of the fireworks, but they hadn't had a bonfire and it was more of a smoky wood smell.

'Jesus Christ!' Malcolm and Derek, who'd been helping Deana in the office just before, came shouting, running around the side of the building. 'Get everyone out! The tearooms are on fire. We've got Deana to call the fire brigade. They're on their way.'

Oh my God! Her lovely teashop. Ellie's heart did a flip. Oh no, had she left anything on in the ovens? On the stove? She was sure she'd turned it all off ages ago . . . Oh shit, she'd left those tea lights on, in the two pumpkins. She had a sinking feeling in her stomach.

361

Was everyone here? What about Joe? *Where was Joe?* She wasn't sure if she'd said it aloud or not.

A rising panic swirled in her gut. She hadn't seen him in ages.

Torchlight flashing across the garden flagstones. James appeared with Deana. 'The fire brigade are on their way. Is everyone alright? Is everyone accounted for?' Deana's voice was heavy with concern.

'Joe. Where's Joe?' Ellie's raised voice was tight in her throat.

'I saw him, Ellie,' James blurted out, 'Just after I seen you. I said you'd gone to the tearooms to get the pan and brush.'

She began to feel dizzy. Chink by chink, her world was falling apart. She found herself running back into the hall, the quickest way to the teashop, her eyes adjusting to the dark, bumping into table corners, knocking over a chair. Deana's voice was harsh behind her. 'Ellie. NO!'

She kept going. She had to get to him. This couldn't be happening. This wasn't going to happen.

As she reached the stairs leading down, her eyes began to sting. The smoke rasped in her throat as she shouted his name, 'Joe . . . Joe.'

* * *

Joe – five minutes before

'James, have you seen Ellie?' Joe tried to stay calm. Think rationally. She was probably fine. Deana was ringing the fire brigade right now. The automatic alert should have gone through to them too. If he hadn't thought it was just the smell from the fireworks they might have acted quicker. Dammit.

'Yes, she was getting me a pan and brush.'

'Where? Where was she getting it from, James? It's important.'

'Umn. The teashop.'

'Have you seen her since?'

'No.'

'Fuck . . . Sorry, James, I'm not angry with you. Okay, take this torch,' he handed the lad the small flashlight he had with him. 'Now go and find the others upstairs. Stay with them and all go outside. Don't come back down. Don't let anyone else come down. Okay?'

'Okay.'

Please God, don't let her be in there. But he'd have to check. The fire brigade could be some time yet. He hadn't even heard any sirens. He tried the light switches in the passageway outside the tearooms. Nothing. Shit. He wished he hadn't given away his torch now. He felt his way down the wall, the smoke making it even darker. The wood panels of the teashop door were warm to touch. The smoke gushed out at him as he opened it.

Get low. Something triggered in his brain. Stay low. Cover your mouth. He took off the Batman cloak, used it to wrap around his face, covering his nose and mouth. It made it tricky to breathe through, but seemed better than the smoke. Staying low he ran in, calling her name.

'Ellie. ELLIE? You in here?' Two pumpkins glowed menacingly each side of the door. No reply. Just an odd crackly noise from the kitchen, the smoke seemed thicker from there. He headed for it.

'ELLIE?'

Keep going. If she was here he would find her. His eyes were streaming now; between his tears and the smoky murk he could hardly see a thing. The air was bitter, acrid in his lungs. Stay low, he reminded himself, pushing through the swing door. Licks of flames danced from the back wall of the kitchen.

He would find her. He was on his knees now. On the kitchen floor. It was damp down there, smelled of smoke and disinfectant. He reached his arms out, feeling ahead of him. She might have fallen, been overcome by the fumes. He thought of her beautiful sunny smile, the feel of her skin under his fingertips, making love to her last night. If she was here he would find her. They'd get out. Together. He bumped his forehead on the metal leg of a work surface. It was hot. Seared his skin. Then the solid coolness of stone against his outstretched palm. So, he must have reached the far wall. No sign of her. She couldn't have been here, then. Thank God.

The wall, the work surface, the shelf. Nanna's book. It'd be there just above him on the shelf. He might be able to reach it. Might be able to save it for her. Held his breath, reached up, felt along the shelf. Squinted to try and see, but his eyes stung and streamed. He knocked down a plastic bowl. His chest felt tight. He'd really better get out of there. Felt again, just in case. She loved that book. Yes, that felt like it, a hard cover. Grasped it. He needed to get out. Crouched low. Gasped for breath. But the smoke was curling within him now, squeezing his lungs, stealing their air. Crawling back. Keep going, keep going. Not far from the swing door now. It'd be better the other side of that. No air. Everything in his chest tight, strangling.

Everything seemed too hard. To move. To breathe. Wasn't sure if he could make it back now . . . If he just lay a while . . .

* * *

Ellie

They were holding her back. Strong arms tight on her wrists.

'You can't go in there, miss. Come away. We're dealing with it . . .'

She could see flickers of flames at the windows. In front of her, the glass popped out from a black-leaded pane.

She clung to the chance that he wasn't in there. Yet somehow she knew in her soul that he was.

Someone was leading her out of the courtyard, back to the others gathered outside the front of the castle now. Blue flashing lights. Sirens. Lord Henry pacing up and down, his Dracula cloak splaying out as he marched. It was all surreal and yet too real.

And then through the main castle doors they were bringing out a stretcher. She ran forward, the grasp on her wrists loosened. 'Joe . . . Joe.'

Saw the floppy dark fringe, his beautiful face so pale. His body there laid out on the stretcher.

Her legs went wobbly.

'Let's get some oxygen here.' A voice shouted. Someone pushed past her in uniform, placing a mask over Joe's mouth.

Ellie registered that he didn't look burned, thank God, just a mark on his forehead. But then smoke could be more dangerous. He wasn't moving. Eyes closed.

Lord Henry came up next to her. 'Joe . . . Are you alright, Joe? . . . What's going on?' he addressed the fireman carrying the stretcher. 'Is he going to be alright?'

'We don't know yet, sir. Can we just have a bit of space to do our job.'

'Of course . . . certainly.'

Ellie and Lord Henry stepped back. Staring. Silent.

Joe was holding something. Ellie saw that now. A book. Why was he holding a book?

Please, dear God. Please, dear God. Please, dear God. Ellie was chanting a silent prayer.

'I shouldn't have said yous was down there.' James was next to her, crying fat, snotty tears.

'It's not your fault, James.' If it was anyone's fault it was probably hers, with those tealights she'd left on. It would have only taken a second or two to blow them out. Ellie felt her own eyes fill. The horrid ache of tears coming in her throat. Yet no tears dropped.

Then Joe's body shuddered, he spluttered. He was struggling against the mask. His hand was lifting to try and get it off his face.

Oh, thank God.

'He's regaining consciousness. We need to get him checked out, though. Let's get him to hospital ASAP.' The paramedics began to load Joe into the back of the waiting ambulance. Ellie didn't want to leave him and began to follow the stretcher.

'Only family in the ambulance, miss.'

'Oh.' But she wanted to crawl in there, cradle him in her arms.

She had to stand back.

She'd drive, then. She'd follow them.

Doris stepped forward, 'I'll drive you, Ellie. You're probably in a bit of shock, pet. My keys are handy,' Doris pulled them from her pocket, 'And the car's just along the driveway there.'

A booming voice filled the forecourt, the tone both anxious and proud, 'WAIT . . . I'm coming in the ambulance . . . He's my son.' Lord Henry, with his Dracula cloak flapping, clambered into the back of the vehicle.

Doris's mouth dropped open and a murmur of surprise buzzed around the castle staff.

Waiting in A & E on orange plastic chairs. Why was it taking so long? They'd been here for an hour or more already, the lady in reception knew they were waiting for news on Joe, and yet there'd been no sign of Lord Henry or a nurse or anything.

And Ellie's mind was doing nasty things. What if there had been permanent damage to his lungs? And how long had he been unconscious? Was there was a risk of brain damage with that? All sorts of things could be happening there behind those swing doors . . . And there was this nagging doubt that it might be her fault. Had she really turned everything off in the kitchen and what about those tea lights still burning in the pumpkins?

'I'll go fetch a cup of tea.' Doris stood up. They'd already toyed with one cup – milky-grey fluid in a polystyrene cup. Ellie didn't really want any more, but she knew Doris just wanted something to do, and it might pass the next five minutes.

Doris was on her way back when the double doors swung open to reveal Lord Henry in his black cloak.

Ellie was on her feet, 'Is he okay?'

'He seems to be. Thank heavens. He's asking for you.'

Relief swept over her like the warmth of sunshine. Thank You God.

A couple of children and a woman were staring at Lord Henry, and an old man across the way looked bemused.

'What the devil are they gawping at?' he said loudly, sounding disgruntled.

'Well, you are still wearing a Dracula outfit and there's fake blood all around your mouth,' Doris pointed out.

'Ah.' He looked down. 'So I am. So I am.' He sat down. 'He's in a bay to the left just through there.'

Ellie couldn't wait to get to him. 'Third on the left,' she heard Lord Henry's booming voice as she stepped through the double doors.

She counted the curtained booths, one, two, three. Pulled the curtain cautiously on the third. She must have got it wrong. This one was empty.

'Joe?' Her voice a question. She didn't feel it appropriate

to shout along the A & E section, though part of her wanted to boom his name. Find him. Hold him.

No answer.

Then she spotted it there on the bedside table – a singed hardback book, its cover browned like tobacco stains, some letters still legible, 'B-e-r . . .' And below it, folded neatly, a black lycra-style suit. The bed was empty. She picked up the book, turned the first few pages, and saw Nanna's handwriting. He'd only gone and saved it for her. Big blobs of her fat tears stained the already singed pages.

Where was he? Had something just happened? Had he been dashed off to Resusc? She knew these things happened, had been a fan of *Casualty* over the years. What if he'd died, bumph just like that? A split second. Taken away from her? Oh Jesus, no.

A big knot formed in her throat. Fat drips continued to plop down onto the Be-Ro book. She'd better find a nurse. See what was happening.

'Hi.' His voice. It was his voice. Or was she just imagining it? Behind her.

Turned to see him loping along towards her in a hospital gown.

'Oh shit, Joe. Don't you *ever* do that to me again.'

'What are you going on about? I've just been for a pee.'

She nearly launched the Be-Ro book at him. 'I thought you were dead'. She hardly dared speak the words.

'Well, sorry for upsetting you and being alive.'

Her body seemed to sink, she needed a chair. He got back into the bed, as she slumped down on the plastic chair next to it in the cubicle. She lay the book back on the side.

'You okay?' she asked, as she came round to the fact he'd just been to the loo. The guilt was heavy on her voice. Remembering her fears of the tea lights, the kitchen equipment.

'Think so.' His voice had a rasp to it. 'Bit tired.'

'No wonder.'

'What do the doctors say?'

'Some smoke inhalation . . . keeping me in overnight.'

She found herself shaking, 'Joe . . . I'm sorry.' She was crying now. The tears hot and heavy. It might have been so much worse.

'It's not your fault.' He lifted a hand to her cheek.

'I left the pumpkins burning.'

'I know. I saw them . . .'

'Oh shite. It *was* my fault, then.'

'No . . . no . . . they were lit, they helped me see . . . they weren't on fire.' He paused. 'Can you get me some water . . . my throat.'

There was a jug on the side table. She poured out a plastic cup. Took it to his lips, which were dry and chapped. She wanted to kiss him there. But instead placed a tender kiss on his cheek once he had taken a sip.

'The fire,' he continued, 'It seemed to be along the back wall by the dishwasher. Might have been the wiring or something.'

'Are you sure? You're not just saying that to make me feel better?'

'Sure . . .' He seemed tired. She rested her hand over his. They both sat quiet for a while.

Then he saw the book there on the side. 'Oh, yes, I found this.' He passed it to her.

'Nanna's book, I saw it a minute ago. Wow. Thank you so much.' Her voice lifted, then dropped, 'You didn't go in looking for Nanna's book, did you? You could have killed yourself!'

'Course not . . . I didn't go in for the book, I went in for *you*.'

'Oh.'

'Ellie, all I could think of in there was you . . . I should have told you this before . . . and then I didn't think I might ever get the chance.' He held her gaze.

The tears were back again fuzzing her view.

'Ellie, I love you.'

She gulped, knowing she was about to blubber. 'I know. I love you too, Batman.'

'Hmn.' He looked her over. 'You're still in your catsuit . . . promise you won't take it off till I get home?'

'Alright.' She'd have done anything for him right then.

As the consultant walked in, he found the young couple indulging in a very full-on kiss. He coughed politely to warn them of his presence. 'Those lungs seem to be getting stronger, then, Mr Ward.'

25

'So, are you ready, pet?' Her dad looked very unlike himself, and, in fact, rather suave in a burly kind of way, all suited and booted in grey pinstripes, and a million miles away from his boiler-suit-and-spanner look.

'Yes, I am.' Ellie smiled across at him as she fastened the clasp of a beautiful silver-and-pearl necklace that matched the drop-pearl earrings she had just put on. A wonderful surprise that Joe had given her the day before; the last time they were to be together before the wedding. Oh yes, she was ready, hook, line and sinker, heart and soul. What she *was* nervous about was tripping over in her very high satin heels and ripping the hem of her ivory lace dress, or stuttering the words she had learned and had to repeat when the rings were being exchanged.

'Well, I'm proud of you, our lass. Coming here, making a go of the teashop and everything, when you didn't know a soul. And Joe, too. I like him – yes, he's not a bad lad. As long as he looks after you right, mind.'

'He will, Dad. I know he will.'

'Well, he seems a decent sort, I must say. I taught him a few tricks to keep the plumbing here flowing yesterday – problem with the new ensuites to the guest rooms. He seemed willing to learn and a hard worker. Anyway, hey, look at us two in our finery, I can't believe I'll be walking my little girl down the aisle in just a few minutes.'

Ellie spotted the mistiness in her dad's eyes. He was never one to be given over to emotion, and seeing him getting choked up made her own heart clench. And a happy tear welled in her eye too. Thank heavens she'd remembered to use the waterproof mascara. Mum would be there waiting with Jay and all their friends by now, downstairs in the castle chapel. Gemma, her maid of honour, had given her a hug and then gone on five minutes before with Ellie's gorgeous little cousin, Daisy, who was flower girl, and Joe's best man's little boy, Jack, who was page boy, all dressed in a cute mini suit that was the same material as the gents' morning suits. Gemma was cursing about having to be nanny all day to her junior assistants, but Ellie had the feeling she was secretly enjoying it all! Why else would you bring Jelly Babies and Dolly Mixtures along with you – though she had mentioned bribery tactics!

The great hall and a marquee in the gardens for dancing later were all set up, ready for the reception. Ellie and Joe had spent many hours, using their newly found contacts and skills to plan and make sure that their guests had a fantastic day. Wendy had agreed to do the flowers and Ellie's bridal bouquet was absolutely gorgeous, scented with white summer roses and soft-pink peonies, greenery swathed artfully around them – like an English summer garden. Ellie was a bit cross with her, in fact, as she would only accept half the true price for it all, and she was sure she'd seen extra pedestals being sneaked in that weren't even on the order list. But Wendy insisted, saying Ellie had given her loads of new business with all the weddings at the Castle now (today was to be the twelfth wedding at Claverham Castle) and it was the least she could do for her and Joe.

The champagne was on ice ready for a Fuck's Bizz welcome drink and a toast to Nanna! And the *pièce de résistance* was a two-tier choffee cake extravaganza, the biggest and best yet, which Ellie had spent two days making and decorating with the most stunning white-and-dark-chocolate flowers. From the detail of the petals, with chocolate stems and leaves that twined around the two sections, to the delicate and edible gold-leaf-effect finish, it was Ellie's best-ever masterpiece – and a true homage to her beloved nanna.

The soft glow of tea lights would light the hall and

tables later, and even the trees out in the garden had fairy lights ready to switch on at dusk, which Derek and Malcolm had helped set up. There were also two large storm lanterns to guide the way in and out of the back terrace. Colin had been kept very busy, with James to help, pruning the roses and trimming the box hedge in the Italian gardens to perfection. There wasn't a dead head within a mile of the castle!

Doris, Nicola and Deana had stayed late after the tearooms had shut one night, making chintzy material bunting, which now adorned the stone walls of the hall so that it looked a quirky, yet oh-so-pretty mix of vintage teashop-meets-seventeenth-century castle. Doris had turned out to be a bit of a whizz with her Singer sewing machine, and had even been found happily humming to herself on several occasions.

And the food for the reception was going to be the best afternoon tea ever! There was a catering company coming in to serve and to bring all variety of dainty sandwiches, mini quiches and savouries, but Ellie had made the prettiest cup-cakes with sugar roses on the top and some fun and funky ice cream cup-cakes – the vanilla icing twirled to look like Mr Whippy 99s' with hundreds and thousands and a chocolate Flake in. She'd also made a batch of lemon drizzles to cut into small squares, and mini Victoria sponges decorated with fresh strawberries to go on all the cake stands. She'd picked up loads of gorgeous china cake-stands in charity shops and flea markets over the past six months, her mum and friends all being on the lookout too. She knew they'd come in handy after the wedding in the teashop, anyhow, and she'd also picked up pretty porcelain cups and saucers all mixed and matched – rose patterns, spotty, willow-pattern, and somehow it all worked. Even the posy jars for the peonies on the great hall tables were recycled jam jars from the tearoom kitchens, with pink silk ribbons and hessian twine tied in bows around them. Wendy had enjoyed making them up.

Ellie had sat quietly with a cup of tea at the close of business yesterday, after Doris and Nicola had gone, thinking how far she had come from the hurt, and rather naïve, girl who risked it all for her dream, for her love of baking and the chance of a different life, a chance to run her own business. Back then, she hadn't even dared to imagine that she might just fall in love too, but, wow, it had happened! And she felt so full up with love that she wanted to jump up and down and shout it from the top of the castle tower every day. And, amazingly, he seemed to feel the same way. She and Joe would have to work hard, and they still had a long way to go until the castle was profitable in the way it needed to be. But it was all heading in the right direction. And she loved seeing the faces of the wedding couples and their families when their reception and special day had all gone well. When the great hall or the marquee looked like the fairytale, vintage, or medieval banquet they had wanted, and everyone had delighted in the food she had made. The cards of thanks for her catering services were proudly stuck on the kitchen pinboard, the kitchen having had a full re-fit after the fire.

'Well, lass.' Dad made a show of checking his watch. 'Time to go.' He crooked his arm in a grand gesture for her to slip her own through and smiled broadly at her, bringing her back from her reverie.

So this was it, she was getting her wedding day at last, and, boy, was she *so* glad it was Joe who would be waiting for her (not tosser Gavin). And to think that all their guests, close family and friends, both new and old, and all the wonderful castle staff who were now friends too, would be there in wonderful support.

'We'd better take it slow down those steps, lass. I'd hitch your skirt up a little if I were you, pet.'

Ellie grinned. 'Good idea, Dad!' She laughed as she tried to tuck some of the ivory lace material in her knickers – which were just a little scrap of lace too, so they weren't holding much up! They made it down the spiral stairwell from Ellie's room, across the cobbles of the inner courtyard and up the grand stone steps, which Ellie spotted were adorned with peonies and roses and ivy entwined along the balustrades.

Malcolm, who was hovering at the top of the stone steps, gave the nod, and suddenly an old organ struck up with a wobbly 'Here Comes the Bride' tune. Ellie chuckled and her dad grinned. Derek was sitting playing on an ancient piano stool, dressed in top hat and tails, that Ellie seemed to remember seeing in the costume display room here at the castle before. He gave her a wink. She and her dad turned left, approaching the chapel.

Ellie now felt a little nervous. Would Joe really be there waiting for her? Or could it all have been just a lovely, but not real, dream. And she'd wake up in her little bed in the terraced house in Heaton, and have to get up and head off to work at the insurance office, just after Gavin had done the dirty on her. Could her life really be this beautiful?

'Just go on in and enjoy every moment, pet,' Nanna's bossy tones played in her mind, as the final chords of 'Here Comes the Bride' played out. Gemma was waiting outside the chapel's arched wooden doors, grinning across at Ellie. She was wearing the long mink-coloured satin dress they'd chosen together. Gemma quickly organised the page boy and flower girl. 'Right, ready, kids? Your big moment is here. We've got to follow Ellie down into the chapel room now, so just keep with me and remember the deal, yeah? There's some jelly babies in it for the prize winner who doesn't step on the dress, okay?' Two little heads nodded seriously; Daisy clutching a flower basket, and little Jack, the page boy, looking so smart with his cream carnation button hole just the same as the men's on his waistcoat pocket.

'Okay?' she mouthed to Ellie, giving her a big thumbs-up. 'You look fantastic, girl!'

Ellie nodded back, feeling a lump rising in her throat. This was really it, the wedding day she'd wanted for so long, but this was *so* the right one.

'Pinch me, Gem.'

'What? I'll hurt you. Your skin'll go all red and nasty.'

'Just the back of my hand, p-lease.'

'O-kay, nutter.'

She pinched, and it hurt, and a bright-pink mark rose up.

'Great, thanks.' Ellie grinned.

'A grade nutter,' Gemma muttered. 'Now, don't copy that, kids, alright? That is just for the grown-ups, 'cos it's a special day.'

Dad was shaking his head, but smiling. So, it was real. Gemma took a second to smooth Ellie's dress down at the back, slightly re-aligning the stylish V, which plunged to her back midway down. The front bodice was fitted, but not too low, with a sweetheart neckline, ivory lace over satin. The sleeves were three-quarters, and there was a sash at the waist that exactly matched the mink shade of Gemma's dress.

'Right, then, pet.'

'Yes.' Here goes. *Woohoo!*

She paused on the threshold as she reached those heavy wooden doors. *Oh*, all the flowers down the pews,

and the satin ribbons the very same shade as the bridesmaids' dresses – they looked so beautiful. And then, all
these people, her friends. Look, there was Nicola, and
Deana and her husband, Bill, two colleagues from her
old insurance office, Auntie Dorothy and Uncle David
and her Cousin Lauren. Hah – Doris and Wendy in *huge*
fancy hats, all dressed in their finest. Mum and Jay. She
grinned at them all, and then her eyes reached the end
of the aisle, and Joe was there looking at her with his
gorgeous smile, dressed in his grey morning suit; tall
and distinguished-looking and her heart did a somersault
and triple flip.

Lord Henry was there at the front pew, just behind
Joe. Their height and stance the exact same. His father
– they were all still getting used to that, but it was easier
now the staff were aware. Oh, and just along on the same
pew, Joe's mum, Sue. It was the first time she had been
back to the castle in over thirty years. She was looking
so proud, with a hanky ready in her hand and a little
wave of encouragement to Ellie. And then she and her
dad made the slow walk down the aisle, with all eyes on
them. They made it to the front and she hadn't tripped
up or fallen, and Joe was there just a metre away, his
eyes giving her a look of awe that made her insides melt
a little.

'Hello, you.'

'Hello, you,' she echoed, smiling back at him.

'You look beautiful.'

Dad gave her a wide smile and wink, as he stepped back and joined Mum and Jay. And it was just the two of them standing at the altar with the local vicar, who was welcoming everyone to the service. She heard the words about 'love and trust' and they sang a hymn, her nanna's favourite, 'All Things Bright and Beautiful', and Ellie made her vows to 'Love him, comfort him, honour and protect him, forsaking all others'. And she heard Joe's loud and sure 'I will' as he confirmed his own vows. The vicar then asked for the rings to be brought forward. There was an embarrassed shuffle as Joe's best mate, Rob, an old college friend, riffled his top pocket for a second or two and then sighed with relief, doing a mock swipe of his forehead as he pulled out the jeweller's box, where the platinum bands Joe and Ellie had chosen lay on navy velvet.

Ellie reached out her hand ready towards Joe, as he took out the smaller band. As he lifted his wrist to reach her fourth finger on her left hand, the sleeve of his jacket rode up a little. She caught sight of his cufflink. Hah – a black Batman symbol on silver. She stifled a giggle, looking up at him, catching those sexy hazel eyes, then gave a tip of her head towards his cuff. He grinned knowingly, and as the wedding ring slid to the base of her finger, he leaned in close and whispered in her ear, 'Just you wait till you see the boxer shorts later.'

She couldn't help but smile.

The afternoon tea reception was fabulous, with speeches, lots of bubbly, and much laughter. Later, there was a fish-and-chip supper, as well as an ice cream van, to serve those wanting to stay and dance in the marquee.

Ellie and Joe had a taxi booked for nine o'clock, ready to take them to the station for their honeymoon breakaway in a country hotel in the Lake District. (And, yes, she had packed her walking boots and cagoule!) Instead of Kirkton Taxis, along came Doris's husband, Clifford, in his prized old jaguar done up with satin ribbon on the bonnet, streamers, a 'Just Married' sign, and rattling tin cans tied to the back bumper. He stepped out grandly, announcing, 'Your chariot awaits.'

Ellie stood on the top step of the castle entrance, in her going-away outfit, a pretty vintage-style floral dress and navy jacket, ready to throw her bouquet in the time-honoured tradition. She turned her back to the small gathering: Gemma, Nicola, Cousin Lauren, and a few others were ready there. Malcolm and Derek stood to one side to watch the happy couple set off. Ellie had never been particularly good at throwing, and from her backwards stance the bouquet hurtled off sideways. Malcolm, star catch at the Kirkton cricket club in his time, threw up a hand instinctively and caught it beautifully. He and Derek shared a surprised glance and grin, as the small crowd cheered.

Shouts of 'Have a lovely time!' and 'Good luck' reached Ellie and Joe as they got into the car.

Ellie looked up at the castle, remembering that first interview day and her hopes for her teashop dream. What she had managed to achieve there made her proud, and finding Joe there too, wow, she could never have dreamed of that. She took his hand, which was warm and sure, sitting there on the back seat, with their friends and family wishing them well, waving them off. There was so much more to come. They could dream their dreams together now.

Acknowledgements

My dream was to become a published author. Last year that dream became a reality, and after over ten years of writing, rewriting and submitting, I finally got to hold a copy of my debut novel, *The Torn Up Marriage* – wow, what a feeling! Now, as the icing on the cake, here is *The Cosy Teashop in the Castle*. So my thanks have to go to Kimberley Young and my lovely HarperImpulse team, especially my editors Charlotte Brabbin and Charlotte Ledger, for giving me that opportunity, and for helping to make my first two published books the best they could be.

Thanks to all my fabulous friends, especially the Barcelona Trio, for fuelling me with prosecco, nibbles and chat when the going got tough! For Julie, for creating the wonderful choffee cake recipe and for letting me go 'undercover' as a waitress in her tea rooms for the day.

For Isabel, for being my test reader on *The Cosy Teashop in the Castle* and for advising me I was on the right lines with a very gorgeous Joe! Louise, through thick and thin, near or far.

The Romantic Novelists' Association – without the support of this wonderful organisation, and the special friends I have made in the Northumberland Chapter, I would never have had the encouragement to keep going, nor had the chance to meet my publisher or my new agent, Hannah Ferguson. So big thanks!

To Northumberland, my beautiful home county, for inspiring me with the most wonderful settings.

Last, and never least, my wonderful family: Richard, Amie, Harry, Mum and Dad, all the wider family too – thanks for your ongoing love and support. Debbie – keep striving for your writing dream, you will get there!

And for anyone who strives to make their dream a reality – Go for it and the Very Best of Luck!

Nanna's Choffee Cake Recipe

Ingredients:

14 oz (400 g) self-raising flour

2 teaspoons baking powder

16 oz (450 g) caster sugar

2 oz (50 g) cocoa powder
– good quality

16 oz (450 g) soft margarine

8 eggs

2 tbsp coffee essence
(such as Camp)

Frostings:

16 oz (450 g) icing sugar

1.2 oz (30 g) cocoa powder

6.5 oz (165 g) butter

1.5 tbsp coffee essence

3 tbsp milk

For decoration:

Dark and white chocolate curls. (Plus, chocolate-coated coffee beans.)

You will also need 4 x 20 cm (8") round cake baking pans, preferably non-stick & well-greased, with a circle of baking paper popped into the greased base.

Turn oven on to 180°C (or 160°C Fan).

For the all-in-one chocolate sponge:

Put 6 oz (175 g) self-raising flour (sifted), 2 oz (50 g) cocoa powder (sifted), 1 teaspoon baking powder, 8 oz (225 g) caster sugar, 8 oz (225 g) soft margarine, and 4 eggs into a mixing bowl. Beat thoroughly (an electric hand whisk is ideal) for about 3 minutes, until all the ingredients are fluffy and nicely blended. Pour equally into 2 of your prepared cake tins. Flatten mix a little with a pallet knife.

For the all-in-one coffee sponge:

Put 8 oz (225 g) self-raising flour (sifted), 1 teaspoon baking powder, 8 oz (225 g) caster sugar, 8 oz (225 g) soft margarine, and 4 eggs into a mixing bowl. Beat thoroughly (an electric hand whisk is ideal) for about 3 minutes, until all the ingredients are fluffy and nicely blended. Add 2 tablespoons coffee essence. Pour into the other 2 of your prepared cake tins. Flatten mix a little with a pallet knife.

Bake cakes for 30-35 mins until nicely risen. Allow to cool slightly then turn out onto wire rack to cool totally.

If they are a little uneven, don't panic. Once turned out just carefully slice any lumps or bumps away, so they will be able to layer nicely on top of each other!

Chocolate fudge frosting:

2.5 oz (65 g) butter

1.2 oz (30 g) cocoa powder

3 tbsp milk

8 oz (225 g) icing sugar, sifted

Melt the butter in a pan, add the cocoa powder, and cook, stirring for one minute. Stir in the milk and icing sugar. Beat well until smooth. Leave to cool until thickened.

Coffee frosting:

4 oz (100 g) butter

8 oz (225 g) icing sugar

1.5 tbsp coffee essence

Make sure the butter is softened, beat through the icing sugar and coffee essence (an electric hand whisk is ideal for this again), until light, fluffy and well blended.

Layering the cake:

Place a chocolate sponge on a circular cake base or stand. Take half the coffee frosting and spread carefully with a knife over the sponge, checking it reaches to the sides evenly.

*Ellie's star tip: If the frosting is difficult to work with and sticking to the knife, have a mug of boiling water to hand, dip the knife in every now and again and, hey presto, the frosting becomes easy to work with!

Place a coffee sponge on top of that. Then spread with half the chocolate frosting.

Layer with another chocolate sponge. Spread with the second half of the coffee frosting.

Top with a coffee sponge. Spread carefully with the remaining chocolate frosting.

DO NOT COVER THE SIDES OF THE CAKE! We should see the layering.

Top with chocolate curls made of both dark and white chocolate and, if you like them, about 10 chocolate coffee beans dotted around the edge.

Enjoy with friends!